SPURN

To my parents (especially Mum) for always believing in me

SPURN

A Walker Saga Book Two

Jaymin Eve

Spurn: A Walker Saga Book Two

Copyright © Jaymin Eve 2013

All rights reserved

First published in 2013

Eve, Jaymin

Spurn: A Walker Saga Book Two

1st edition

Chapter 1

Talina

Talina floated on her back facing toward the half-sun. She barely noticed the expanse of sparkling blue and green waters surrounding her. Instead, she focused on the peace and quiet as she lay semi-submerged in the depths. Her one and only aim had been to escape the endless squabbles of her family. And she had finally swum far enough. She'd reached the edge of the territories, but despite the push of the drifting currents, she wasn't quite brave enough to cross out of Earon's quadrant. After all, it was a punishable offence to enter any of the other clan areas.

The four moons were just beginning their slow spread across the pale pink skies of Spurn. They

1

were the force dictating the measured ebb and fall of the tides. Talina loved it when the weak light of their half-sun was washed away by the bright moonlights. Sighing, she turned over to lightly tread water. It was probably time to stop hiding and face her mother. Gladriel had been in fine form today. As head of the Earon clan she took herself and her duties far too seriously.

Talina hated confrontations, and she hated being around other Spurns; that is, with the exception of her brother. If only she could escape forever, but there was nowhere to swim. The four clans divided their world, each with a distinct hierarchy and private quadrant.

Earon was the second strongest, and with her mother as the leader she should have loved her life. But instead, she hated it. In Earon, she was nothing but a half-breed.

She duck-dived beneath the water. It took a few moments (far longer than most Spurns) for her gills to kick in and the instinct to breathe through her mouth to cease. Talina hated her differences; they drew attention, marked her as weak. And on Spurn the weak were eaten, luckily not by each other, but there were plenty of other predators in the waters.

Still, she had to admit there was truly nothing comparable to a glide through the ocean. She

2

didn't even care that her webbings were small and fragile. She ducked and dived with the currents, searching deeper until the strength of the moonlight waned. There was a fine line in the deep water between light and eternal night. Talina had never been able to venture any deeper, not without assistance. Her defects, her weaknesses, prevented it.

Talina, be back at our pontoon before half-moon. Do not make me tell you twice.

She flinched as Gladriel's voice echoed through her mind. Her mother was the one Spurn she was forbidden to block out. She had the capability, but it wasn't worth the drama.

Rising once again, she swam closer to the surface. The protective clear lenses over her eyes flicked, clouding her underwater vision, before settling back into place. Glancing to her left, a pod of droltines swam alongside. The playful pink creatures with large fins and spout-shaped noses were a very distant cousin to Spurns. She danced with them in delight until they moved off in a different direction.

Talina groaned as her stomach rumbled; she hadn't eaten that day, refusing the morning's ration of cucreamer. Normally she loved the sweet, pink fruit, but for some reason, earlier she'd been unable to stomach any food. But with the distance she had traveled, her energy had depleted significantly. Through her lenses she noticed a small stock of krillonia, the shrimplike planktonic crustacean that was her favorite. Gliding in the midst of the dense cloud, it was simple enough to open her mouth, expelling the water through the small gills on her neck, and take in the sustenance.

Satisfied for the moment, she increased speed toward her home pontoons. A flash in her peripheral vision brought a broad smile to her face. A familiar image darted out of the gulfstream to fall in beside her.

Raror, where did you come from?

She opened her mind to speak with her brother. He was the only one never to judge her, and she loved him dearly. His emerald-colored hair, long enough to secure him as a future leader, streamed behind in the ocean depths. The visible veins beneath his skin were more prominent than ever; he had to have been swimming long and hard to get that amount of pump.

Earon was called to Silver City for a meeting of council heads. Mother sent me.

The deep rich timbre of his voice echoed through her mind. Without fail it evoked memories of the many nights he had protected her, rocked her to sleep and comforted away her hurts throughout the years. His voice was the sound of

4

safety. Talina had only been to the underwater city once. It was difficult for her to make that distance; the water pressure at that depth played havoc with her senses. But Raror was often there. It was the neutral ground where the four clans discussed all issues.

What has happened to bring everyone together?

He didn't answer immediately; they'd just reached the edge of Earon's pontoons, and needed to slow.

Some strange occurrences. Three Baroons and a Gerk have gone missing, and there have been disturbances on the Sacred Isle.

His eyes widened, nostrils flaring. In a world that was predominantly water, the one and only section of land was protected and off-limits to everyone except the Keepers.

Cucreamer and wood are missing. The rationing systems have been thrown out, so we've had to redistribute. The vote found the Gerks will receive less.

Talina's pulse raced as panic threaded through her mind. Who would risk the wrath of the gods by stealing from the Sacred Isle? She pushed that terrifying thought aside to focus on the caste system which she despised.

Why is it always the Gerks who are treated like lesser Spurns? They are no different. Hair color should not dictate status for life.

Raror shrugged.

Talina knew that while he sympathized with her point of view, he failed to understand why she was so soft-hearted. The way the majority of other Spurns had treated her had resulted in her possessing an unparalleled empathy. But the castes were a part of life on Spurn. The Gerks, or Grays, were mostly found in positions of servitude. They controlled less territory, and had less power and status. It had always been that way.

They dodged the pontoon pets, cat- and dog-fish swimming lazily in the waters surrounding their family home. Talina gave a quick pat to Toto, her favorite little friend, whilst keeping an eye out for Earon's guardian, Chamandia. The large water dragon had never liked her, and since just one touch of its scales or breath of its venom would find you writhing in agony for days, it was worth the vigilance.

In sync, brother and sister surfaced. Talina sucked in a deep breath. This was the fastest way to activate their interior respiratory valve to switch from gills to lungs. Unlike other Spurns, she found this a more comfortable state.

6

Instead of moving forward she stared in dismay toward their floating pontoon. Returning home was never a pleasant experience.

As Gladriel was head of Earon, their dwelling was the most lavish in this quadrant. Constructed out of the trees that grew on the Sacred Isle, the timber slats were layered over each other, and the pontoon had small decks off each level.

The clans were granted a certain quota of the lagoona trees. The leaders then divided this between the individual families. So it was no surprise that Gladriel's house was three stories of floating opulence. Talina's room was at the top, in keeping with her low family status. Only those of high standing scored a room near the water. Behind their home were low rows of tethered pontoons, spreading as far as the eye could see. The emerald flags of Earon swayed lazily in the cooling breezes. The majority of their community lived here, with just a few lone Spurns scattered throughout the quadrant.

Raror was already at the edge. Talina watched as his lithe muscles rippled, and he shot himself up out of the water and onto the higher decking, a feat her weaker body had no chance of achieving. He lowered the ladder for her to climb. With a sigh, Talina grabbed the bottom rung and pulled herself up. As she climbed, the fine webbings between her fingers disappeared, and each digit emerged. She was the only Spurn whose webbing completely disappeared when out of the water. Her long emerald hair trailed behind her, but unlike the pure color of the other Earons, Talina's was flecked with black throughout.

According to Gladriel, this was courtesy of her unknown father, who was not of Spurn. They'd had a brief affair before he disappeared, never to be seen again. Spurns rarely stayed in long-term relationships; they tended to have mating seasons, and then moved on.

Raror reached down, and hooked Talina under the arms, dragging her onto the middle decking – his level.

"Gladriel has requested us downstairs, Talli." Raror spoke aloud, his lispy voice courtesy of the Spurns' tongue structure and vocal cords, something she also lacked.

Talina groaned and hung her head. "I just need one day without her constant disapproval."

Raror pulled her into a tight hug; she shivered slightly against his skin. It was always so much colder than her own, but she appreciated his gesture. Spurns were not normally a demonstrative people.

"Come, we might as well find out what she wants. Get it over with." He clasped her hand and led her downstairs.

Talina kept her head lowered, not making eye contact with any of the Earons scattered throughout her mother's vast quarters.

"Nice to see you, Raror my son." Gladriel, shifted in her bright pink coralline chair, a living entity made by microscopic sea creatures that continued to grow even outside the ocean.

Gladriel lifted her emerald hair over one shoulder; it was free-flowing down to her knees, as any good ruler's would be. Then Gladriel turned her cold yellow eyes toward Talina.

"And you. Take a seat, and do not speak unless I require you to."

Eyes downcast, Talina scurried along before falling down to sit cross-legged on the floor. She had chosen a back corner, where no one could come at her from any side but the front. Raror took his appointed seat next to Gladriel in a smaller coralline chair. The rest of the floor space was taken up by the heads of the minor family units within Earon.

"Thank you all for gathering so quickly. My son has returned from the city with grave news of thefts of cucreamer and wood from the Sacred Isle."

A gasp rippled throughout the room. They all understood the gravity of the situation. Cucreamer and wood, vital to their existence, only grew on the Sacred Isle, and Spurns could not survive without that small stretch of land.

"However, in the time since the meeting at Silver City, there has been a capture on the Isle."

Gladriel's slightly pointed teeth gleamed as she smiled around the room. She looked proud, as if she had made the arrest herself.

"Foreigners, from a distant planet, apparently. And the chosen of the clans are to convene for the trial."

Whispers and murmurs echoed throughout. The last foreigner to visit from another planet was Talina's father.

Talina sighed; she knew what this announcement meant for her. Raror would be gone, and life was almost unbearable without the protection of her brother. Nothing that she couldn't handle, of course, but the constant taunts and loneliness would wear her down after a while. Plus Gladriel loved to leave her with all the worst jobs. In particular she hated de-barnacling the base of their pontoon.

As if Raror had heard her thoughts, he raised his head to glance in her direction. A small smile played on his lips.

What was he up to?

He straightened his shoulders and met Gladriel's gaze. "Mother, I cannot attend this trial with you." He spoke without hesitation.

The rest of the gathered members looked up at him in confusion. More and more lately he had been taking on the responsibilities of the clan.

Talina waited for her mother to explode, but Gladriel simply smiled out into the expanse of the room.

"Talina will accompany us, Raror; you do not need to worry about your promise to her."

Raror continued to stare at the troubling smirk displayed by the head of Earon. Talina could tell by his expression he felt the same way she did; Gladriel was up to something. And right now she was not keen to be going on this adventure. But, as always, she had no choice.

Later that night, as Talina stepped into her water-pod for her nightly respite, and everyone else had either returned to the water or to their pontoons, she heard screeching.

"No," she breathed.

Surely Gladriel wasn't up to her old tricks. She'd promised Raror she would stop. But Talina knew Raror was away visiting his mating partner, and clearly Gladriel was taking advantage of his absence.

Stepping out onto her balcony, Talina dived headfirst over the rail into the cool water. She shook hard, her anger bristling over.

How could she do this? But Talina knew her mother was pure evil.

She continued to swim towards the largest moon, staying close to the surface. No one else would be able to hear the droltine's cry, but Talina's hearing was better than most. Finally the isolated barge came into view. Mesh netting surrounded it on all four sides, a barrier to keep them contained.

With her head above the waterline, she gripped the closest section of netting.

"Gladriel!" She would probably pay for it later, but Talina couldn't help the anger that spilled out in that one word.

A single screech was her reply.

Talina's clenched fists tightened on the barrier. She would have to enter her mother's lair.

Diving over the top, she descended into the sparsely lit water. All the way down she continued to hope she was wrong. But there was very little doubt.

Gladriel came into sight then, her emerald hair surrounding her. At first it looked as if she was alone, but within moments the droltine came into view. It was tethered to Gladriel by a simple twined rope. And she was systematically pulling it forward, send hot shock waves into it and blowing it back.

STOP! Talina mentally screamed at her mother.

Gladriel turned, a sneer gracing her features.

Hello, daughter, come to join me while I train our next guard and scout?

Talina shuddered with anger. She could taste the fury as it ascended from the pit of her stomach. The swirl of energy that always lived inside her was tumultuous, and her vision started to blacken around the edges.

No, I can't lose control again. She silently begged herself to hold it together. *You have to stop, Gladriel. You cannot treat our beautiful friends so cruelly.*

It is in our nature, daughter. I need this one's co-operation and I need it to be tough. There is no other way to achieve this.

And she turned to shock the poor animal again. It screeched in pain, shying away from its torturer.

Talina noticed the spattering of red where the droltine had endured Gladriel's training.

The water started to swirl around Talina and she knew it was almost too late; her power wanted to be released; Gladriel must be stopped. The water heated as it formed turrets.

Slowly her mother turned back toward her and noticed the energy surrounding them.

Talina! What are you doing? You must control yourself; you are weak.

Talina barely registered the insult. She was reveling in the flow of power, the confidence that she was the baddest thing in the water and that she could end Gladriel's reign of terror. The blackness was descending over her vision again, but she registered Gladriel's fear. Her mother trembled and dropped the tethered droltine, holding both hands up in a pleading gesture.

I promise I will let her go and never do this again. Just stop this.

A smirk crossed Talina's face; Gladriel knew she was about to become the victim; she was practically begging for Talina's mercy. It was time to give some of the torture back.

That last thought was enough to shock a semblance of control into Talina's system. She paused on the brink of sending out a devastating wave of power.

No, she refused to be like her mother, abusing the powers granted to her.

Instead of attacking Gladriel, she sent a powerful force through the water that blasted apart the mesh cage.

If I ever catch you doing this again, Gladriel, I swear I will not stop at disintegrating the mesh.

Talina turned then and left the area. She needed to get away from her mother before the anger brimmed over. She needed some hard swimming to calm down.

Her power needed release, and she'd never be able to control it if she couldn't work off this pent-up energy.

As she swam she decided not to tell Raror what had occurred. It would only create drama for him, and she hoped that was the last time Gladriel would commit such cruelty. Her fear of Talina's powers might just keep her in line.

The next morning Talina and Raror sat with their legs hanging off the side of her top-level balcony. Eighteen pontoons had been separated from the collective to head for the Isle. It would take them seven days powered by wind and seahorses to reach the land. Earon's quadrant was the second largest behind the Baroons; blue-hairs were top of the food chain.

Talina rested her face on the railing. She stared out into the half-sun lighting a pink sky.

"You know, despite the fact Gladriel is probably going to have me sacrificed, I'm really excited to see the Isle."

Raror glanced at his sister. He'd always thought she looked like a mystical creature. The differences that marked her as weak among Spurns seemed beautiful to him. The thin lines of hair covering the ridges above her eyes and the flicked-out strands along her eyelids framed her brown eyes perfectly. Most Spurns had eyes that ranged from gold to marmalade, but always in the yellow tone, which made Talina's unique.

The black flecks through her hair, which she was so clever at hiding, transformed her emerald locks to that of the brightest polished stone. She was taller than almost everyone on Spurn. Only Ladre, the Baroon's leader, topped her height, though Talina was leaner and less muscular. But more than all of this it was the innate goodness that shone from her; she was not like the rest of them, operating in the animalistic environment of eat or be eaten. She had imparted much of her gentle qualities onto Raror, and he believed himself to be a better Spurn for it.

"Don't you worry, little sister." He patted her warm arm. "Remember? I will never let Mother hurt you."

Talina nodded and Raror turned back to gaze at the sea. A long time ago he had made the promise – to protect her from all of those that aimed to harm.

And on Spurn, that was everyone.

Talina really enjoyed the journey, she didn't see Gladriel once, and there was nothing more calming than the great expanses of the ocean. They were due to make land the next morning, and she wondered if she would get any rest that night.

This was the most exciting thing to occur in her nineteen-year lifetime. She'd never seen land that formed above the water.

Then she noticed the moons were already at full sky. It was later than she thought. She left her balcony.

Generally, Spurns required exactly five hours of closed-eye respite, whether above or below the water, but Talina functioned better on six or more. She opened her pod; it was half-full of water, a calming level for her. Shedding her white mesh covering, she stepped in. Lying back and closing her eyes, she allowed the pontoon's rhythmic movement and water in her pod to calm her energized thoughts. Surprisingly, she had no trouble drifting off.

The next morning the Earons gathered together.

"Isn't it the most beautiful thing you have ever seen?" Talina held Raror's arm as she bounced in excitement, a euphoric emotion that she rarely felt.

They were standing on the balcony, waiting for Gladriel's command to start swimming.

"It's so strange, as if something has broken the ocean and there is a crack in it." Raror was wide-eyed, the clear lenses flickering off and on as his eyes adjusted to the air.

The sand was white, with just a tinge of gold. It was unlike any color Talina had ever seen. The sunlight sparkled off the grains like the precious jewels they were.

Earons, take to the water now. We are to make our way to the edge of the Isle and wait.

Their leader's voice echoed through her mind, and without hesitation Talina dived into the depths. She let the water flow over her, and as her gills kicked in she took off. Speed-swimming was her favorite thing to do. To her left, Raror kept pace, although, if he needed to, he could almost double her velocity through the water.

Emerald hair streamed in the currents as their collection of members approached the golden sands of the Sacred Isle. For the first time in her life Talina was shocked to see the ocean floor tapering up. It became shallower until at last she could put her feet down and stand above the water line. She wobbled precariously, but as her lungs kicked in she found her feet on the squishy sand, digging her toes in for extra stability. Gladriel, who'd been the first to stand, shifted once or twice, but managed to stay straight at the head of their group.

"Do not move too quickly. It will take time to get used to the stillness of land." Her lisped words echoed.

Talina glanced around her. Judging by the tumbles already being taken in the shallow water, Gladriel was correct.

She turned when she heard a clamor behind them. A foreign pontoon, blue flags flying, indicated that the Baroons had arrived. They were in the process of tethering to a nearby station. Her heart skipped a beat at the possibility of seeing Ladre, their intimidating leader. She swung back as Gladriel spoke again.

"We have permission to move onto the land. Take it slowly. Start on all fours for balance." She waved everyone forward, and then turned away to concentrate on her own journey. Talina could see that their leader was still slightly off-kilter, but otherwise she made it onto the flat sand without drama. Realizing she would be left behind, Talina took her first hesitant step.

Her muscles made their usual adjustment for the sway and ebb of the ocean, but for the first time there was no movement from below. She over-balanced and sprawled headfirst into the shallows.

Raror moved to help her up, but he was just as un-coordinated as she was and splashed into the water next to her. Dragging herself forward on hands and knees, Talina crawled onto the still dryness of land. Her head started to sway, and an instant nausea rose as her body tried to compensate for the lack of movement it was so used to.

"I think I'm going to be sick." Raror dived past her to heave his morning cucreamer all over the sand.

He wasn't the only one.

Talina flipped over onto her back and, using the half-sun as an anchor, breathed deeply for a few moments. Finally the nausea abated enough so she wasn't about to join the hurling ranks. Sitting up, she straightened her shaky legs before pulling herself up to stand.

She guessed that this was how it felt when learning to walk for the first time. Balancing without the movement of the ocean required different muscles and a center of gravity that Spurns lacked, but eventually most of the Earon clan was able to stand and move further along the sandy beach. Talina loved the delicious texture between her toes; it tickled as it scrubbed her feet.

Once walking became easier, she was able to observe her environment. And she wasn't the only one; most of the Earon clan was trying to walk and take in the vast wonders surrounding them, which meant there were plenty of tumbles, golden grains flying up in small clouds all around her.

The sand started at the water line and drifted gently up a curved mound. From there on, it looked to Talina like a mix of sand and swathes of green vegetation. She knew that the entire island was only fifty miles wide and ten miles long. At least eighty percent consisted of the lagoona tree plantations, which she could see stretching out into the distance in long straight rows.

It was simply incredible to see. Everything looked so free and unencumbered with no water surrounding it. She was distracted at just that moment as Raror stumbled and fell down next to her. A grin spread across her face as she reached out a hand to help him to his feet.

"This is not exactly how I pictured this experience." He shook his head, dispelling the masses of sand that had accumulated in his long straight hair. It was such a warm day that already sections of the emerald tresses looked dry.

"We need to get you to water soon, Raror."

Talina frowned as she examined him. She had never forgotten the story of the Baroon, the blue-haired Spurn who had become lost on this island. They had found him almost at the water's edge. His hair, which looked to be reaching for the water, had lost all color and was brown and shriveled. From that day on they'd been warned to never let their hair dry out. It was a living entity that was essential for each one's survival. Cutting a Spurn's hair was tantamount to cutting off an arm.

But Talina knew that she was different.

When she was younger, she had allowed her hair to dry completely – with water at the ready just in case – but she had only experienced mild discomfort and a dry mouth.

Raror touched her arm. "I'm sure they will have water available when we reach the buildings."

Eyes crinkled with worry, she continued to shoot glances at Raror. The walk felt like it was taking forever, but eventually Talina noticed a small lagoona-clad building in the distance. Progress had been slow and members of the clans were staggered along the beach.

Already standing under the eaves of the building were the Yetles with their sunlight-yellow hair. Behind the Earons were the Baroons. They marched in a coordinated line. None of them had land-sickness, and their dark-blue hair was sand free. And at the very back, farthest from the meeting place, were the Gerks, the smallest group, their hair shorter and seahorse-gray.

Although progress was slow, the Earon clan finally finished their trek across the warm sand to halt in the shade of the building. Raror sighed in relief as a cool spray rained down on their group. The entire perimeter of the building was furnished with shooting jets that delivered a constant stream of briny ocean water. Talina strained to see where this water came from, and eventually noticed a few Gerks off to one side pumping a large handle. It was attached to some type of water well.

"Talina ... Raror, it's nice to see you again."

Talina spun around at the sound of a familiar voice. Ladre was the first of the Baroons to arrive. He was her secret fantasy, and was so much better than the average Spurn – taller than she was by at least two inches, with the darkest blue hair, and a skin tone that was pinker than most others. She had admired him from afar, since ... well, it felt like forever. And, most importantly, he was always kind to her, even going out of his way to offer her jobs in Silver City, preventing his clan from treating her as less and always stopping for a chat. Despite the fact he was considered the most powerful Spurn alive, he was honorable, and she wished that there wasn't such an unbridgeable gap between them.

As he met her stare, a familiar heat flooded her cheeks. Among Spurns, this only happened to her and only when she was around Ladre. She knew that Raror had discreetly asked others, and not one Spurn had ever experienced this warm-face sensation. *Perhaps they were too cold-blooded?*

"Ladre, it's good to see that your clan has arrived from Silver City." Raror lowered his head slightly, showing the Baroon leader the respect due to his position.

Not that Talina had ever seen Ladre impose his position on others, unlike Gladriel, who imposed hers all the time.

My son and I have to step inside for the initial meet-up. Everyone else stay on the beach.

As if she'd heard Talina's thought, her mother issued her harsh order.

Raror touched her arm briefly before stepping under the overhanging eaves to enter through the open doorway. Ladre, who would definitely be expected inside, hesitated before leaning closer to Talina.

"Are you not joining us for the meeting? The clan leaders have been called." His hairless face, and dark-yellow, almost ochre eyes looked confused. Normally daughters of leaders would be included in all important clan decisions.

She shook her head. "Gladriel likes to keep her mistakes as far away from her as possible."

Her deep brown eyes widened in shock and she covered her mouth with both hands. *What was she thinking saying something so honest?* Being around Ladre made her feel flustered, and when her mind was muddled she said stupid things.

Understanding replaced Ladre's confusion and, with a genial nod, he left her there, leading his delegation into the building.

It took a few moments for Talina's cheeks to cool again.

The remaining Spurns stayed in their clan groups, sitting under the spray. A few made their way back to the ocean, finding it uncomfortable to stay on land. But there was no mingling between the hair colors, and Talina hated that more than anything.

Frustrated and bored, she moved away from the collective to explore their surroundings. The longer she was on the land, the more it felt right. She loved the vast expanses of ocean, the quiet, the freedom. But there was that other side that apparently craved the stillness of land.

She made her way through a small section of lagoona trees. She knew that she shouldn't wander off. The woods were patrolled by Baroon Keepers, and their job was to make sure nothing was disturbed.

Each stick of tree was precious, and all allocations viewed and voted on. It was a versatile material, with both thin and thick stems that were quite pliant and springy, yet never deteriorated in the salt water. The older plantations had stems that extended high in the sky, with just a few scattered leaves up top. The leaves were pretty useless and were mainly utilized as stuffing for day beds.

While wandering without direction, she accidentally stumbled through a line of closely growing stilt bushes and into a clearing. Before her was a small building surrounded on all sides by the densely growing bushes. Curious as to what this secreted area was, she crept closer. Two spear-armed Baroons stood at the entrance door, their backs to her.

Talina crouched down and moved back into the shelter of the trees. *Is this where they were keeping the prisoners?*

Moving slowly around the structure and being careful to make no noise, she examined the building. The lagoona wood layering the walls looked newer, less salt-pocked than usual. There was a small window high up on the back wall.

Most Spurns would have no chance of reaching it, but with a little help Talina might have a shot.

She hesitated.

She didn't usually go looking for trouble; she'd already spent far too many moons being disciplined. But something urged her forward.

After a quick search, she found a rock that wasn't too heavy to move. Back straining, she dragged it beneath the window and stood on the rock, using the wall to balance herself. She still had to stand on her tiptoes to be able to see in through the barred window.

From what she could see, it was definitely an open-planned prison, and two of the four small cubicles were occupied by a collection of strange humanoids. They had the same basic shape as Spurns, but ... with no webbings or gills ... and their skin was the wrong color.

Her eyes were drawn to one of the females in particular. A stunning redhead, she was statuesque and much taller than Talina. She stared in amazement at the pale ivory of the female's skin and her green eyes. Talina couldn't believe what she was seeing ... green eyes ... crazy.

But the reason this female, in particular, stood out from the rest of her group was the amazing red markings that framed the left side of her face and tracked down her neck. Also, she strode around the small prison, so sure ... confident. This was a woman who was afraid of no one.

Talina was instantly jealous; she'd always wished for one ounce of the composure and attitude this female so effortlessly displayed. But that would never happen.

Putting aside her feelings, she examined the prisoners more closely. They had hair on their faces, just like her own. Twin lines above their eyes and flicked-out blackness along their eyelids. Were they from the same land as her father? Excitement and panic flooded her. She needed to break in there and speak with them before they either disappeared or went to trial.

The redhaired female turned to face someone in the other occupied cell. Talina shifted her view to observe him, a giant man with broad planes and flashing dark eyes. He was unlike any of the males on Spurn, but for some reason Talina found his chiseled jaw and muscular physique attractive.

She had just started to observe the rest of the inhabitants when strong hands grabbed her, pulling her backwards away from the window.

Chapter 2

Abigail

Even though our current adventure wasn't exactly going to plan, I was enjoying the mini-meltdown happening in front of me. Lucy stood at the bars of our prison and, from where I sat, it looked like she almost had her head through the slats. She was yelling as loudly as she could. And, for a small person, it was damn loud.

"What the eff? Seriously, where the hell are you hiding, fish-boy? You better get your ass back in here." Her blond curls stood on end; she'd run her hands through them so many times.

The 'natives' were out of sight at the moment, and I wasn't sure if that was a good or bad thing. From the moment we had arrived on Spurn, landing on stunning white beaches in the weak sunlight, we'd been taken captive by the locals. I hadn't had much chance to observe them before they threw us into the prison. But they were ... different.

"Why is it every time I turn my freaking back someone is throwing me in a cell? I swear to God, if anyone comes near me with a knife or a taser or anything resulting in the marking of my skin, I will rip their face off and wear it as a mask for Halloween," Lucy continued her tirade.

Samuel, my brother and Lucy's boyfriend – mate – whatever the current term was – looked torn between amusement and desperation as he attempted to calm this five-foot-nothing fire-storm.

I chuckled again; she was just so amusing to watch. She was now storming back and forward, swearing like the proverbial sailor.

Lucy and I grew up together on Earth, the youngling planet my parents stashed me on for safety, and I knew her better than anyone. She was scared. Word-vomit is her go-to for fear. And I couldn't blame her; she'd just recently escaped captivity, where she was tortured by Olden, our old compound leader on Earth. We had no idea what awaited us in the hands of these strange hybrid humans. I don't know exactly what type of welcome I had expected, but immediate imprisonment ... well, it was a little less friendly than I had hoped.

Absentmindedly, I rubbed the now non-existent scar on my chest where Olden had stabbed me. I still wondered if it had been another inch to the left whether I would be here to tell this tale.

Yeah, I know my father is a kick-ass god, but considering I'm just a half-Walker whose longevity and powers are unknown, I won't be thinking of myself as indestructible yet. In fact, Josian, god-like father, had once believed I was the only half-Walker in existence. But my aunt Francesca, a.k.a. the crazy soothsayer, assures us there is one on each of First World's youngling planets. And it's my job to find and gather them. Hence the reason we're sitting in a prison on the youngling planet of Spurn.

"Aribella, do something to stop her before they come back." Samuel, who rarely spoke, had decided that now was the time to start ordering me around.

I was getting used to being called 'Aribella', which I'd recently learned was my given name. But for most of my life I've been Abigail, Abby to my friends. Well, friend. Lucy was really all I'd had.

Lucy gave Samuel a shove before I could throw him the rude hand gesture his arrogant command deserved. In annoyance, I pushed long masses of curls off my face. At some point I'd lost my hair-tie and I was really missing my braid. The blood-red color of my hair, threaded through with black flecks, was even more potent since my power-enlightenment. It was thick and shiny now, without any help from me. Definite bonus. I stared down at the diamond mark on my right wrist. Unlike every other scar, blemish and dot, it had not disappeared during my Walker enlightenment. I now wore the birthmark of each of my parents' lines.

"Abbs, can you open a doorway and get us out of here?"

I glanced up to meet Lucy's beautiful baby blues; they pleaded with me to give her a different answer to the question she'd asked a dozen times that morning.

Closing my own emerald eyes, I attempted to draw from my power again. And again there was no response. I could still feel its endless depths, but it was quiet. Instead of the thick string of energy I'd normally feel, all I was getting were wispy strands of fairy floss. I knew there was another way to access the Walker doorways, but unfortunately my father hadn't had time to teach me.

Sighing, I opened my eyes to look at my desperate best friend. "Sorry, either something has blocked me or I've worn out my powers. I got nothing."

Her face fell, the panic in her features more pronounced now.

I'd felt off-balance ever since leaving my home planet, First World, and opening a doorway to transport us all to Spurn. It was as if my energy was taking a vacation, getting a little rest and relaxation. Perfect timing, of course.

Movement from the adjacent cell caught my eye. Brace and Lucas were back against the wall, deep in conversation. For some reason those two had been seen as bigger threats than we were and had been separated from us.

I'd briefly wondered how Samuel, who was in our cell, felt about that. It was hard to read anything on his coldly chiseled face. He looked just like our beautiful mother Lallielle. But since we had different fathers, and I favored mine in looks, there was no real resemblance between us.

Samuel had been held captive in the same place as Lucy for an entire year and the ten words he'd spoken to me since discovering I hadn't died eighteen years before have been forced from him out of politeness.

As I turned to look at him, he dived forward and yanked Lucy away from the bars.

I spun around to see what had prompted his action, hands at the ready to combat any threat.

A Spurn stood between our two cells.

Lucy wrestled with Samuel, and it was lucky he had a hand covering her lower face. I smiled. At least now she had another protector to save her from her big mouth.

I examined the newcomer with great interest. The male was shorter than all of us except Lucy. All of the inhabitants so far had been petite but with lithe muscles framing their entire bodies. He was shirtless, with a simple webbed loin cloth wrapped around his waist, just covering the very essentials – which I assumed were the same as ours. His skin was pink, but in a translucent manner, as if muscles and blood reflected through the skin. On top of that I could see blue veins throughout his entire frame. His general shape was humanoid, but slightly off-kilter. It was mainly noticeable when they moved, as if their joints were more flexible or something.

His skin was smooth and shiny, as if a layer of oil coated the outside. He was hairless except for an incredible mane of blue hair on his head. It was long, almost to his knees, and one solid color. He was barefoot, and his toes looked long and slightly webbed, a membrane connecting each digit. At first when they had captured us, I'd been more worried about the trident-style weapons they carried, rather than their differences and powers. But now I wanted to know what secrets they hid. I was also curious why no one had spoken to us yet. There had only been an initial capture and search before we were deposited into these cells.

Even as I thought this, the man opened his mouth to speak.

"You have disturbed the Sacred Isle, and you have stolen from us. The leaders of each clan will converge here for your trial. I am to inform you of this and then there is to be no contact." His voice was deep and slow.

His lisp spoke of a vocal structure far different to our own as he read us our rights – of which apparently we had none.

I moved forward and clutched at the bars of our cell. How was I supposed to find the half-Walker if I was stuck in this room the entire time?

"Wait a minute. We haven't stolen anything." I gripped the bars tightly, barely two feet from the Spurn. "We had just arrived from First World when you captured us. You didn't find anything on us, right?"

His shiny yellow eyes widened, looking even more alien with their lack of lashes and brows. He hadn't expected me to answer back but something told me he'd registered my comment. With one last look, he turned and walked away.

Sighing, I banged my hands against the bars, wishing desperately for an axe, or energy ball, or something to get us out of here.

A few boring days later, I'd just finished my small portion of a sweet fruit they had given us. The rough-skinned produce and its juice was all we'd had to eat or drink since arriving, but for some reason I hadn't felt hungry or thirsty.

I paced our tiny cell and then slumped back into my mesh, closing my eyes. This was the only way to escape Lucy and Samuel's constant face-sucking. They were driving me insane with a combination of both nausea and jealousy. It would have been nice to have my own distraction from the boredom.

My eyes flew open as an explosion of voices broke the silence. The noises drifted in through the small window at the back of the room. I jumped off my mat. If I sat there any longer I think my butt imprint would become permanent.

"Can you hear what's happening out there, Red?" Brace had moved to the front of his cell. His question was perfectly acceptable until he added, "You should step away from that window."

He didn't look worried, but his tone was stern, commanding me to obey ... *not likely*. Ever since he'd dropped that dream bombshell on me and then refused to elaborate, our conversations had been a little heated.

I crossed my arms over my chest. "I'm fine here, Brace, but thanks for your concern." I love an over-the-top use of sarcasm.

Brace was a pain in both my butt and my heart. When I was on Earth, he'd appeared in my dreams, and neither of us knew why. He'd recently informed me that he had dreamed of me too. But that was all the information he'd given.

Since meeting in the flesh we've had major unresolved chemistry. I alternated between wanting to kiss him senseless and restraining myself from punching him in the kidneys.

The problem was I knew something was up with him.

I couldn't put my finger on exactly what it was, but I didn't fully trust him. Yes, he'd saved my life, and given me a hell of a first kiss, but he was hiding something.

I hate secrets.

My curious nature struggled to accept or leave them be and I was determined to figure out what his secret was.

That's if he didn't keep distracting me with his face. Brace was ... gorgeous. There was no other way to put it. Every other man paled in comparison … well, for me anyways. And Lucy was more than vocal about how hot he was.

On quiet nights, when I examined my feelings closely I had to admit that he might already own my heart.

I was still facing him, but my refusal to move had his chiseled features dropping into stern lines, highlighting a dark captivating beauty. His brown hair was short again but it still fell messily across his forehead. He was a giant man, and in this cell he almost reached the roof. Six and half feet easily. He shifted slightly to one side as Lucas moved to stand next to him.

My eyes flicked across to the blond; he wasn't as tall or as broad as Brace, but he had an icy beauty that was interesting all the same. Lucas, who is the next Crown Emperor of First World, had decided to join us for this planet-jumping journey. I still didn't know what his end game was and I was pretty annoyed to be surrounded by such secretive men.

Mostly, I went out of my way to avoid Lucas since he believed I was his to-be-crowned Empress. And even though I'd done my best to set that straight, he was still here. Besides, any interest

I could have in Lucas disappeared the moment Brace entered my world. He eclipsed everything else.

"Abby, you haven't moved," Brace said, his tone still stern.

I shook my head in his direction, my full lips curving up. I hated being told what to do.

"I might just have a quick look," I said as I moved closer to the window.

I was tall enough that if I grabbed on to the bars and pulled myself up I'd be able to see out.

"Abigail, get your ass away from that window." Brace was right at the forefront of his cage now. He gripped the wooden slats. "Samuel, Lucy ... get over there and stop her."

Lucy laughed out loud. "Brace, I've seen Abbs fight. Trust me when I tell you, I'm not getting in her way – my nose is just too perfect." She crinkled said perfect nose.

She was referring to our fight classes on Earth, where I may have broken a few of the girls' noses.

"All four of those incidents were accidents," I said in my defense.

She snorted.

As soon as I was under the window I reached up to grip the wooden slats. I only had to pull my body weight up a few inches to see out. I paused at a loud banging noise. Spinning my head around, I could see Brace slamming his crossed arms into the wooden slats.

"I'll come for you. Don't mistake me, Abigail. And I'm going to be ... annoyed ... when I get over there." For some reason, the depth of his tone sent a thrill of excitement through me.

What was he so worried about? I was just going to have a little peek. What's the worst that could happen?

Damn it, I had to stop saying that.

I threw a look over my shoulder; it was pure challenge. Yeah, I did feel pretty safe in my barred cell. Lucy had sat down at this point, pulling Samuel with her.

"This is great. Wish I had some popcorn, though." Her hands were clasped in front of her, face alight with delight as if she'd just settled in to watch her favorite movie. "Ten bucks on Abby."

I grinned, none of the First Worlders would have a clue what 'ten bucks' was. They didn't use money; their world ran on a much more efficient barter-for-skills system.

Another burst of noise from outside drew my attention again. It sounded like there were a lot of Spurns arguing out there. I couldn't quite make out the words, especially with all the lisping. I still had a grip of the slats, so I slowly pulled myself up. Swearing echoed around the room behind me.

Ignoring the noise, I enjoyed the familiar burn in my muscles. I was going crazy locked in this little cell, so even a small physical release was welcome.

Once my eye level was above the ridge I could see a large group gathered. There were many Spurns with the same blue hair we'd already seen, but for the first time there were also Spurns with green, yellow and gray hair. They stood around a crouched girl.

My observations were cut off as strong hands gripped me around the waist. I was almost yanked off the bars, but at the last second managed to catch hold again.

"I swear to the Walker gods, Red, you're going to be the death of me."

At the sound of his voice, I let go in shock and Brace and I tumbled down.

Using his nicely muscled chest, I dug my elbow in as hard as I could to push myself up to stand. He groaned and I looked toward his old cell. There were large holes in both doors. Brace-size holes. I turned my eyes toward the angry towering-over-me man.

"How ... what did you do?" I stuttered out.

He shrugged, but his expression was burning – I felt like prey, and I wanted to run, fast.

"You know I can manipulate energy, and my power levels are no different here."

"What. The. Crap." Lucy, showing no fear, punched him in his thigh, which was the easiest place for her to reach. "Are you telling me that you could have gotten us out of here straight away?"

She pulled her fist back to hit him again, but Samuel gathered her up in his arms before she could.

I laughed. "Violent little thing, isn't she?"

Truth be told, both of us had a slight tendency to hit first, ask questions later, courtesy of the world we grew up in. Brace's expression lifted from burning anger to mild irritation. I might have even seen a small flicker of amusement as he held his hands up in surrender.

"Yes, I could have broken through these little wooden slats. But I figured Red was hoping for a more diplomatic solution, considering we need to stay here until we find this half-Walker."

"You're lucky you're hot, Brace, because I'm not finding much else to like about you right now," Lucy said, continuing to shoot dirty looks at him, but she was at least no longer trying to dodge around Samuel to punch him again.

"Let's leave now, before we are recaptured, and see if we can find someone to talk to about our situation." Lucas had moved to stand in the center of the room.

With an exasperated snort, I elbowed Brace as I pushed past him.

Lucas smiled when I reached his side. "Probably better to keep that little temper under control when we step out of here."

I ignored him by walking past without a second glance. Screw saving Brace. Those Walker gods better save me from impossible, arrogant know-it-all men. I was just about at the barred door to the exterior when Brace strode past me – someone had his speedy pants on. Stepping to the front, his boot smashed into the heavy wooden door. It flew off the frame to land outside on the sand.

Show-off.

"He gets to smash things, but when I do it I have a bad temper," I muttered as I followed him out.

The weak sunlight was back, but I knew from our few days here it was soon to be replaced by four-strong moons. Their moonlight was blue tinged and as bright as daylight back home.

We didn't make it more than ten steps before Spurns came running from all directions. We were surrounded within a few moments.

"Do not move or I will be forced to end you without a trial," a tall blue-haired man lisped in a low tone.

He was a pillar standing before the masses of four-hair-colored Spurns. A few of the five-prong trident-style weapons were pointed in our direction – they looked like big forks. I was intrigued by the strange texture of these weapons – they looked like coral – and they were brightly colored.

"There has been a mistake made here. We are not thieves or criminals." Lucas, as a future Emperor, had the best diplomacy skills. He had both of his hands held up before him. "We're travelers from another world, simply looking for adventure and new experiences. You cannot hold us prisoner any longer. We have rights, and we demand to be released now."

The Spurns muttered.

"Hair is short."

"Unnaturally tall."

A nervous energy was building amongst the smooth-skinned, shiny pink people.

"What is this world you have journeyed from?"

It took me a moment to understand her lisped question. Spurn speech was difficult to follow, especially if they spoke fast. The green-haired woman – well, it was more of an emerald, similar tone to my own eyes but darker – who'd spoken, was waiting impatiently.

"First World is our home planet; it's far from here, and is only around sixty percent water, vastly different from your own." At Lucas' words, another series of mutters and gasps spread through the group.

I hadn't realized First World had even less water than Earth. Interesting.

"That's why we disturbed your Sacred Isle. We cannot breathe under water," I added as soon as there was a lull in the Spurn chatter.

The tall blue-haired Spurn turned around. "Is any of this true?"

"Yes, Ladre sir. Our initial examination determined they have no gills. And they weren't found with any of our wood or cucreamer either." Our guard stepped forward to speak.

He locked eyes with me briefly, and I smiled in appreciation.

Shifting my gaze, I examined Ladre closely, trying to find his 'gills'. Eventually I spotted tiny slits on the side of his neck. They were subtle, almost flat and did not lift or flap as he spoke. Just for underwater breathing?

Ladre turned back, catching my blatant examination.

45

"I can see that you are not Spurns." Clear lenses flicked over his eyes as he spoke. "But your arrival coincides at a time of great unease; we've had thefts off our Sacred Isle. This is why we have treated you as criminals; you were discovered here right after this event."

No 'innocent until proven guilty' on Spurn; though they hadn't just killed us, so maybe that was a little unfair. I also wondered why there was no real surprise that we just happened to saunter onto Spurn from First World. If 'aliens' had strolled on to Earth from another planet, I was pretty sure the leaders would have a few questions. Were we not their first 'alien' visitors?

"They cannot be allowed to roam free on Spurn, doing this adventuring." The emerald-haired woman stepped forward, her movements awkward but controlled. "They cannot traverse the waters. They are unknown, and that is dangerous. We should just kill them now and save the future trouble."

I was distracted by Brace, whose entire body had tensed. The muscles in his chiseled jaw started to twitch. Tick ... tick ... tick. He was not a fan of this woman. And here I was, finding her so delightful. His sooty fringe of black lashes lowered briefly as he fought for control. I placed a hand on his arm to calm him before he blew them all up or whatever he was planning. I still didn't know exactly what his First-World powers entailed.

His eyes locked me in, his gaze intense.

As I pulled my hand away I reminded myself to breathe. My distraction had at least resulted in him looking a little less murderous, but it had left me all girly and flustered as usual.

"Quiet, Gladriel. I know you have history here but your first instinct should not be to kill." As Ladre turned back to us, he missed the flash of hatred that shone in her cold yellow eyes.

If I was him, I'd be watching my back for sure.

I examined her more closely. What was up with her attitude? What had we ever done to her? Or was she just a bitch? I knew it happened; sometimes people are just ass-hats.

"We can't leave yet; the energy we used to arrive on your world is currently unavailable to us," I said, not without a little annoyance. "So instead of killing us, maybe you can just house us for a short time. You know, as a second option."

"I will take responsibility for them while they are here. Until they leave, they will be by my side." An emerald-haired male appeared from the middle of the group.

Gladriel spun around. Her pink features flattened into irritated lines. "Raror, what are you doing?" she hissed at him.

"They just said they cannot leave, and you say they cannot be allowed to roam on their own, so logic dictates that they will need an escort while they are here." He stepped closer, his hair flowing behind him.

Ignoring the drama, I continued to observe closely. All of the Spurns had long hair, at minimum to mid-back, but those who spoke out and carried an aura of being in charge had hair that reached to their knees. There were four distinct hair colors, but no variances within their tone. And all of the four hair colors were exactly the same shade, none lighter or darker, none with streaks or fading. *Did they age?* I could see some discrepancies in their appearance, but there were definitely no very young or old present.

It was like watching an intensely three-dimensional movie. I had so many unanswered questions, but clearly flicking to the end wasn't an option. And, although it had taken awhile, I found it less challenging now to understand the lisping way they spoke. Well, I'd at least stopped wanting to say 'Huh?' after every second word.

Gladriel appeared frozen, her eyes mere slits across her face. Her features remained stone-like as she turned around to speak again.

"My son has decided that the Earon clan will house these other-worlders." She spat the words at us. "This is about Talina," she muttered.

If I hadn't had Walker hearing, I'd probably have missed it.

Who was this 'Talina'?

My heart started to race as a woman stepped up to Raror and smiled.

Could it actually be that easy?

She was different from the average Spurn, taller than most – though still shorter than me. She had striking features. Her smooth skin was creamy rather than pink like the rest of the Spurns. Her face was round rather than elongated, and she had long lustrous emerald hair with flecks of black. Unlike the others, she had brown eyes in a sea of yellow, and eyelashes and brows, whereas the others had none.

Lucy caught my eye, her head starting a continuous nod in the unusual woman's direction – in case I'd missed it the first five times she'd done it.

I laughed silently; subtle just isn't in Lucy repertoire. And, if I wasn't mistaken, we might just be staring at my half-Walker.

Chapter 3

When most of the arguing had subsided, they led us out of the clearing and toward the beach. During our time I'd noticed a few new Spurn characteristics. They were very cliquey, mainly staying in their hair-color group. My half-Walker was the only exception, sometimes crossing paths with Ladre, the blue-haired leader who'd first confronted us. Was something going on there? They certainly exchanged lots of quick flicking glances, but there was definitely no touching.

As we arrived at some small lowset buildings, most of the inhabitants dived under the eaves. I wondered why until a face full of salt water assaulted me. Judging by the misty spray pouring from all sides of the structure and the relief on their faces, they needed to stay wet.

Whilst I enjoyed my observations, documenting as much information as I could, most of my attention was focused on Talina. I was afraid to lose sight of her. I probably didn't have to worry, though. In between glancing at Ladre, she would often catch my eye, as if she was keeping tabs on me too.

Everyone turned as Ladre moved onto the first step of the building.

He cleared his throat, and all noise ceased. "We are still going in to have a council meeting. We must discuss other options now for the destruction and theft off the Sacred Isle, if it's not connected to these foreigners."

Pink faces shone with respect as they faced him.

With one last smile at his people, he turned and stepped inside.

Gladriel climbed onto the top step. "Raror, you must stay and mind your ... new friends. Do not let them wander; they are not welcome on this isle." With a toss of her head that made her emerald hair shimmer, she entered the building.

Small groups broke away from their clans to follow them into the structure. And just like that we were no longer prisoners or suspects, which was suspiciously trusting of them.

"Well, she's a pleasant piece of work, isn't she?" Lucy's eyes crinkled in annoyance as she glared after Gladriel.

"Yes, I am very sorry; my mother is not the most even-tempered Spurn. She doesn't like strangers, and unfortunately many of the collective reflect her attitude."

We spun around to face the half-Walker. Talina had wasted no time approaching us, stopping a few feet away on the sand. Her voice was soft and gentle, without the lisp.

"So what are you really doing on Spurn?" she continued, her question more prying than her soft manner of speaking indicated.

"Well, there's a high possibility that we're actually looking for you," I replied. I was on a deadline, no time to pretend otherwise. "We need to tell you about your father and explain a rather crazy situation."

Her eyes widened. I could tell my words had shocked her. But I had her interest and complete attention. And also Raror's, who was at her side in an instant.

"Talli, there is no need for you to speak about this. I promised you I would look after them until they could leave. Let's not stir anything up." He had to look up to meet her eyes.

It was hard to distinguish expressions on his hairless features, but I guessed he was pleading with her.

She laid one of her pale hands on his arm, her fingers lacking the obvious membranes that I could see between each of Raror's digits.

"Raror, I have suffered my entire life for weaknesses that are not my fault. If it wasn't for your protection, I have no doubt my half-status on Spurn would have resulted in my death."

I doubted that. Walkers were hard to kill. But, who knew? Judging by what I'd seen of Gladriel, she was a woman who would definitely eat her young.

Talina must have noticed my expression. "On Spurn, it is survival to the extremes. My mother *would* have been the one to kill me if it wasn't for the strength of Raror."

She had just taken a reasonably accurate guess at my thoughts ... unless.

"Can you read my mind?"

I had to constantly remind myself that people on worlds other than Earth had this ability. Josian had worked with me to develop a strong shield of protection, but maybe they could circumvent that here.

She shook her head, the breeze lifting the flowing emerald locks. Her hair was amazing; it almost appeared to be moving with a life of its own.

"I have not attempted to. That would be unforgivably rude. If you are worried, do not be afraid. Whenever I have brushed your mind, I have felt a strong barrier. In fact, all of you appear to be well protected."

I glanced at Lucy. She remained a puzzle. No one had figured out why her thoughts were safe. Being from Earth, and without active energy, she should have no shields.

Talina continued to stand before us in a meek and timid manner, as if she expected us to start yelling at her. I hated to see anyone so downtrodden; it was as if she'd been kicked every day. Shifting my heavy mass of salt-ridden curls, I tried to think of something to say that might make her feel better. I remembered her words to Raror earlier.

"You know, Talina, I think the rest of Spurn has it the wrong way around."

She frowned, the confusion evident on her face.

"You aren't the one with weaknesses; it's them. They just haven't realized it yet."

"What exactly does that mean?" a blue-hair who had been lingering nearby lisped at us.

"Well," I drawled in annoyance, fixing the interrupter with my famous glare. "Where should I begin? From my very short observation, all of you seem to linger under these ocean-mist things, and yet I see that Talina remains here and is looking remarkably dry."

I shrugged, letting them deduce the rest. Talina smiled. I think it was the first time I'd seen any solid emotion from her.

"Yes, I can remain out of the water indefinitely, but if the average Spurn allows their hair and body to dry out they could die," she said, sounding far too innocent, as if she would just give an honest answer to anything we asked.

Judging by the angry glares, the other Spurns did not look happy to have that particular vulnerability exposed to us.

"Bang!" I said loudly. "Number one way you're weaker. And number two, Talina's sturdier on land."

From the way she moved, she was obviously more co-ordinated than they were.

She nodded. "It's strange. This is the first time I have ever stepped foot onto solid land and, whereas I fall behind in the ocean, here I'm comfortable and, well, not a freak."

I found it amusing that on this planet her similarities to First Worlders was a disability. We must have looked like true aliens to the other Spurns.

"And how does any of this help the half on a world that is predominantly water?" The freaky lenses flicked over his yellow eyes as he spoke.

Their attitude was really starting to annoy me, especially the way he referred to her as 'the half' as if she didn't even warrant a name.

"Well, fish-boy, have you ever considered that she won't always live on this world?" Lucy, who'd been standing close by, challenged him.

"We are not fish, you other-worlder imbecile."

Lucy tossed her blond curls. "I disagree: you have gills, flippers and are slimy. Sounds like fish to me."

He shifted forward, to do what I have no idea, but he stumbled before he reached Lucy, sprawling at her feet. Lucy let a brief grin cross her lips, before turning her head in a disdainful manner. His friend dragged him up quickly, and they left without incident, moving to the other side of the building. Our men, who had tensed for a moment, relaxed again beside us.

Another smile graced Talina's impassive features. "Thank you," she said, "but you will find yourself in many challenges if you continue to defend me."

Lucy and I shrugged. That was nothing new for us. Brace looked at Samuel and in sync both snorted with laughter. Come on. We weren't that bad.

"Shut it, douche-wads." Lucy kicked sand in their direction.

Talina shuffled backwards, as if unsure of what we were doing or afraid of our joking. I patted her arm, meaning to be reassuring, but instead I was shocked at how cool she felt to touch.

"That's amazing," she said, rubbing her bicep, "you're even warmer than me, and I'm warmer than Raror."

Gee, fish-boy must feel like an ice cube.

"So what can you tell me about my father?" She finished her words in a rush and there was a glimmer of hope in her brown eyes. They were not the same liquid chocolate of Brace's. They were much lighter – but still lovely.

"Let's sit on the beach." I indicated the way with my hand.

This was going to be a bit of a story, and I really wanted to move away from all the curious eyes.

She nodded. "We have to stay close to the ocean for Raror."

57

Right, I'd forgotten all about our 'guard'. He was standing a short way from us, but I could see the unhappiness on his face. He didn't object when we turned to leave the main group, only pausing at a distant but unbroken thrashing sound from the tall trees to our right. No one moved or showed any sign of worry; they just faced the noise, waiting to see.

Should we be panicking? Was this an attack?

I couldn't exactly take comfort in the Spurns' calm faces. I was pretty sure they only had two emotions: nothing and angry. Eventually, as the forest rustling grew louder, I could also make out the sound of heavy panting.

A blue-haired Spurn stumbled into sight.

He was bleeding heavily from a large jagged wound on his right side. His blood, which was almost purple in color, had soaked his loin cloth.

He lurched in a swaying motion as he reached the group.

"Tell Ladre ..." he gasped, "tell him the creature ... it's back ... Jonah dead." The words were disjointed but understandable.

The group didn't hesitate. A few dashed into the building, and others took off in the direction from which the bleeding Spurn had come.

"You girls stay here. We'll see if we can assist." Samuel leant down to give Lucy a brief kiss.

Brace locked me in his gaze and nodded. Lucas smiled his usual charming, obnoxious grin before falling into line. With Raror leading the way, our three men left us standing there on the beach.

I looked at Lucy. "Did they just? – seriously – did that just happen?" I knew I wasn't making much sense, but I was annoyed.

"I'm not sure, Abbs." She shook her head. "But I think we were just dismissed to sit on this beach like little women and, like, knit scarves until the heroes return."

Talina looked at us in confusion. "They are just protecting you, right?"

I shook my head, hands on my hips. "No way, not on our world. We girls have the right to kick butt as much as the men. We don't sit on the side-lines for anyone. Come on, let's go," I said, waving my arms in a forward motion.

In my experience, men usually got into more trouble than they prevented.

Talina hesitated briefly, but with an almost unheard sigh she pushed her beautiful long hair over her shoulder and joined us.

We stepped around a few female Spurns who were crouched on the ground tending to the injured male.

Before we could set of, our journey was intercepted by the council streaming out of the building. Since we had no idea where to go, we simply fell in behind them, although it was frustrating keeping to the slow pace of the less co-ordinated Spurns. I breathed through my exasperation, taking my time to observe our surroundings.

Lucy must have been doing the same. "Where are the waiters that bring you those little drinks in coconuts with umbrellas?" she asked as we jogged past gorgeous expanses of white sandy beaches. The grains twinkled enticingly in the sunlight.

I sighed, giving her a half-smile. "Yes, why didn't we land on one of those islands in the 'Caribbean' that we read about in the compound. Instead our island paradise is full of blood-thirsty fish-people who want to kill us and use our bones for their soup or something."

"Word, Abbs. Aunt Frannie has a lot to answer for."

I thought I heard a tinkling laugh from my other side, but when I turned, Talina was silent. As a group we dashed between huge plantations of trees. They were tall, with thick trunks and a few scattered leaves up high. They reminded me of bamboo but with thicker stems.

The weather was balmy, the sunshine not hot, but everything still felt warm. As we finally burst free of the trees, we could hear shouts ahead of us. We'd ended up at the easternmost point of the land. At first all I could see were endless oceans, where the water looked calm, blues and greens intermingling across the vast expanses.

More shouts drew my attention and I saw a group of men standing waist-deep in the shallows. All around them were ominous trails of what looked suspiciously like blood.

"What's out there? What are they fighting?" Lucy asked as she stood next to Talina, both of them scanning the scene.

My eyes widened as I caught sight of Brace and Lucas. They were further out than everyone else, towering head and shoulders above them. Suddenly, from the darker depths of the water, just beyond the blood, rose ... well, a freaking monster.

"Uh, Talina. What the crap is that?" I gulped.

In sync, the three of us took a step back.

"I don't know. I have never seen anything like that in the waters before. It is almost like our water-dragons but ... it has been changed." She brought up both hands to grasp at her face.

The creature had many limbs, like an octopus, but it was scaly with a mix of colors: dark stormy grays and dirty greens. Its head was massive, with a long snout and rows of sharp and lethal-looking teeth. It was twelve feet tall, and at least that in width. Snaking out one of its limbs, we simultaneously gasped as it wrapped the length around Lucas, its movement so quick there wasn't time for Lucas to react. As it lifted him into the air, I took off toward them.

Must have taken a crazy pill today.

"Why do you always have trouble remembering to run away from the monsters?" Lucy cursed as she grabbed at me and missed.

I sloshed through until I was thigh-deep in the water, surrounded by four-hair-colored Spurns. In front of me I could see Ladre and Brace working together to free Lucas.

Ladre gripped his trident and dived down to stab at the creature. Its green goopy blood sprayed around, adding another layer to the film of muck surrounding us.

Brace shot off small energy balls. The moment he released one, he already had another gathered in his hands. In a perfectly co-ordinated move, Ladre stabbed in deep and Brace shot an energy ball from his left hand straight at the beast. With a strangled roar, the creature flinched and the tentacle that had been holding Lucas retracted. He dropped with a splash into the deeper water.

"Get him out now," Ladre ordered over his shoulder.

Three blues disappeared from sight – diving below the surface. They made no ripples as they traversed through the waters. I was amazed and slightly jealous.

The beast turned its attention to Brace. From all sides the tentacles moved forward to surround him.

Something inside me snapped.

Panic and anger flooded my system, and suddenly I felt it. My energy pulsed at me, responding to my emotion. I shoved my way past those blocking my path. I'd had no Walker fight training – there hadn't been time before we left – so I did the only thing I knew – drew from the endless pit that existed inside me.

I was only a few feet from Brace. With his giant height, the water was waist-deep, though for me it sat just below my shoulder. My energy hummed – comforting and familiar – and a warmth spread through me, I wondered what looked like right then. Dirty, tired, in the same stink-ass clothes for a week – all of that paled as the energy flowed through me.

"She's magnificent ... glows ... the marks are glowing." A Spurn close to me spoke out loud. Other words surrounded me, but I barely registered them.

As if he sensed my presence, Brace swung around with fires of hell burning in his narrowed eyes.

"Pretty sure I told you to stay on the beach, Abigail."

I was always Abigail when he was really pissed off.

He was just snaking out an arm to grab at me when he had to dive under the water to avoid an attack. Two tree-like limbs thrashed about, attempting to encase him from either side, while a large spike stabbed out from the center of the creature.

To my left I noticed the Spurns gliding past with Lucas in tow. Out of the corner of my eye, I registered that they had dragged him up onto the beach, where Lucy immediately jumped on top of him to stop him returning to the ocean.

Figuring he was okay, I turned back to the creature.

The energy I'd gathered was starting to ache. It wanted to be free; I could feel it pushing against my restraints. But I needed the perfect moment, and I couldn't really step any closer because the ocean floor dropped away dramatically.

A shadow in the water startled me as Brace emerged, streaming water from him. Luckily, I'd already dived away, so when his long arms swiped through the free air, he just missed me. He intended to drag me to shore, and I needed to use this energy first.

My dive took me into the salty depths, but luckily I found my footing again and rose spluttering from the water. Two feet from me, Brace groaned as he ran his hands through the dark wet strands of his hair. I noted the frustration on his face, but before I could say anything Lucy shouted from the beach.

I spun around.

Samuel and Lucas were holding her back as she tried to get into the water. Her eyes were frantic. It took me a moment to decipher her words over the noise.

"Abby, turn around! That thing is heading straight for you."

Too slow, I swung my head in time to see the large slimy green limb as it smashed into my side. Its power was incredible. The force knocked out my breath and a few ribs, I think. I was flung far out into deeper water, managing to keep my energy ball from dispersing as I sank, breathlessly, into the depths. My two swimming lessons on First World had given me enough skills to scissor-kick my legs, slowing my descent but not reversing it.

The water looked depthless; I could see the darkness beneath me, where the weak light of the sun did not reach. It was eerie in the quiet expanse as I continued to fight the current.

Then strong arms encased me. I struggled before noticing the emerald hair that surrounded me. Looking to my left, I saw it was Raror.

As soon I stopped fighting he dragged me toward the surface, minute trails of bubbles dispersing from the tiny slits down his neck. The water surrounding us grew steadily lighter until finally I was free.

I gasped in a couple of breaths, my aching lungs thanking me with puffs of relief.

Raror's freezing cold hands released me before grabbing my right leg and dragging me through the water. When I looked around, I could see why.

We were in the shadow of the creature.

Brace was close beside us and he had hold of one of the tentacles, while he hacked at it with a medium-sized knife. With a roar of pain, the creature snagged him with one of its many limbs, lifting him into the air above its core.

Raror powered us through the water like a mini-speed boat. I needed to help Brace before I was too far away. Ignoring the stabbing pain from my ribs, I reformed my heavy sphere of glowing energy.

I pictured it as a large torpedo.

I waited a moment ... and another... just for that perfect opportunity.

The creature reared its head, and I was staring into a huge expanded jaw that had opened to devour Brace. Its eyes flashed with at least twelve large dark globes. I knew this was my best chance; the creature had allowed a moment when its core was unshielded and vulnerable. Closing my own eyes and drawing on my control, I set the energy free, depleting myself as much as possible.

A hoarse scream left my mouth at the burn of release.

"Red, what's happening over there?" Brace bellowed from his position above the creature.

Despite the fact he was about to become monster food, he seemed to be more interested in what was going on with me. At this point I could barely keep my head up. As water splashed in my face, it took every effort not to fall forward and drown. A large burst of light forced my eyes closed. I didn't even move to see if I had missed or hit my target.

I was semi-conscious enough to feel the rough sand as I was dragged from the water.

"What happened out there, Raror? What's wrong with Abby?" Talina's cool hands, though warmer than her brother's, help to position me on the beach.

"So I'm guessing you're going to be a little low on energy for a while again, Abbs," Lucy said as she moved to cradle my head on her lap.

I could sense her worry as she stroked my hair, which felt like it weighed a thousand tons. My lashes flickered, but my lids wouldn't obey my command to open.

"Urghhh." I managed a slight moan.

A shadow fell over me. The weak light behind my eyelids disappeared.

"Did he make it back to shore?"

The voice sounded like Lucas'. But it was hard to tell since it was minus his usual flirty arrogance. Maybe getting attacked by a huge sea-monster had given his over-confidence a much needed deflating. He had to be asking about Brace, and just hearing his worry gave me a shot of panic and adrenalin. I had no problem forcing my eyes open then.

"Brace?" I said out loud, not caring what Lucas might think.

From my current position I could only see Lucy. She wasn't even looking at me, but was staring over her shoulder toward the water. I began to struggle, like a turtle that was on its back and couldn't get the right way up again. Another shadow fell across my face.

"Sorry, Red, you're going to have to find another way to get rid of me." The sound of his beautiful accent sent a wave of relief through me.

He moved around me to stand with a leg on either side of my hips. It was hard to tell against the sun-glare behind him, but I was pretty sure he was scowling.

Big surprise.

Able to finally move my head, I drank in the sight before me. In that moment I was consumed by a single thought, one I'd never tell him: Brace was the closest thing to perfection I'd ever seen. Soaking wet, his dark hair slicked back off the perfect planes of his face, black fitted shirt plastered to muscles. Muscles which I guessed were honed from hard work, not enhancing drugs. He was like a god rising from the sea. I forced my right arm to move, lifting my hand to check if I'd started to drool. It was hard to tell with the sea water still dripping from me.

"So, I'm pretty sure that someone has a little problem with obeying a direct command." Brace's eyes flashed; they almost looked black.

I narrowed my own eyes.

Oh, no, the hell he didn't. Direct command?

69

Someone was about to learn I wasn't one of his soldiers.

Without thought, my leg flew through the air in an attempt to crack Brace right in his jewels. But as usual the smug ass anticipated my move and now had a hold of my calf muscle, keeping my leg suspended in the air. Luckily he didn't lift it too high. I was pretty sure my ribs would pop right out of my chest if they received more abuse.

"You're going to have to move quicker than that, Abigail." His eyes promised me to-be-determined punishment.

Bring it on.

My entire body tightened at the thought of our battle.

I couldn't help the images that flooded my mind. I might have only had one kiss in my life, but my imagination needed no help.

Brace let me go before bending from his lofty heights to haul me over his shoulder. I groaned as my ribs protested. But I was surprised that they didn't feel quite as bruised as before.

"Thanks for the assistance out there, Red. But it would save my nerves and sanity if you could stop risking yourself. I had it under control." He patted me lightly on the butt.

I kicked out at him again.

Groaning, he wrapped an arm around me, limiting my movements.

I twisted until my face was close to his. "Why do you care, Brace? What have you dreamed about us? And why did you kiss me?"

The questions spilled from me. They'd been burning a hole in my mind for days.

He looked sideways at me. "Because you are mine." The statement was short and it just about stopped my heart.

I shook my head, dispelling some of the water in my heavy hair. Had I heard that correctly? I twisted around, attempting to see more of his expression.

"You're mine to protect, Abigail, and I will not let anyone or anything hurt you again."

I ignored my surge of disappointment; I should have realized this was just a duty to him.

"I'm no one's to protect. I look after myself," I said.

I felt, more than heard, his second deep groan.

"That's where you're wrong, Red." Now I could barely hear him. He'd turned away to speak into the breeze. "You are mine."

He ignored any further attempts at conversation. I turned my attention back to Lucy and Talina, who were following behind us.

"Did I kill it?" I asked.

Talina shook her head. "There was a lot of blood in the water. You definitely hurt it, but it took off, faster than any of us could follow."

Her worried tone said much more than her statement.

Sighing, I closed my eyes, and pretty soon the rhythmic movement of walking, and that intoxicating scent that was all Brace, had me drifting in a half-sleep state.

Chapter 4

I was standing in my room on First World staring at four pale-pink walls. Lallielle appeared in front of me and I realized I was dreaming.

"Mom!" My voice sounded a little disjointed. This was different to my dreams on Earth.

She stepped closer to me. Her long black hair flowed down her back and her green eyes, lighter than my own, were shadowed with concern.

"Aribella, thank the gods. I've been trying to dream-span you for days." She sounded almost the same, maybe less vibrant, a little more one-dimensional.

I couldn't move toward her, but speaking was easy enough.

"We were captured as soon as we landed. We've just managed to convince them to let us free ... or kind of under house arrest." I still couldn't move. "Have you spoken with Dad?"

I needed to ask him about my powers.

Lallielle shook her head. "No, I've tried a few times, but wherever he is, I cannot reach him."

No wonder she'd been upset; she hadn't been able to reach anyone.

I sucked in a breath. "Is that normal?"

She shook her head and shrugged.

Great answer.

Since I didn't know how much time we had, I decided to tell her about my energy.

"So my powers have sort of shorted out ... since I opened the initial portal. I've only been able to use them one more time." I raised my brows, the only thing I could move. "They're kind of temperamental."

She gasped. "I don't like that, Aribella. You're stuck on Spurn?"

Her face was turning into one big wrinkle of concern. She was probably flashing back to the time she couldn't find me on Earth.

"This must have something to do with your halfling nature. Not even Josian could guess what we were going to produce."

I laughed. "Don't you worry about that. You produced all kinds of awesome." I'd teased half a smile out of her. "And, yes, we are stuck here for the foreseeable future, although I've already found the halfling. Tell Frannie that planet one was as easy as she promised me. Although the natives are a little blood-thirsty and there's a crazy-ass creature in the water."

"Aribella," she admonished me. "I'll let her know, and if she has any additional advice I'll pass it on next time I manage to contact you."

"Why couldn't you contact me until now?" Were everyone's powers crapping out today?

Her image froze then.

I waited an extra second, before trying to move forward again. I swore angrily as I was once again contained. The scene began to fade, and with a pop, I was back inside my own head. But at the same time I wasn't there alone. My mind flooded with a repeated phrase and even though I had only heard it just one other time, I had no problem recalling every word.

Children of Gods, born unknown and alone,
the seven are needed to eliminate. Take heed,
for baby will not live till four and one year
unless removed from the world here.
The youngest and strongest to collect.
Lost and alone, a god-man is the key.
Gather the Halflings, stone and fear.
The end of days is written in mineral.

75

It was a warning – or prophesy, if you could call it that – from Francesca. I wanted to open my eyes and stop the chanting of words but I couldn't.

How had I jumped from Lallielle to this? I guess, if I was honest, until this point I hadn't really spent much time thinking about these words. I didn't put much faith in prophesies. Although most of what was there made sense, it was about the seven half-Walkers and how we were the key to preventing the end of the world. But gather the stone and fear? Written in mineral? It was too vague, and that was part of my pet hate of soothsayers. Just give me facts, not this crap that can be interpreted in twenty different ways.

I wrenched my mind free from the chant and forced my eyes open. I didn't have time to get lost in those words. I needed to do my job, and that was to collect Talina and move on to the other worlds.

Sitting upright, the last echoing vestige of the words faded from my mind as I stared at my surroundings.

I was camped out on the ground, but it was soft. I realized I lay on some type of mesh throw rug. The room looked like a living area, and if my slightly queasy stomach was any indication, the ground was shifting under me. I stumbled to my feet, my right hand pressed firmly against my chest. My throat tightened, unexpressed tears and emotions brimming, threatening to burst free.

I was out of the dream but there was something wrong with me. Had the words affected me somehow or was this manipulation from an outside force? After a few deep breaths, I calmed and distracted myself by walking around the small room, stumbling occasionally from unexpected lurches.

The floor was timber. It was smooth, with an oily feel under my bare feet. There weren't many pieces of furniture. The main piece leaned against the back wall and I realized it was a strange-looking couch. It was bright blue in color, but the material was unusual, and appeared brittle enough to collapse if someone were to sit on it. Moving closer, I reached out to gently drag my hand along the arm, pulling back as my finger-tips caught on the rough material.

"It's made of coralline." A voice sounded from behind me.

I spun around to face Talina, who was standing in the open doorway.

"I wanted to check on you and see if you had woken yet." She smiled as she stepped inside. "The coralline grows in our waters. It's part of a living ecosystem. Once we remove it from the sea, parts of it petrify, but the rest continues to grow and change. It's the basis for most of our furniture."

That's what it reminded me of: coral – the way it grew in peaks and ridges, with many little turrets. Of course, I'd only ever seen pictures. The pollution on Earth had destroyed most of the fragile coral structures throughout the world, or so we were told. Never having set foot out of New York, I kind of just had to take their word for it. And from my experience their 'word' wasn't worth much.

"Where are we?" I managed to croak out, my voice husky from the salt water.

"You're on Gladriel's pontoon." She blinked rapidly.

As with the other Spurns, she had a clear lens which occasionally flicked up and down over her eyes.

"This is part of my area. We were no longer welcome on the isle; everyone had to make their way back to their territory. We've been traveling for about ten leagues."

My heart stuttered.

We weren't close to land. We were smack bang in the middle of the freaking ocean.

I pushed back my damp curls and without much thought reached for the comfort of my energy. In that moment I understood my previous emotional outburst. My energy felt empty, and I felt empty too. I was grateful Talina didn't notice my distress as she started talking again.

"Sorry about the wetness in here. The pontoons are designed to distribute a constant stream of humidity. It's enough that most Spurns suffer no discomfort, but you will probably feel damp."

Now that she'd mentioned it, I was slightly itchy and kind of wishing I hadn't swum in my clothes and let the saltiness dry on me.

"Where are my friends?" I croaked again, unable to clear my swollen throat.

"It's almost meal time; they're upstairs on the decking, waiting for us. I'll show you the way." She waved me forward as she moved toward the doorway.

I placed a hand on her cool arm to halt her for a second. "Did you collect our bags from the guards before we left the Isle?" I was not staying in these clothes a moment longer.

She shook her head. "I'm sorry, Abby. They won't release them until you leave Spurn; they seem to think that's incentive for you to behave and to get off the planet in a timely manner."

I croaked out bits of laughter. There was nothing in our bags but clothes and a couple of first-aid essentials.

"I will get you some netting. It is quite easy to learn the wrap."

I paused, looking down at Talina. She was wearing a pale blue netting now, but besides covering the essentials, the rest of her skin was bare.

"Are you telling me that everyone is wearing this?" I gestured to her skimpy attire. "All of my friends?"

With a slight grin, Talina nodded. "Uh, yes. Gladriel insisted that if we are to house you, then you must conform to as many of the Spurn customs as possible." She lowered her head. "Looking at the males of your clan, she might have actually done us all a favor ... for once."

My heart almost stopped beating. My face went burning hot as I mentally pictured Brace in one of the loin cloth garments. My feet began to move all by themselves. I was just about out the door when Talina's voice halted me.

"Would you like to change first, before you leave? Gladriel will not allow you to dine unless you are dressed appropriately. She is quite the sea-witch."

My arm caught the door, halting my pace. Looking back over my shoulder, I saw Talina hadn't moved and she still had that grin on her face.

"Yeah, sure, that would be great." I was calm; I would not go breaking my neck to see Brace shirtless.

Talina turned to rummage through a large wooden trunk tucked away in the corner. She emerged with two long strips of black material. I forced my feet to make their way back to the center of the room.

"This color will look stunning with your hair and red marking." She turned to me, holding the material aloft, her warm eyes sparkling.

She didn't ask me about my Walker marks, but I could hear the curiosity in her voice. She possessed such an obviously kind nature. I wasn't a horrible person, but if anyone messed with me or those I considered mine, I was inclined to go all psycho. Talina appeared to be a genuinely gentle soul. Could she really be half-Walker? I didn't get the impression that kind and gentle was part of their ... our nature. I could open my necklace and test it for sure, but I didn't want to scare her away before having the chance to explain everything.

"Okay, strip off your clothes." She gestured for me to throw them into a nearby bucket. "Stand tall and hold your arms out to the side. I'll hose you down and then we can get these wraps on."

She produced a large smooth device, like a bucket, but it was in the shape of a half-clam. I discarded my clothes and was turning around to face Talina when she dumped the entire contents of the shell on me.

"What the hell, Talina?" I spluttered as the clear liquid ran down into my mouth.

It didn't taste like water. Actually, it was similar to the fruit we had been eating here. I was amazed and grateful that it cleared the last clogging from my throat.

"Oh, sorry, Abby. I should have warned you. We don't generally wash, since we are always in the ocean, but the juice of the cucreamer fruit is our only means of fresh water."

"I guess that explains why we haven't needed anything to drink since we arrived here," I said, sardonically wiping the excess liquid off of my face.

It wasn't sticky. In fact, when I looked down I realized I was clean, as if it had literally sucked the dirt off as it flowed over me.

Once I was reasonably dry Talina showed me a simple but effective manner of wrapping the soft strips so they covered everything. It was pretty ingenious; they were secure and actually really supportive. She led me over to a reflective surface against the side wall. It wasn't a mirror, more like another of the giant shells, but it did echo a slightly distorted version of my image back at me. My red and black curls hung loose down my back, and the meshy wraps offered more coverage than a swimsuit. My mark was obvious, even all the way down my hip and thigh. I liked the mesh. I felt liberated, no clothes weighing me down, and they were amazingly soft and light.

Standing there, hair flowing free, Talina and I looked like Amazonian woman.

"Okay, let's leave; Gladriel doesn't like it if we're late for dinner." Talina's creamy features paled to a sickly white and her eyes widened.

Every time she mentioned her mother, the brown of her lovely eyes dulled and she retreated even further into herself. I didn't like it. I wondered what the odds of me making it through a dinner without punching Gladriel in the face were. Low, I'm sure.

I followed her from the room and we moved out to a central landing with a curved wooden stairwell that went both up and down. She led me up to the next level. We emerged out onto an open deck. The moons were in the sky, spanning the four corners. They cast that lovely blue tone. I liked it. It was as if the world was washed clean each night.

The first person I saw was Samuel. He stood stiffly against the railing, staring out over the expanses of the water surrounding us. In the distance, following in a line, looked to be many of the strange flat-bottomed pontoons. Samuel turned at the sound of our footsteps on the wooden decking. Before I could catch myself, I laughed.

He stalked over to me. "Don't even say it, Aribella. They gave us no choice."

He crossed his arms over his broad and bare chest. I didn't bother to look closely. You know, brother and all that. But I did notice the series of faded scars criss-crossing his arms. They were similar to Lucy's but so much more detailed. Some were the faded pale pink lines of aged scars, others were still a puckered red. I hadn't expected these physical reminders of his year-long imprisonment. For some reason I'd thought First Worlders healed all injuries.

"Abbs, I'm so glad you're awake. It's just spectacular out here. You have to come and see everything." Lucy bounced over to us.

She was wrapped in baby blue, which matched her eyes. Talina obviously liked to color-co-ordinate. Her curves were highlighted in a really obvious way; she looked like a mermaid from the ocean, blond curls flapping in the winds. I noticed Lucy's wraps were a little more detailed, hiding most of the red welts on her back. She stopped right before me. Taking a step back, she gave me a once-over. Lucy loved fashion. She never stopped trying to dress me like her own life-sized doll.

"Hot damn, Abigail. You look smoking. It's not really fair. These wrap things are designed for tall or thin. Not those of us that are ... curvy ... yeah, let's go with curvy." Both hands were planted on said curvy hips, lower lip jutted out in an exaggerated pout.

"So what has been happening since the Isle?" I ignored her, while continuing to look around.

I loved this area. The deck was huge, with a few different levels hidden from view. I couldn't see Brace or Lucas. Not that I was looking for them.

"We dragged your unconscious butt through the water, and Gladriel grudgingly let us board her pontoon. We're traveling back to the Earon's territory; apparently Spurns don't mix in each other's quadrants for too long. They end up having a hair-color dance-off or something."

I laughed at the mental images.

"What's an Earon?" Had that been mentioned before?

Talina took my arm, her other already clutching Lucy. She led us over to an outer deck that spread out over the side of the pontoon. Samuel didn't bother to follow. He just moved back to where he'd been before. This outer section had no railings, and it felt like we were flying above the water. There was a soft bedding spread out, like the one I had slept on till I woke.

"We are Earons." She ran her hand through her emerald hair as we sat.

The ocean was calm now, which helped settle my queasiness.

"There are four clans on Spurn. Baroons are the blues, the top clan, with the most territory and numbers. Earons are second; Yetle, the golden third; and the Gerks, the grays, are the smallest and least powerful clan. As the leader of the Baroons, Ladre holds dominance over basically all of the clans."

"Do all of you live on these boat things?" I gestured to the flat-bottomed barges that surrounded us.

"No, not everyone." Talina shook out her long hair. "Ladre spends most of his time in Silver City, a place under the sea, in the center of the four territories."

Seriously?

"Let me get this straight." Lucy sat forward, her face alight, eyes sparkling. "You can live under the sea? Do you just swim down there? What anchors it to the ground?"

"Why don't you all live there? Is there any way we can visit?" I added my questions.

Talina looked at us. "Hold up," she said, laughing. "Silver City is a huge underwater structure, built by the Spurns many moons ago. It is encased in a large tensile bubble, blown by the monstrone species."

I raised my eyebrows, but she continued before I could speak.

"They're an underwater species, mammalian, like Spurns, but they cannot breathe above the water. They are extremely rare. I've only ever seen one in my life. The strongest swimmers can make it down to the city without assistance, while the rest of us use the tube," her eyes flashed, "and before you ask, if we have time, I'll take you there and you can see it for yourself."

Lucy and I sat straighter. That would be a once-in-a-lifetime experience.

"The tube pumps essential air and nutrients down to the city, which means, if allowed, you can visit." Her wistful expression was trained on the horizon. "I have only been there once. I find it uncomfortable down there."

"So what's with you and Ladre, of the blue-hairs?" Her fascination with the only Spurn taller than herself had not escaped my attention.

Talina's pink skin darkened and her head dropped to a point where I couldn't see her expression anymore. She answered me while looking down.

"Next to my brother, Ladre is the best Spurn. He has all the power, but I've never known him to abuse it." A disdainful laugh escaped her. "And if you truly understood the nature of my race, you would understand how special he is."

"You should tell him how you feel." Lucy's eyes locked on Samuel as he continued to stare outwards from the side railing. "Life is short, Talli, and the worst that can happen is a bit of rejection, which won't kill you."

I could tell Lucy had to restrain herself from leaving us to stand beside Samuel. My friend was not an individual anymore; she was now invariably tied to another being. I just wished that her choice wasn't such a damaged man. I could tell that she was struggling to ignore his current distress. She noticed me watching her and smiled.

"It's just been a stressful few days for him. He doesn't like to be imprisoned, and seeing me in danger just wigs him out," she answered too softly for Talina to hear.

Reaching out, I squeezed her hand.

"I can't." We both swung around as the words burst from Talina. "If it was just rejection then that's something I could deal with. But it can never be."

I had a terrible feeling this was one of those insurmountable segregations of their society.

"Baroons will never mate with those outside; they are afraid to mar the purity of their clan." She was looking up again now, her voice flat. "And even if once-in-a-land-sighting they did deign to 'slum it', I'm a halfling, which is basically worthless here."

"The clans never inter-marry?"

"What's inter-marry?" Talina tipped her head to one side.

I laughed. "To be married is like being mated, but for life, and you aren't supposed to be with any others but the one you marry."

The 'supposed' part was what many Earthlings forgot.

She shook her head, the masses of emerald hair cascading out onto the wooden deck. "No, we never do that on Spurn. We have mating seasons, and some couples will be together for a few of those, but there is nothing like marriage here, we are a species of clans and family but our true nature is more solitary."

I was just opening my mouth to speak when male voices drifted over to us. The lisping of Raror was clear across the deck.

"... there's no fishing here. We don't eat our brethren."

My heart beat faster as I waited for them to approach. I wanted to pre-picture Brace in the loin cloth, but I didn't think I could mentally do it justice.

Talina stood. "Gladriel is requesting us for dinner," she said formally, her face falling.

I jumped to my feet in one easy motion. These mesh wraps allowed such a range of movement. Lucy was already at Samuel's side. He took her face into his hands, and as their lips touched in what even I could tell was a fiery kiss of passion, I turned away.

Only to find myself staring at a massive expanse of muscular sun-kissed chest.

Every speck of moisture that had been in my mouth disappeared. I tried to swallow once, but my muscles wouldn't obey me. Brace and Lucas were side-by-side, directly before me, laid out like a gift-from-the-gods. They were twin bookends, one so dark and dangerous and the other icy blond. However, it was Brace my eyes were glued to; it was Brace that for the fiftieth time took my breath away.

"Abby, you should look into procuring more of those garments for your wardrobe back on First World," Lucas said, speaking in his usual mix of formal and modern.

I tore my eyes from Brace to note Lucas was wearing a plain white wrap, which looked extra crisp against the dark honey tone of his skin. He was lean, but with prominent and well-defined muscles. His chest was virtually hair free; that, or they were so blond I couldn't see them.

"I have to disagree with Lucas," Brace interrupted, drawing my attention again. "I think there's a bit much of your flesh on show."

I managed not to drool over him as I flipped him off. That level of bossiness should be such a turn-off, but it wasn't dampening my interest at all.

Brace's responding grin was dark. But his eyes never left my face. The intensity had me squirming a little. His mesh matched my own in color, and right then all I could do was take as many mental pictures as I could for the future.

You could say that I was very aware that he was an oversized man. More heavily muscled than Lucas, but thankfully just falling short of being bulky. I hate bulky. His height saved him, allowing his grace and agility to carry his muscled chest and arms. But without looking top heavy.

I followed the muscles down, over his fifty-ish pack abs and muscled legs. His skin was tanned, not as honeyed like Lucas', but still shades darker than my own ivory tone. I caught a smirk from him. Clearly he was enjoying my perusal.

"Are you going to lick him?" Lucy's low words in my ear startled me out of my daze. "He does look lickable." She finished with her hands on her hips.

"No!" I blurted out in shock.

Well ...

No ... I shook my head ... no, I wasn't going to lick him.

"Lucy, you're not allowed to say any man is lickable, unless that man is me." Samuel didn't seem to have the same over-the-top-possessive streak that Brace was capable of; his words sounded semi-serious, but I was pretty sure he was joking.

Lucy winked at him, and her expression was hot enough that I wanted to blush.

Glancing back at Brace, I was relieved to see he hadn't reacted to Lucy's comment. I hoped he was far enough away not to have heard. Although, as I took one last glance ...

No, Abby, no licking.

"If you could all follow me downstairs, we have been requested." Talina stood next to Raror at the highest point of the stairway.

I managed to keep my tongue and eyes to myself for the journey down to the lower levels. More often than not, Brace's looks clouded my judgment, and I'd forget all the secrets and weirdness. But there was to be a confrontation between us in the not too distant future. I was at my limit of secrets.

Stepping into a large wood-paneled room on the bottom level, I realized that the water movement was much stronger down here.

Gladriel was waiting for us, already seated at her own little table. It looked to be made of coralline. She waved a hand, gesturing for everyone to take a seat on the ground. There were separate padded meshes laid out.

Raror and Talina sat on either side of her while the rest of us fell down in a rough circle.

I watched with interest as a bevy of emerald-hairs entered the room and placed little tables before us. More followed, handing around bowls. I wasn't surprised to find them filled with the pink fruit; it was a light pastel shade with a creamy seed-filled center, the way I remembered a melon from years before. But then we received a second plate, a type of slimy-looking salad. It held an array of green-toned weeds, which I had a sneaking suspicion was going to taste very salty.

"I apologize for the limited variety of nourishment," Gladriel started, her arrogant tone not sounding at all sorry, "but we do not eat other than krillonia, cucreamer and the blanch weeds."

I decided to try the weeds first. That way I could wash them down with the semi-sweetness of cucreamer fruit, which I already knew was edible. The first bite was as predicted: salty with a crisp and crunchy texture, and a tang in the aftertaste. But it wasn't half bad.

Before I knew it, I'd finished my entire portion. Lucy, looking a little green around the edges, offered me hers. Eagerly I grabbed it; I was starving. I still felt restless. My energy was depleted. I could feel the depths, but I wanted to fill it with something – anything – to staunch the aching hollowness. Before I knew it, all three of my bowls were empty and I was semi-content.

Sitting back, I noticed Gladriel had not touched her portion. She was staring at me, her yellow eyes cold.

"Why have you visited Spurn, and why do you wear that mark?" Her words were hasty, one running over the next.

I sucked in a breath, needing a minute to figure out the best way to broach the subject.

"Well," I finally said, "I'm here for Talina."

Silence echoed around the room. No one seemed willing to break the fragile air, but I had their undivided attention. Finally, Gladriel spoke.

"Talina?" Her pulse was visibly pumping in the pink skin on her throat. "How can she be special ... wanted ... needed for anything of importance?"

"Mother, for the last time, stop this." Raror was on his feet, the air around him echoing his anger. "Stop blaming Talli for your mistakes and hurts. It is not even Spurnian to keep holding on so hard to the wrongs you feel."

I expected Gladriel to rise to her feet in her usual wave of anger, but instead she shrank in on herself at her son's words. Raror faced me, and with a sigh of resignation spoke.

"I have known since her water-birth that Talli was both beyond-this-world special, and someone I would love more than my own self."

Talina's lashes fluttered at these words. She pressed one of her hands against her cheek, hard enough that her nails would be cutting small crescents into her lightly pinked skin.

"She's made me a better Spurn, and has given all of us a welcome insight into humility, empathy and sympathy." His words rose to a crescendo now.

I felt an urge to move back on my mat, but his will just wasn't strong enough for me to obey.

"I tell you this now, Abigail of First World, so you understand: I will never let my sister go without a battle."

"Raror, please." Talina's gentle voice drew our attention. "Please let Abby tell her story. I still do not know anything, and I long to understand."

Raror deflated as if the wind had died in his sails. He sat again.

And suddenly I had the floor.

I jumped right in this time, before we were interrupted by more angry family members or ... maybe pirates? It was a water world; it could happen.

"I'm a halfling, the same as you, Talina. And in fact our fathers are from the same race of ... people." I just couldn't bring myself to say god, at least not before giving a little more explanation. "I've only recently found this out myself. We're half-Walkers."

Talina nodded. "Yes, Gladriel has explained my father was Walker, and that he was from another world, but that is all she knew."

I shot a glance at Gladriel. Her gaze was fixed and I realized she was staring without focus into the center of the room. Her cold features showed no emotion.

"Walkers are an immortal race; they wander amongst the worlds, as they have no planet of their own. They're the very reason we all have stories and a history of gods."

"No ... No ... No. This can't be right," Gladriel whispered to herself over and over. Her head whipped up to lock me in that eerie yellow gaze. "Almastore was not powerful; I sensed nothing from him in the time he spent on Spurn." She sighed. "But he also assured me that there could be no child from our union, that damn liar."

"Walkers are very powerful, but I don't know much about them either. I spent very little time with my father before I had to leave to come here." I brushed my hair back from my face. "I do know that they can manipulate energy and can probably mask their own power, and that they have always believed that they could not have children outside their own race." I gestured to myself and Talina. "As you can clearly see, they were mistaken, but it's still extremely rare. Apparently, their halfling children, and there's only one on each planet, will only be carried to term by the most powerful woman on each of the youngling's planets."

A flash of arrogance crossed Gladriel's face.

"And that's what has led me to Talina. My job is to gather the halflings, and then together we need to contain the Seventine."

97

"What are the Seventine?" Raror spat out.

I blinked at his tone. Someone was not happy. "They're the anti-Walkers, basically. Created and contained in the origin, someone is releasing them. Which, according to – well, everyone – will spell disaster for all the worlds. The half-Walkers are all that can stop them." I wasn't sure I believed that, but the story had to be good or Talina would never leave.

"Thank god." Talina's words surprised me.

Instead of freaking out, she showed relief.

"Thank the gods. I finally have a purpose outside of the hell that has been Spurn."

It didn't look as if I was going to have much trouble convincing Talina to leave.

"Talina! No!"

Her brother, on the other hand, was going to be a far harder sell.

Talina locked eyes with Raror.

"You can't leave me, Talli. I'll have nothing without my family."

As she moved across the room to comfort him, he trapped me in a gaze of despair.

"Where is your proof of this? Why should we believe you? Why should I just let you take my sister away? For all we know, you are trappers, and have come to collect people from each of the planets. I know, once she is gone, there is no way

98

for me to protect her. I promised." He turned back to Talina. "I promised I would protect you always; how can I do that if you leave Spurn?"

I had no idea how to reassure him.

I looked to Lucy for help. She was the one most people instantly liked. They found me odd. But she just shrugged, her blond hair bouncing against her bare shoulders. My eyes moved again, searching for assistance. They locked on Brace and Lucas. In unison, as if they had been mentally discussing it, they both pointed to their right eye and traced the mark.

I needed to bring out the Walkers' origin stone, the moonstale crystal, to prove at least one part of my story.

"I can show you that we're from the same race, and you'll understand the meaning of my mark," I said as I reached for my world necklace.

It was the only personal item I had retained. Talina and Raror faced me, their heads tilted to the side in identical movements.

I hesitated with my hand on the clasp. Since my enlightenment, I hadn't stood so exposed in the light, and I remembered that last pain intimately. I also wondered what would happen to my permanent mark. Pushing that flash of doubt aside, I flicked open the clasp and let the yellow light bathe the room.

99

Chapter 5

The light filled the section of room where I was standing. It was always the same: the glittering crystals and my cravings for them. They were so hard to focus on. The shiny depths continually shifted and changed, even within the small cavity of my locket.

"Talli!" Raror's strangled gasp stole my focus.

Talina's eyes were huge as she looked around. Clearly she had no idea what was happening. I immediately moved a step closer. Her mark was different to mine, thicker, more tribal in design, and it was black, standing out starkly on her skin. She locked eyes with me, and a connection flowed between us. I could hear her voice in my head; it sounded like an inner monologue of panic.

Why is everyone staring at me? ... Abby's marks look stunning but why are they glowing so ...?

The words were faint and disjointed, but I picked them up like a radio wave. And then they were gone. Had she heard anything from me? As a precaution, I added another level of protection around my mind. Even with depleted energy, the shield protecting my thoughts never wavered.

"Get her a mirror or something," I said over my shoulder as I took another step closer.

"Abby, your marks are glowing red, and swirling even more than usual," Talina said in a half-whisper.

I sucked in a breath as she repeated the words I'd inadvertently picked up from her thoughts.

"Talli," Raror said again, capturing her attention, "you have marks too. Her story is true ... you are ..." His lisping was worse when he was upset. "You're going to leave me."

She shook her head. "No, I will never leave you here with Gladriel."

He shook his head, regaining his composure. "Right, you can't leave. I know the marks are there, but we have no way to verify any of the other information."

Raror faced me again. "We need to convene before the council to discuss this; Ladre would not

101

be happy for you to just stroll in here and take Talina away."

I was about to protest when an emerald-haired Spurn entered the room. He was carrying a smaller version of the shell mirror I'd used upstairs. As Talina stared at her new reflection, I realized Gladriel had not moved. She was still seated, and had now commenced eating her portion of the meal that she'd neglected earlier.

My jaw tightened and my hands clenched into fists. *Bitch.* I gave Talina a few moments to observe and feel the thrill of her marks before I slammed my locket shut. My anger flowed over. I wanted Gladriel to care for Talina, to show her just a minute portion of love and kindness. I must have been flashing back to growing up under the heartless Olden's 'care', because suddenly I was taking this treatment very personally.

Could Gladriel not see the damage she was doing, the damage she had done to Talina? Fury continued to build inside me, and my energy started to respond. I felt the burning heat.

Closing my eyes, I struggled internally, but it quickly reached the point where I couldn't contain the mass of energy pulsing within me demanding to be released. Where had it all come from? A minute ago, I'd felt empty.

Eventually, I had no choice but to let free my emotions, my pain and anger, my need for Gladriel to see what a sea-bitch she was. It forced itself from me in a burst of light. I closed my eyes, and instead of fighting the pull of power I encouraged the release. Relief flooded through me and I reveled in the power as it flowed. My head fell back, I arched my neck, floating in endless waves of energy.

"Abbs!"

Words started to penetrate the field of power I was releasing.

Lucy screamed at me, "Abby, shut it down, whatever you're doing."

Strong hands gripped my arms, and I dropped my chin and my eyes flew open.

Brace held one side and Lucas the other. Between them they blocked some of the visible stream of silver light emanating from me. With a strangled breath I started the difficult struggle to slam the lid back on the power. After a moment I realized that half my trouble was the addictive nature of the power. It felt good; I felt strong and invincible. I knew that I needed to let that feeling go. Like a junkie, I eventually weaned myself off it, and as the light abated the room fell silent.

I looked around. Brace and Lucas still held my arms, but no one moved. Everyone appeared to be

103

in the same trance-like state, as if they had been frozen in their last movements, staring off into space.

Panic consumed me. What had I done to them?

Brace shifted then. Shaking his head, he stared down into my shocked face.

"What have you done, Red?" He echoed my thoughts. For the first time he seemed disarmed, as if he did not have control of this situation. "What was that energy-release all about? I just saw some of your life." He shook his head again.

"What?" I whispered, my voice low and tight. "I don't see anything?"

"What were you trying to achieve when you released your energy?" He reached over to nudge Lucas.

The tall blond shifted but otherwise didn't respond.

I let the words fall over each other in panic. "I was annoyed at what a cow Gladriel is. She treats her kids like crap. I wanted her to see the damage she's done. How horrible it is to grow up without love ... family."

I shifted my gaze. My heart rate settled as Samuel and Lucas started to stir. They blinked their eyes twice, although the room remained silent.

I turned back to Brace. "Since I don't actually know about Talina's life, I must have projected my own."

"This isn't a power that I'm aware of." Brace looked calm, which was awesome. His calmness would keep me from freaking the hell out. "But it's a little remarkable. The scene was so real. I caught a brief glimpse of you as a young girl; you were asleep."

I glanced about. "Do you think everyone is seeing the same thing?" I didn't like my personal life being broadcast.

"It's like Lalli," Brace said all of a sudden, before locking me in his gaze. "This is a take on Lalli's power of dreaming. You're simply able to project dream scenes out in the open, while people are awake." He laughed, in a short derisive manner. "That's a very strong power, Abby. A little scary."

I agreed. What I had just done was completely debilitating. I could take out each one without them having the smallest chance to defend themselves.

"Why are you not still under the projection?" I asked him, without any real hope he'd answer.

He'd hate for me to accidentally learn something personal about him.

He closed his eyes briefly. "I'm going to tell you, Red. I don't think it's possible to keep my secrets for much longer. You and I ..." He sounded semi-serious for once. "We need to start working together."

I felt a flash of annoyance when Lucas' groaning interrupted us. Brace finally seemed to be opening up.

Lucas pulled back from gripping my arm. His icy blue eyes locked with mine.

"Abby, that was interesting. I don't know how, but I'm pretty sure I just saw part of your battle on Earth."

His eyes rested on my chest, and for once I think he was looking for the knife wound, not my breast size.

I flicked the briefest glance at Brace. He shook his head. Either Brace had missed the last part, or everyone had seen a different section of my life.

"Anyone want to tell me why I just relived our intro to puberty, Abbs?" Lucy yelled at me from across the room. "I wasn't that keen on it the first time around; I certainly didn't need the replay."

She didn't sound angry, just confused like the rest of us, me especially.

"What did you do to me?" Gladriel was on her feet now, her voice low.

She barely even lisped as she stalked across the room. Her long hair moved on its own, twisting around her head until it stood out in thick tendrils.

"What's with the freaky hair?" Lucy whispered.

"Their hair is like a limb; it has an ability to move all on its own," Samuel replied.

Gladriel halted before me.

"How dare you use your witch magic on me. I am the head of Earon. I am the ruler in these waters, and I will see you put to death for this."

I only had to look once into her yellow eyes; she was serious and absolutely furious. Anger bristled off her in waves, and the room started to fill with Earons.

"Mother, calm the hell down." Talina moved over and inserted herself into the space between me and her angry mother. "Abby did not do that on purpose. It's just like those times I have lost control of my powers and it lashed out." She stood tall and proud for once, and I was finally seeing the Walker in her. "It's the reason I always stay as isolated and unassuming as possible. I am afraid I will hurt someone again." She looked back at me. "Is there any possibility we are going to find someone who can teach us to harness and control this power?"

I shrugged. "I hope so. My energy is temperamental to say the least, and I have no idea what I just did. Some weird spin on my mother's power." I glared at Gladriel. "I was trying to show you that your actions have hurt Talina, relegated her to a life of being nothing more than a joke here. And you had the ability to prevent much of this, especially within Earon."

Talina lips lifted in a soft smile as I continued.

"But I know now you're never going to care. You're cold-hearted, and you're a bitch, and there's no changing this."

Gladriel's expression didn't shift. Either she hadn't registered the insult, or she didn't care.

"Word, Abbs," Lucy chimed in as she moved closer. "But why did we see your life?"

"Because part of Talina's pain is also Abby's. Their halfling status has molded their lives," Samuel answered.

I raised my eyebrows to acknowledge his insight.

Lucy blew me a kiss.

I didn't need it. I already knew she loved me, but it was always nice to be reminded. I returned her gesture.

"Leave us." Raror waved to the Earons standing in the room.

Their eyes flicked to Gladriel, but when she didn't contradict him, they left. With a huff, Gladriel followed.

"Awkward ..." Lucy said.

I burst out laughing.

Talina joined me with a few chuckles. The men looked at each other, small smiles on their faces, but refrained from joining in.

"So, Abby, tell me what this plan is for Talina and the rest of the half-Walkers once you rescue them. If she is granted permission to leave, when will I see her again?" Raror's questions dispelled any lingering laughter.

Someone clearly didn't want to waste time on humor.

"I'm sorry, Raror. I knew when I was sent to find these girls I'd be disturbing lives, but it's so much ... worse. I honestly hate to be the bringer of this news." The naked pain on his face made me uneasy and a little sad. But I continued to explain: "Despite the fact the Seventine have been imprisoned for endless millennia, someone has decided it's an awesome idea to start releasing them."

Brace shifted next to me. He didn't usually fidget. Something was making him uneasy. I focused on Raror again.

"My aunt is a soothsayer; she foretold that the halflings would be the ones to banish them. That's about all the information we have as well."

"You haven't mentioned where you will be taking her until you gather all of these halflings."

I paused. We'd never discussed what to do once I found the halflings. I thought I'd be wandering around forever, only to return home empty handed.

"We should leave them at your parents' house on First World, Abbs," Lucy said. "The place is huge, and Lalli will keep an eye on them."

I nodded. "I think my parents' home is the safest. That way I can get around to all of the planets as quickly as possible." I had another thought. "We live on the ocean, Raror. You can come with Talina, if you want?"

Talina's face lit up.

He hesitated, before finally shaking his head. "I can't. I have responsibilities. I am the next successor to rule Earon. With everything that's happening here, I can't abandon my people."

"What's happening here?" Lucas asked.

"Besides finding you on the Sacred Isle and the mutant creatures that shouldn't exist, we also have incidences of missing wood and fruit."

Talina and Raror's expressions indicated this was the gravest of crimes.

"We've also had a few Spurns go missing in the water, which is not a common occurrence." He looked grim. "But even if we assume that was the work of that creature, there is something in the waters, a new type of darkness."

His words reminded me of Francesca's warning just before we left.

"You might find this is a ricochet from the release of the Seventine. Apparently, First World's energy travels to the youngling planets, and since the Seventine is pure negative energy, this is influencing the planets."

It didn't hurt to let them know the seriousness of the situation. I wanted Talina to be happy to leave; kidnapping was not part of the plan.

"Have they already been released?" Raror asked, his features falling in lines of horror.

I shook my head. "No, not all of them. The information we have is that one or two are free. But it's any moment until the others find freedom. Each subsequent release will only throw the balance of these worlds even further off. It's going to get worse before it gets better."

"Why haven't they just freed them all? This has been bothering me for a while?" Samuel draped his long arms over Lucy's shoulder.

She cuddled against him.

"I get the feeling that it's not that easy to release them," Brace said. "It either takes a lot of time or requires lots of energy."

I raised questioning eyes in his direction.

"That's what Josian always indicated to me whenever we discussed possible scenarios for our journey."

The doubt must have shown on my face, considering the way Josian had treated Brace before we left. I couldn't imagine my father discussing anything important with him.

"So when do we leave, Abby?" Talina looked like she was both excited and hardcore freaking out.

She reached out and took Raror's hand, squeezing it tight.

He growled. "Talina, no, I have already decided that we must travel to Silver City and discuss this with Ladre. I know you hate Spurn. I know you have always dreamed of an escape, but this story is borderline crazy, and we don't know these people."

Gee, don't sugarcoat it for our benefit, Raror.

"That will probably work out for the best." I interrupted their intense stare-off. "At the moment my powers need recharging, and I can't access a Walker doorway until this happens."

"How long will that take?" Raror asked. "We will only need a few days to reach the city."

"I'm going to say a week, but it's only a guess. My powers seem to require an intense charge or some form of motivation to work correctly."

The previous dream scene had demonstrated that I had the power levels. I just couldn't figure out how to use them.

Talina's eyes were crinkled at the edges as she turned to me. "Sorry for the extra stop, but I know Ladre will understand, and then I will be free to leave. Plus, this is a big deal; not everyone gets to visit the city under the sea."

I smiled back at her. She was right; it was an amazing opportunity. If only Raror wasn't scowling and mumbling under his breath at me, it would be perfect.

"Alrighty," Lucy interrupted. "I'm not sure about everyone else but I'm tired as hell. I think we should get some rest if we're cruising ... *under the sea, oh, under the sea, nothing is better, down where it's wetter ...*" Her eyes twinkled as she started to sing. Her voice was awkward and off-key, but endearing somehow.

Uncontrolled laughter spluttered from me. I remembered that song from when we were kids. Everyone else looked pretty confused, which only made the pair of us laugh harder. Nothing like an inside joke to break the tension.

"I'll show you where you can rest for the night, since I assume you do not sleep in the water." Talina words broke through our laughter. She waved us toward the room exit.

"Uh, no, we don't sleep in the water, or on a water bed, thanks," Lucy said, her laughter turning to astonishment.

I followed along with the brief hope we wouldn't drown in our sleep that night.

I woke early the next morning. The half-light of the sun shone through the small round window. We had camped out on the meshy beds on the floor in the same place I had woken yesterday.

Lucy was on my right side, but she had snuggled into Samuel. I almost couldn't see where she ended and he started. Observing them, in a completely non-creepy way, I really thought they fit well together. She'd confided in me a little while before that they, despite her best efforts, hadn't had sex. Apparently, Samuel was an old-fashioned sort of man; he was waiting for the perfect moment or some crap. Lucy told me she was continuing to work on changing his mind, one skimpy pair of underwear at a time.

This wasn't the first time they'd slept next to each other. But here they seemed more comfortable than they had in our previous prison. Samuel had an arm protectively around her, and he looked relaxed in the pose of deep sleep. It softened the anger and pain he carried around with him every day. And I could really see Lallielle in his features.

My heart panged at the thought of my parents; I'd been missing them a lot the last few days. Josian's booming roar and hug every morning, and the gentle nudging of Lallielle as she forced me into a normal First-World life – well, even that seemed less annoying in retrospect.

Pulling myself to my feet, I moved across the room without disturbing anyone. I did notice that Brace was already gone, but everyone else was still sleeping.

Talina had left us new wraps on the chair. Before changing, I used some of the cucreamer juice to rinse out my mouth. Its absorbing ability worked the same way as teeth-brushing, removing all morning breath and cleaning my teeth. Talina had demonstrated its hundred and one amazing uses before she'd left us to go sleep in her water-pod. Yep, that's right, a water-pod.

With a quick glance to make sure no one was awake, I managed to shrug off my old wraps and get re-wrapped in pure white mesh – it took me a good ten minutes to get all the important parts covered. Honestly, wearing no underwear should make me feel all kinds of vulnerable, but instead under the wraps you couldn't even tell.

I stepped over the sleeping people to make my way upstairs to the top deck. Of all the things my power-enlightening had brought me, the best was the feeling inside. I felt so alive. I was stronger, required less sleep, could think and process faster and my memory was almost perfect. There were definite benefits to being a half-Walker.

Stepping out onto the deck, I was captivated by the beauty of the endless oceans. Breathing deeply of the clean air, I loved that there were no buildings, no clouds of smog, no Gangers or Burbers, or any other weird and wonderful creatures in sight. Just silence and tranquility. I was fast becoming an eighty-year-old lady.

"Morning, Red, how did you sleep?"

I glanced over my shoulder. Brace was making his way from the top of the stairs to stand with me on the edge of the pontoon. He was wrapped in white mesh also, his skin looking extra tanned against the wraps. I had to contain my sigh of pure appreciation.

"Yeah, I'm surprised at how comfortable it is to sleep on the floor," I said as I turned back to the view, mainly to prevent any untoward touching.

My fingers were itching to run across the expanses of skin that towered next to me.

I clenched my hands together and closed my eyes, trying to move past this unnatural obsession I harbored for Brace. I couldn't explain my fixation with him despite my best efforts.

"I'm interested in seeing this underwater city," he said as he stood close.

I could feel his warmth. And, damn, why did he smell so good? It was like clean fresh air combined with a spicy sweetness ... like donuts. Okay, maybe not exactly donuts, but it gave me the same feelings. I attempted to focus on the conversation as I opened my eyes to the beauty of the ocean.

"I can't even picture a building under the water. The dynamics seem impossible." My life had taken a dramatic twist from my days on Earth. "But what will we do if they don't let Talina leave? I mean, I always knew it was going to be difficult; imagine if aliens just popped in from another planet, and told you about a crazy mission and you needed to leave immediately. I know, if it was me, I'd have a few reservations."

Brace's expression didn't change. Maybe that wouldn't have been odd to him.

"I think that we'll deal with that if it happens. I'm sure that Ladre is a reasonable man. We should be able to convince him," he said.

If only Ladre was a man. Spurns were a whole other kettle of fish. I chuckled internally at my poor joke.

"I need us to book in some time to talk, Red."

I lifted my face to meet his serious gaze.

"It's important that I explain to you what's been happening."

His velvet eyes told me he'd made a decision and was ready to divulge some of his secrets. One of the things I loved the most about Brace was the intensity of his gaze, despite how unnerving it could be.

"I've always trusted you, Abby, trusted in our relationship. You're the girl of my dreams; I just never expected to be so torn between my family responsibilities and ... everything."

"Why do you think this has happened? Why have we been starring center-stage in each other's dreams?"

He shrugged. "I have a few theories, and – " He smiled before I could interrupt him. "I will tell you. Just try and have some patience. It will probably be a long conversation."

Patience ... I don't think so.

I couldn't tear my eyes from him. For the first time Brace was almost talkative, and I wanted more. More of this beautiful creature that was so unlike the secretive one-dimensional dream-man I knew.

"You know you can tell me anything, Brace." I decided to be brave despite my discomfort at being vulnerable. "There's a connection between us; a reason why we've been in each other's lives, in a manner, for a long time."

"There's more than a connection, Abigail. You must feel what I do. This is not just a weak link or a crush. This is much more. It feels ... epic."

I savored his words and nodded. My breath caught in my throat.

"Yes." I dropped my gaze slightly. "Yes, I feel the same way. But is this intensity just because we're young, and First Worlders and Walkers feel emotions strongly?"

Or ...

I paused, my features freezing at my next thought. Was Brace my mate?

"Don't sell this as some teenage infatuation, Abigail." He leaned in closer to me, pausing when his lips were just breaths from my own. "This is beyond all that."

I closed my eyes as his lips hovered over my own, his breath caressing my face. I was waiting for an interruption. The moment was just too perfect and these moments are always interrupted. Surprisingly there was no disturbance, but he also didn't close that final distance.

My eyes flew open.

He was still close, his eyes locked on my face.

He smiled at my confusion. "Sorry, Red. I'm just savoring the moment."

My heart was beating so rapidly it felt like one constant beat. I understood exactly what Brace was saying. This delicious moment before his lips actually touched mine was filled with anticipation and butterflies and pure delectable want.

Then he closed the distance, and I realized I was so wrong. There was nothing comparable to the actual kiss. The last time we kissed there had been a tinge of anger and desperation. But now he started slow, light, his lips just brushing my own.

And then he deepened the kiss.

I opened my mouth as his tongue flicked out. I swallowed a groan at the intensity of his lips on mine. Even with his height, we still fit perfectly together. My arms lifted of their own accord, and I rested my hands on the strong, bare muscles in his chest.

Despite the slow beginnings, his kiss moved rapidly past light and teasing to hot and heavy. My breath came in pants, and he was breathing heavier than usual. I gasped as a familiar voice sounded behind us.

"I told you we would be interrupting, Sammy." Lucy's words echoed out over the expanse of ocean.

We both paused, but didn't pull away.

"Ignore them," I whispered against his lips. "They're like monsters under the bed: if you don't acknowledge them, they aren't real."

"If you want, I can kill them. That's what I usually do with monsters."

I chuckled, unsure if he was kidding. Upon opening one eye, I could see Lucy and Samuel paused in mid-step, as if they'd frozen there and weren't sure whether to move forward or backwards.

Reluctantly, I untangled myself from Brace. I heard him mutter as he reached out to capture my hand, but his words were too low to understand. I'd noticed recently that he was quite the toucher, a bit like Josian, my tactile father. I had never thought I was so physical, but I was starting to think I actually liked it a lot.

"Come on over. We were just discussing the weather." I grinned at my best friend.

121

Lucy bounced over, throwing her arms around me in a hug, not caring about Brace at my side.

She seemed extra bright and happy this morning. And, like the rest of us, she was wrapped in white mesh.

"Sammy and I are practically meteorologists, we discuss the weather that frequently." She nudged me.

Samuel and Brace gave the typical guy-nod of 'good morning'. Some of the strain that had been between them since Samuel's return from Earth was dissipating. And Samuel made no comment at all about me and Brace, but then I hardly expected him to come across the heavy big-brother. He barely acknowledged me at all, let alone played the brother card.

"You and I are due some serious girl-talk, Abigail," Lucy said, leaning in close to me.

She clearly thought I'd been holding out on her.

I put my free arm around her and gave a squeeze. I was apparently neglecting everyone since they were all trying to book in some talk time. Things had just been so crazy busy lately.

"I'm not sure I'm okay with you two discussing girl things, or whatever you women do," Samuel said, looking uncomfortable.

I snickered. "I'm not sure I care what you're okay with. And, trust me, I have zero interest in Lucy discussing your weather, its size, shape or ability to rain, storm or hail."

Lucy cracked up laughing then, doubling over as she almost fell down. It only took a few seconds for me to follow. We had to hold each other up as we laughed. Eventually, we composed ourselves. Although, every time I saw Samuel's face and his current shade of red, I wanted to laugh again. Brace's lips were curved into the smallest of smiles, but he didn't comment. Instead he reached out to re-capture my hand. Lucy's eyes followed the movement, but for once she didn't make a suggestive comment. Instead she turned to Samuel.

"Sorry, baby, you're just an easy target. You should relax a little." She moved closer into his side.

"I assure you, Lucy. I'm a thunderstorm where you're concerned. Huge ..." His eyes twinkled. "And I can bring any weather you'll ever need, want and desire."

She patted his arm. "Oh, I know, Sammy. I more than know."

I shook my head a few times trying to dislodge the mental images our metaphors were bringing.

"It's a real shame that there're some things you just cannot un-hear," I said with a frown.

"Yes, I wouldn't mind some brain bleach." Brace squeezed my hand.

"Here you all are." Talina walked into view, followed closely by Lucas.

And as the blond Emperor-to-be smiled at me, I was hit again by the connection between us. If Brace was my destined mate, then what the hell was this tie between me and Lucas? It seemed to intensify the more we were around each other and, although he kept his distance, he continued to stare in a way that told me he was just biding his time.

The moment Lucas walked closer, Brace's smile faltered and his relaxed features hardened. He already had my hand, but he continued to tug me closer. I was sure that was his way of establishing ownership. But I was not a piece of property. I freed my hand before gathering a small portion of self-respect and moving out between the two of them. I wasn't going to be the rope in their tug-of-war.

"I have arranged some cucreamer for you to eat before we journey to Silver City. Mother has agreed to let us have our own pontoon," Talina said, looking relaxed and more confident.

"I'll bet she was glad to get rid of us for a few days," I said, returning some of her enthusiasm.

124

She smiled and nodded. "Yes, most definitely. But I do feel we are the winners in this escaping situation."

I was suddenly unable to contain my excitement at seeing a city under the ocean. Like what the hell? When would anyone expect that to happen in their life? And if I didn't think about how much water would be above us, my claustrophobia would stay uninvited, something to worry about only if a crack suddenly appeared above our heads.

Chapter 6

After breakfast, Talina and Raror ferried us through the cool water to a smaller flat-bottomed pontoon. I tried not to think of the possible monsters lurking below. Thankfully it didn't take long to reach the side. Behind us the rest of the Earon convoy continued without pause, forming a long line of tethered boats sailing off toward the horizon.

Using a rope ladder, I climbed up onto the top deck of the two-level vessel. Almost immediately the heavy water exited from my white mesh wraps, leaving them light and damp.

"We will be at the tube entrance to Silver City in about four hours. I found a few extra seahorses to ferry us," Raror said.

He had just launched himself up out of the water and onto the top decking, without any need of a rope ladder.

I leaned over the side to examine the seahorses. There were four out in front, just visible beneath the crystal-clear water. They looked a little like a mix of dolphin and octopus, large gray creatures with at least eight legs. Their back four tentacles were attached to small ropes on the front underside of the pontoon. I continued to watch as we started to move.

"They are strong and amazingly smart. Cacaol is one of my oldest friends." Talina was next to me; she pointed to the smallest one out on the left.

"Can you talk to them?" I asked, fascinated by their graceful play through the water.

She shook her head. "No, they have no vocal cords to speak, but that doesn't mean we can't communicate. They have a form of sign-language that is pretty easy to understand. And they comprehend most of our words."

She waved to her friend, and I saw two of the long limbs shoot up out of the water. Talina laughed and blew a kiss down to her.

I smiled, looking at Talina's happy face. "Spurn is pretty amazing. Where we're from, no one could comprehend a world without land. Some people have never even been in the ocean before."

I was starting to wonder if, in the end, Talina was another person I'd have to convince to leave. She had more here than she realized.

"I can't imagine that. There is nothing comparable to the silence and majesty that comes from dancing through the oceans, riding the currents, seeing the beauty that lies beneath."

"Stop," I said with a sigh. "You're making me so jealous. I'll never get to experience that. You're pretty lucky to have almost the best of both worlds."

"Yeah, I guess I've never thought of it that way. I've always hated my defects, the things that made life so hard for me here." She looked away, the breeze blowing her emerald hair back in one long thick stream. "Now I have to start believing in that which makes me special, unique. If I'm to accept your story then there's no other like me in all of the worlds."

"That's it, girl. Embrace your differences, and flip off all those who don't recognize all that's awesome about you," Lucy said, hearing the end of our conversation as she walked up behind us.

Talina smiled. "Flip off?"

Lucy waved a hand in her direction. "It's something we do on Earth, and it basically means go eff yourself."

"Eff yourself?" Talina parroted again.

128

I laughed. She was never going to understand Earth slang, and since we had no idea what the Spurn equivalent would be, we couldn't explain.

"I think that's their way of saying take a long dive into a shallow sand bank." Raror put an arm around his sister.

Comprehension crossed her features.

"I'm not sure I'll ever be confident enough to tell anyone that, but I'll work on it." She looked petrified at the thought.

We moved as a group to sprawl on the meshy beds spread along the top deck of the pontoon. It was nice to have some down time; it seemed as if life was reasonably relaxed on Spurn. Swimming and lying around. As I lay back to stare into the pink skies I realized there were no clouds. I was pretty sure I hadn't seen any since we arrived. Just the pink half-sun days and the four blue moons nights.

"Does it rain here?" I said, reaching my hands behind me so I could prop my head up.

"What's rain?" Talina and Raror asked at the same time.

My eyes widened. The water planet had no rain. That was weird ...

"When water falls from the sky," Lucas answered. "We don't get a lot of rain on First World. I hear it's more common on Earth."

"Water has never fallen from our sky. That would be amazing to see." Talina's voice sounded wistful.

How had this world ended up being mostly water? What was their water source?

"You'll get to see rain when we leave Spurn," I said, ignoring the reappearance of Raror's scowl.

He seemed pretty confident that she wouldn't get permission to leave. What did he know that we didn't?

It didn't take long for the men to become bored and decide to jump in the water. They were all strong swimmers, and Raror promised they'd be able to keep up with the boat. Lucy, Talina and I stayed to continue the glorious task of getting a tan. The wraps didn't cover too much skin so we had plenty of the half-sun exposure. It was weak enough that there was no chance of burning.

After an hour I rolled over onto my front, cradling my head in my arms. Lucy shifted next to me.

"I'm going downstairs to check Sammy hasn't drowned," she said, getting to her feet.

Talina nodded, before following her. She probably didn't like to be out of the water for too long. I felt better knowing she'd be looking after Lucy in the water.

"Mmm, hmmm," I mumbled drowsily into my arms.

My mind drifted. The sun felt so good, recharging and regenerating me.

Eventually boredom kicked in. I got to my feet. I wasn't very practiced at lazing around. I was ready for some swim time.

I made my way down the stairs, and then stepped out onto the open deck area of the lower level. Leaning my head over the side, I expected to see everyone swimming alongside the pontoon. Instead, they were all sitting in a huge side net. Okay, that's how they were keeping up with the seahorses' speed.

The net ran almost the full length of the pontoon with the majority dragging in the water, which was perfect, considering I wasn't the strongest swimmer. I could just lie back and be pulled along for the ride.

"Just jump in, Abbs." Lucy kicked her legs out in front, her hands tangled in the side netting so as not to be thrown out accidentally.

With a shrug, I jumped off the side, landing on my butt. The cool water immediately enveloped me and my weight pulled the netting down. I went completely under. Spluttering, I launched myself above the water level, coughing out the salt water I'd swallowed.

Reaching out a long arm, Brace hauled me over to sit on the edge with him. We were on the opposite side to everyone else, and with the sound of water rushing past, it felt semi-private. I could see Lucy and Samuel laughing together, and Lucas flirting with Talina, a skill which seemed as easy to him as breathing.

"You know I can't remember the last time I got to relax and just have fun," Brace said as he lay back, letting the water run over his body. "My life is family obligations and following orders. I'm about ready to walk away from that for a while."

"I know what you mean." I was trying really hard not to plaster myself to his warm skin, but the bumpy water kept throwing me into his side. "Earth was just training and survival. Having fun was not on our schedule. Until an hour ago I'd never sun-baked. I'm eighteen years old and that was my first chance to lie in the sun." I looked up at him. "Want to tell me how old you are?"

Although he'd mentioned being twenty-two before, something told me that was not entirely accurate.

He ignored me, flashing one of those brilliant smiles. "It's about time you acted like a teenager."

He hauled me into his arms and threw me across into the deep center of the netting. Once again I found myself submerged under the water, but at least this time I'd closed my mouth first. I was about to propel myself up, ready to kick some butt, when I was distracted by the scene before me. My vision under the water was almost as clear as above, and the world below was incredible.

Glittering and shifting beneath us were creatures: at least a hundred different fish species. One of the smallest drifted close to me; it looked like a black puff of cloud. I could have reached out and touched it.

There were also huge beasts, with lots of teeth, gliding lazily along. Those I definitely did not want to touch.

I would have sat there for hours observing the diverse ecosystem, watching the different species interact and chase each other. But I wasn't a Spurn, so I couldn't breathe under water and eventually my burning lungs forced me to rise above the surface.

Brace grinned at me from where he was perched. "I wasn't sure if you'd decided to live under the sea or if my skills had scared you a bit too much, Red."

Without thought I launched myself at him, practically landing on his head. As we wrestled in the water, I was determined to dunk him. Our scarcely clad bodies touched everywhere and there were far too many electrical jolts running between us. Our play was sexy and tempting in all ways, but more than that it was fun. I'd never roughhoused with anyone before. It wasn't Lucy's style; she hated her hair getting messy.

My competitive side couldn't let him win. Although with his strength and limb-length advantage I wasn't having much luck, even when I utilized all my speed and flexibility. Brace captured me a few times, but I always managed to free myself. After a while we declared a truce. We lay back side-by-side, letting the water cool our heated skin.

"You're deceptively strong and devious, Abigail." Brace glanced sideways, his brows raised. "You'd have made a good ninja."

I laughed. "Don't let Lucy hear you say that; she thinks she's a ninja."

As I relaxed against his side, I couldn't believe how comfortable this was. Of course it was unbelievably nerve wracking and the electrical current continued to buzz, but I felt a strange sense of contentment. As my body relaxed, so did my brain.

"Do you think we've had the dreams, and feel this connection because we're true mates?" As the words fled my mouth I realized what I'd said.

Had the filter between my brain and mouth suddenly become defective?

I was about to hang my head in shame and sink beneath the water to escape his probing gaze when my pride kicked in. No ... No way was I hiding. I might not have meant to put that out there so soon but I deserved to know. Or, more importantly, I needed to know. I'd fight for anything that was real, but I had no time to waste on games.

"I think it's slightly more complicated than that, Abby. But, yes, I think there's a high possibility you are my mate." He smiled then, his serious expression lifting. "A term I'm coming to enjoy."

I really loved it when he smiled.

"You're kind of pretty when you smile," I said, unable to stop myself again.

"Tough and manly, Red," his brow furrowed, "I'm manly."

I patted his arm in a placating manner.

"So where do we go from here?" I couldn't tear my eyes from his. This was the conversation I never believed I would have. "Do we have a choice in this mate thing?"

"Do you want another choice?" he asked as he flicked his gaze toward Lucas.

I followed his direction and noticed a pair of icy blue eyes watching us both closely.

"I want ..." I shook my head.

"You want?" he repeated.

I want you.

I almost blurted it out. What the hell was with my mouth today? I attempted to cover the awkward silence.

"It's a lot to take in when I've basically been raised in a world where soul-mates and one-true-loves don't really exist," I diverged.

"Nice segue, Red." He smiled. "You can try and fight it, and you can run if you want." He touched my face, his expression almost reverent.

I was lost again. He really was the most beautiful man I had ever seen. He should make me feel insecure, make me wonder what he wanted with someone like me, but instead I felt powerful and strong around him. Like I could do or be anything. When he locked me in his gaze I felt the perfection. He continued speaking, unaware of my thoughts.

"But I won't give you up. I don't even think I can stop ... being with you. I can't stay away."

"I assume you've already tried to fight this." I thought of the time he'd disappeared after our journey to Earth.

He nodded. "Yeah, I'm not too proud to say I attempted to run like hell. I have so much sh ... unpleasant things in my life, I don't want to drag you into it. And I don't like things that are outside my control. Plus, you're young, with many things to experience. You deserve a chance to grow. But it is what it is, and I'm not strong enough to give you up."

I looked away; I needed to catch my breath. But I found no relief as Lucas captured my attention. For once he watched me seriously, his expression ... intense.

"What's the connection there? I'm not sure I understand." Brace's words were soft but drew my full awareness.

I could see in his stare a brutal vulnerability, a sense of helplessness. I didn't understand my connection with Lucas either, and I didn't like it. And I had no answers for him.

The rest of the time went quickly. We had lunch of the same old fruit and salty salad. I was really starting to crave meat and flavors of a different variety. Just remembering the foods of First World had my mouth watering.

Talina eventually announced that we had arrived. We stood on the front deck, waiting for Raror to receive permission to enter.

I turned to Talina. "You said earlier that your powers whack out of control at times. What exactly are your powers?"

Her brown eyes crinkled. "I'm not really sure. I try to never use them. But they are definitely water-based. Sometimes, when I'm in danger, they take over. I create waves, whirlpools, water jets. And I'm strong. I can keep anyone out of my mind, and no one can manipulate me."

"These half-Walker powers are too unpredictable. How the hell can they expect us to fight these Seventine?" I was frustrated with our lack of information.

No wonder Raror was holding strong to Talina staying here. He must see we were crawling our way through the dark.

Talina's face paled. "I'm excited to leave Spurn, although I'm not sure what to do about leaving Raror. But, to be honest, I really hope the Walkers have a better plan than gathering the halflings, and we will do the rest."

"Well, Josian, my father, is out finding Walkers for the battle. Hopefully they have an idea. I'll definitely ask him when we get back home."

"Josian will never let anything happen to you, Red," Brace said from where he stood beside me. He hadn't been far from me all afternoon, and I was kind of hearting the hell out of him. "And neither will I."

138

"Well, not all of us have a tall, dark, and hot-as-hell-man to watch our back, so I think I'll keep on worrying." Talina's comment was more like Lucy's style, who must have agreed since she high-fived her.

"You two have to stop hanging out so much," I said drily. "Luce's starting to rub off on Talli, and one of you is enough."

Lucy rolled her eyes at me, sticking her tongue out for extra measure.

"Alright, we have been granted permission," Talina said, pointing to where Raror glided through the water.

The pontoon had drifted close to the tube – a clear round structure that stuck out of the water at a forty-five-degree angle.

"It looks like one of those huge slides that used to be in amusement parks before they all fell apart." Lucy jumped up and down, her curls bouncing.

We'd always been sad that we'd missed our chance to go on the roller coasters.

Talina towed Lucy and I across first, leaving us to hold on the tube edge while she ferried the rest. Raror's presence was comforting as he waited with us.

As soon as everyone arrived, he spoke.

"It is quite a distance down to the city. The tube has grooves fitted throughout the base, so you should be able to descend at whatever pace you're comfortable with. I will go first and wait at the bottom."

With that he launched the few inches out of the water into the open shaft of the tube. And then he was gone.

Glancing up, I gulped audibly. How was my claustrophobia going to hold up in the little slide?

"Abbs and I will go down together." Lucy reached out to hold my hand under the water. "Otherwise I know your butt will bail halfway," she finished quietly.

I flashed her a look of gratitude.

"Alright then, move around to the front, and we'll boost you up." Samuel waved his hands; he trod water effortlessly.

I moved first, and Lucy followed as we made our way around.

Samuel gripped me on either side of my waist and without any strain lifted me up and into the small opening.

The moment I was resting on the angled tube I started to freak out. The sensations started. I felt like the space was closing in on me. I breathed deeply as my pulse raced and sweat broke out along my body. I closed my eyes, which helped

140

immediately to quell some of the sensation. Using my hands, I felt the deep, almost ladder-like grooves along the base of the tube. There was no way you could accidentally slide down it. I started my descent slowly, going feet first with my eyes remaining closed.

"I'm right behind you, Abbs." Lucy's voice echoed near my ear.

Since I was already borderline having a panic attack, her voice didn't scare me at all.

"You'll be fine. Just keep moving along."

Soaking up her comforting presence, I continued the slow plunge.

"Open your eyes." Her command came after what felt like ten hours but must have only been minutes.

I shook my head vehemently. "No! Hell, no, Luce. I'll freak out, and there's no way for me to escape. I'm sure you don't want a screaming, fighting, biting Abby on your hands."

"Just trust me, weirdo. Open your eyes."

"Well, when you put it like that ... No!"

She poked me in the back, and then continued for the next five minutes.

"Lucy!" I finally yelled, my eyes flying open. My body had decided I needed to see so I could punch her.

I froze.

"Holy sh ... crap in a bucket," I trailed off.

We were about halfway down the tube, but I didn't have to worry about my claustrophobia. I definitely didn't feel enclosed. I was floating in an endless sea, as if we were part of the ocean, the clear plastic providing no visual barrier. It was well lit, even this far down. I felt as if I was sitting in the center of a fish tank. There were creatures everywhere, and even more fascinating were the many Spurns, mostly blue-haired ones, but a few of the other colors were present as well, racing through the waters. Others drifted lazily in the currents, their amazing hair flowing behind them in a graceful arc.

"Hey, what's the holdup down there? Keep moving." Samuel's impatience jolted me.

Lucy turned around and yelled something back. I was pretty sure it had four letters. I began to move again, my eyes never leaving the beauty of the scene before me. The light started to wane the further we traversed from the surface. But there were these floating jelly blobs everywhere. They glowed, illuminating vast areas around them.

"This has got to be the most amazing thing I've ever seen," I said, my voice drifting behind me.

I was sad to see we were coming to the end. I wanted to sit there for at least another twenty hours. Sticking my legs out, I dropped a small distance to land in water. It was only calf-deep, like a moat, creating a barrier around the impressive construction before me.

The dome was large enough to just cover the Silver City, which was not really a city; it was more like one large building, combining wood for the structure and growths of coralline for texture. It wasn't huge, probably about fifty square feet, and appeared to have two levels. The shape was square, with coralline formed turrets and huge towering wings off either side of the building. It had an open plan, no proper roof or covered-in walls. But considering there was a huge clear sphere protecting the entire city, there wouldn't be much weather down here.

I turned to Raror. "What exactly is this bubble made of?"

It looked like plastic, but I wasn't sure they had that on Spurn.

"It's water. When it was created the monstrones formed molecular bonds between water and carbon molecules, creating a solidified structure. And that's the secret to its survival: it's water, and it exists in water. It cannot be destroyed easily."

That was a relief.

Raror was better informed than I'd expected. I had to stop thinking they were less intelligent because of their animal halves. In fact they seemed able to create far more than humans had ever dreamed of.

I took a step forward, moving through the clear waters of the moat to step up to the large front entrance. The water continued through the building, ankle height, and the floor still moved as it had when we'd stood on the pontoon. We weren't anchored to the floor, but since under our feet was covered in sand I couldn't see below.

"I think I'm dreaming. I'm pretty sure my theory long ago in the alley where we both died and were living in an alternate universe actually happened," Lucy said, standing next to me. "Nothing has been the same since then." She tore her gaze from the view to smile at me. "And I couldn't be happier."

"How amazing is it to see the ocean surrounding us." We couldn't be too deep; there were lots of Spurns swimming outside the protective tube.

How much water pressure could their bodies withstand?

I was suddenly thrown forward as something hit me from behind. I landed on my hands and knees in the shallow water. To my right, Talina sprawled next to me.

"Oh, damn, Abby. I'm so sorry. This place does it to me every time. I feel like I'm drunk on sea wine down here," she said as Raror reached her side to assist her up.

He kept an arm tightly around her.

Lucy reached down to help me. She was surprisingly strong for such a small person.

"It's probably from your water powers," I said to Talina, who looked mortified. "If your affinity is water, possibly this much around you throws your energy out of whack."

I reached down to rub the pain out of my knees. As I straightened, a firm hand landed on my back and gave it a gentle stroke. The warmth and leap of desire in my belly told me immediately that it was Brace. His magic hands stroked away the hurt where Talina had hit me.

Did he realize that he was creating an entirely different set of aches? This chemistry was going to drive me insane. I wondered for the first time what it would be like to hear Brace's thoughts. I wasn't too keen to have anyone in my head. It was the last security I had and I loathed letting it go. But to hear his thoughts ... I had a sudden craving to know what he was thinking.

So I dropped the energy around my mind.

I shivered at the feeling of exposure, almost as if I suddenly stood there naked. Ignoring this, I projected a tentative word toward Brace.

Hello.

Everyone around me, except Lucy, groaned and clutched their heads.

"Aribella, put your energy back around your mind," Samuel wheezed next to me, holding his forehead with both hands.

I quickly yanked it back up.

"What ... what happened?" I said. "I was testing my telepathy."

"Well, we heard you loud and clear," Lucas said drily. "Your 'hello' echoed around my mind until I felt like my head would explode."

Whoops.

"Maybe don't try that again until Josian can tell us what just happened. It was like you projected energy along with the word. It was not pleasant," Samuel said, looking dazed.

Lucy shrugged. "Sometimes being a little old Earthling has it benefits. I didn't hear a thing."

Samuel's expression shifted. "Just because you're from Earth doesn't mean you aren't affected by energy. It's very odd that you seem to be immune to all this."

It was at this moment that I had a horrifying thought. One I should have had long before. Lucy, being from Earth, would be bound by the evolution of that planet, which included a lifespan of at most a hundred years. I would outlive her and I couldn't do that. That was not cool with me. There had to be something that Lallielle or Josian knew that could change Lucy's fate. I pushed my sudden nausea and horror away for now. There was nothing I could do until I spoke with my parents.

"Ladre is waiting for us. We should move into the main hall," Raror said from inside the front room.

He continued to help Talina.

We followed as they led us through room after room. They were all open plan, but still gave the impression of individual space. There were scattered tables and chairs throughout. I had the feeling of small dining rooms, or gathering places. But each room was empty. Eventually, the smaller rooms tapered off. We finished up in one huge cylindrical space. Along the back wall, sitting around a large coralline table, were five Baroons. The center one was Ladre, their leader.

"Hello, welcome to Silver City," he said, waving us over. "Please have a seat. We have much to discuss." He turned his head slightly to indicate his companions. "I have gathered some of the council to hear your story, and then we will vote on whether Talina is free to leave."

147

Talina, who had been watching him longingly, suddenly frowned.

"I was unaware that I was owned," she started. "Surely this is my decision. "

Ladre's eyes clashed with hers. "You are an important part of Spurn. As Raror reminded me, you are the daughter of the Earon leader and have duties. It is not as simple as you think."

Talina glared at her brother, who shrugged apologetically. I knew then he would use any means to keep her on Spurn.

Ladre continued. "You are needed, Talina."

Her eyes widened and shimmered at his strongly spoken words. "But first, before we discuss this further, there is someone who has been waiting to meet you."

I paused at the sudden disjointed nature of his words. He had been speaking fine a moment ago, and now he sounded like a puppet. I took half a step forward.

"Wait a second, Red." Brace held out a hand to stop me. His eyes narrowed as he perused the area. "Something's up with Blue there. He no longer appears to be in control of himself."

I wasn't sure if Brace knew something I didn't or if he'd just noticed the strange behavior. As he spoke, the men fell into defensive mode. They

148

moved in front of us, and as a group we drew closer together before backing up in steady steps.

"Yes, but who besides Aribella, with all her super powers, has the ability to do this." Samuel's features were schooled in tight worried lines.

"Do any Spurns have powers to hypnotize or mentally manipulate others?" I was pretty sure I hadn't done anything this time.

Talina shook her head. "No, I have never heard of anyone who would be capable of that."

Ladre hadn't moved yet. He was still standing, his hand out in a gesture to sit, his expression blank.

"Ladre is the most powerful of any Spurn. Who could have done this?" Talina's voice broke.

She was fidgeting, and I knew she was very close to running back to Ladre.

Raror, who must have sensed the same thing, tightened his hold on her arms.

The other Baroons around the table continued to sit, expressionless and silent.

"Well, well, you are slightly more aware than I gave you credit for." The low deep voice came from behind us.

We spun around.

"I didn't think First Worlders were too fast on the uptake. They definitely weren't the few times I decided to stop off on your ape planet." The giant man framed in the doorway continued to speak.

Derision rolled off him in waves, and I recognized this level of arrogance. I knew immediately what we were dealing with; he was a Walker. His white-blond hair was long, and was secured at the nape of his neck. His eyes were such a dark blue they looked violet. He had the same broad-plane features as Josian. I guessed that many of the old Walkers would look as if they'd been carved from stone millennia ago. But unlike Josian this man had no warmth, no sparkle in his eye that spoke of empathy or care.

"Damn it, you Walker freaks just keep popping up everywhere we turn lately," Lucy commented. "No offence, Abbs," she finished, without turning her head.

I actually laughed a little.

"How dare you address me? You are even less than First World; you are from Earth," he muttered, as if she was some crap on the bottom of his foot.

Brace moved forward slowly, edging me out of sight. I assumed he was trying to hide the red Walker marks on my face. It was probably a good move, considering halflings were not supposed to exist. The man started to pace before us.

"When I arrived on Spurn, for ... well, my own important reasons. I was surprised when my old buddy Lanster," I was pretty sure he meant Ladre, "informed me that there were visitors from First World here. Now he didn't exactly understand the significance, but I know First Worlders can't just jump worlds. So I got to thinking." He paused and faced us again, energy rolling off him in waves.

It made my stomach ache, and I wanted to take a step back.

"That maybe you little travelers had a Walker aiding you. And, well, we just can't have our Walker secrets paraded around for any lower life-form to utilize."

His face fell into a pose of exaggerated apology. "Sorry to say, but it's my duty to make sure that you don't leave here with any information you shouldn't."

I wasn't sure if I should step forward or not.

"Of course we have the power on First World to travel. I am the Emperor. I control the royal stones." Lucas spoke up.

I groaned; he should not have mentioned the laluna to this Walker.

The blonds' face grew even colder, although a slight red flushed his cheeks.

"No one controls the lalunas, you pathetic ape. They were gifted, in error if you ask me, to you

151

unevolved entities. The fact that these objects, which are to be honored, are in your filthy grips, well, I and all Walkers should hang our heads in shame."

"Oh, for eff sake. Someone shut this ass-hat's mouth. Every time I have to listen to something more moronic than the last thing he said, my brain cells commit suicide in protest." Lucy, as usual, had absolutely no sense of self-preservation.

Samuel and I both dived to cut her off, but we were too slow. Her words seemed to linger in the air for a few moments, and then, before I could blink, the Walker was standing in front of her.

"For that, mortal, you shall die." He smiled down at her, a smile of pure cold-blooded killer. He would take her life in that instant and not think twice about it.

"Stop!" I screamed.

He whipped around to lock on me with his dark, violent eyes.

I stepped around Brace and faced the Walker. "Leave her alone. I am Walker; I transported us here."

He moved at super speed again to stop in front of me.

"What witchery is this? How are your marks on display?" He reached out a hand, his grip gentle as he cupped my face. "You are of my clan." His tone held a sliver of respect.

A storm of energy was brewing behind me. Brace stepped forward, his skin glowing, a light emanating from within. He was taller than this man, and I watched with shock as the blond Walker took a step back.

"Abernath's ..." he said in shock. "You are of Abernath's house. Why have I sensed no energy from any of you?" His arms shook, but he stood his ground. "How are you masking your energy?"

When we didn't answer I felt his anger building. Brace had moved to stand in front of me, and the glow he emitted made my eyes ache. What the hell were his powers again? Glow-worm.

"Just leave now, and no one needs to get hurt." Brace's words were soft and deadly, though serious enough that the threat behind them wasn't even close to being veiled.

"You don't scare me, son. You're just a baby compared to all I have seen and done. Despite your family," a calculated look crossed his face, "I will have my answers, and since you appear to be hovering protectively around the redhaired beauty, then I think she is my ticket."

I had no idea what was going on. How could he know Brace's family?

"If you touch her, I'll kill you. Don't think because you're Walker that you're safe." Brace sounded so sincere that I actually believed him for a second.

The man grinned, and then he laughed out loud, head thrown back, in the same manner as Josian.

"Lesson one of the day: don't underestimate your superiors. We are superior for a reason."

Brace nodded once. "If I meet anyone superior, I'll be sure to keep that in mind."

"Excellent," the man said, and then, in a slow-motion movement, he brought his hands together.

"Boom," he said.

And the world fell apart.

Chapter 7

Strong arms enveloped me as the walls of Silver City dissolved. Water crashed in around us. As the pressure encased me, I inhaled one big breath before I, and whoever held me, were sucked out in a huge tidal wave and I blacked out.

The sound of steady dripping was the first thing I noticed as I roused from my semi-comatose state. My head was forward, resting against my chest. As I lifted it up, the faint throbbing that'd been plaguing me turned into a pounding headache. I tried to lift my arms to rub my temples, but they didn't respond.

It took far longer than it should have for me to realize I was tied down, arms and legs secured to the chair I was sitting on. I yanked hard on my tethers, twisting my wrists, trying to break the bonds.

What the eff? What was I tied down with?

I peered in a disorientated manner around my prison. I was in a large room. The walls looked like they were made of bulky stone blocks, each one varying in color and texture, like you'd expect in an old castle.

And the air was warm, not damp like it was on Spurn, but rather warm like it was on a sunny spring day in New York: crisp, clean and beautiful. I swear I could hear birds chirping from somewhere to my left and that incessant dripping.

There were no windows in this room. A wooden door was the only break in the expanse of gray and brown stone.

I noticed that my energy was back swirling inside me. This told me that at least I wasn't on Earth.

Open a doorway and try to escape? Or wait and see?

I could open one, but being tied down made it kind of hard to walk through it. I'd be smarter to save my energy. At some point a better opportunity would present itself.

"I see you're awake, and still tied up. Are you sure you're a Walker?"

Tall, blond, and deadly appeared before me. And, no, he hadn't used the door. Nope, he just popped in somehow. So of course I shrieked loudly.

"Give a girl some notice ... cough or wear a bell or something," I managed to splutter out, my heart beating so hard it was about to exit my body.

He cocked his head to the side, the slightest smile gracing his lips. He was examining me.

I began to wiggle my tightly bound hands. They felt like they'd been tied together and then attached to the back of the chair. I could lift them up a little, but I couldn't move them apart from each other.

"What creature are you, baby Walker?" He stepped closer. "Who is your father?"

Should I tell him? Would it make a difference to whether he allowed me to live?

"Why are you holding me captive? Is this normal behavior between Walkers? And aren't you worried that my family is going to uber-pissed by this little 'hostage situation'?"

He threw his head back and laughed. "Your ape-like speech is actually endearing. Usually I find it ear-piercing, and want to kill whoever is speaking."

"You're so arrogant," I sneered. "What the hell makes you so awesome?"

What a giant asshole. This guy was getting on my last nerve; he was like a cartoon character he was so obnoxious.

"The mere fact I have existed for close to a thousand years is reason enough. I have seen cultures rise and fall. I have seen the evolution of man." He laughed. "In fact, I have participated in many of these historical events. I am everything and everywhere, seeing all, and have decided that no longer shall the worlds, any of them, continue down the same destructive path."

Oh, great. He was bat-nuts crazy. And I was tied to a chair in the room with him.

"A mass culling is required on all of the worlds. I have started with Spurn. Weed out the weak, the unworthy. I'm doing the worlds a favor. They will be stronger. It's survival."

I could see that he honestly believed he was working for the greater good. And unfortunately he probably could 'go mad with power', as they put it.

"I think that if the worlds wanted your opinion on their current path, they'd have probably asked for it."

He stared at me without saying a word. I tightened my energy around my mind, and hoped he couldn't break in. He flicked his fingers then, and the ropes binding my hands and feet fell free.

"You're no longer my prisoner. If you can find your way from here, without the use of Walker doorways, then you're free."

I rubbed my chafed and bleeding wrists together. The ropes had cut me during my struggle, but by the time I looked again the skin was starting to heal. Within moments there was just creamy unmarked flesh. No sign of any injury.

"You're quite magnificent." His words washed over me.

I leaned back from all the creepy he was emitting.

"Is the Abernath your mate?"

I was confused for a second before I remembered him calling Brace that.

"What's an Abernath?" I demanded as dozens of thoughts flickered through my mind.

His eyes widened in surprise. "He hasn't told you of his family?" His expression grew calculating. "The Abernaths are the most powerful clan. Even without his marks displayed, the power he released was impressive. He has to be a high-ranking member."

I'm a little slow at the moment, but is he saying what I think he's saying?

"Brace ... is a Walker?" I spluttered out, my words almost incoherent.

Pain and anger flooded through me. I felt betrayed at the highest level. Why hadn't anyone told me this? Why had Josian kept it from me?

The Walker interrupted the flood of betrayal that was dragging me down. His laughter echoed around the stone of the room.

I got to my feet in one blinding lunge of anger. I was standing before him so quickly that I realized for the first time I'd utilized Walker speed.

"Answer me," I yelled, my energy bubbling over.

He was a liar. He had to be, otherwise I was the world's biggest idiot. I was going to kill Brace when I got my hands on him.

"You said his name is Brace?" A flicker of ... fear maybe ... entered his eyes. "Then he is Que's son. The Princeps of the Abernath line." He lowered his head until we were almost at eye level. "I think I was lucky to escape with you when I did."

My head hurt again as I thought back to the moments in Silver City before I blacked out. "What did you do in the city?"

All I had were disjointed memories, flickers, images – all terrifying.

"I dissolved the bonds that formed the water dome," he said, his tone casual.

At that moment my heart stopped beating. As it stuttered to life again, the full repercussion of his actions flooded me and I dropped to my knees. I attempted to suck in some air. My protesting lungs were starving, but nothing was responding.

"You killed my friends," I stammered out through gulps. "They couldn't have survived that."

He shook his head. "I have no idea. Brace will have survived; nothing would take out an Abernath. But the rest – collateral damage."

"Noooo!" I screamed long and loud.

Sobs broke from me as I stumbled back to my feet. I couldn't escape the mental images; all that water crashing in on them. Lucy, especially, could not have survived. My energy filled me up, expanding my insides until it was forced from me, along with continued screams of outrage.

I shot everything I had into the blond Walker. My energy was irrevocably tied to my pain. The walls began to shake as dust fell from the roof. The stones groaned as they began to shift free. The room around me was crumbling to the ground.

Despite the depth of my pain, the ache in my heart and the burning in my eyes, I could not sustain the flow for long. I collapsed again, and as I fell forward my arms cushioned my face before it hit the floor. At that moment the walls came down. I waited to be crushed under the heavy stone cciling, but nothing landed on me. I sobbed uncontrollably. I was so tired and the shock of my loss crushed my ability to fight. Bruising grips encircled my biceps and lifted me to my feet.

"Your power is remarkable, baby Walker."

He held me up off the floor, and my exhaustion was such that I let my head hang limply.

"And I've changed my mind. Since you're such a surfeit of secrets and intrigue, I'm going to keep you for a while. If anything, you're a good bargaining chip with the Abernaths."

And as quick as that I was back tied to the chair. And he'd disappeared again.

I tried desperately to direct power toward my tethers, but I was empty and the wisps did nothing except float around me. Accepting a semblance of defeat, I dozed for a while, my thoughts dark, my heart heavy. I tried to block Brace from my mind, but I couldn't rid myself of those moments – playing in the netting and the stolen kisses. I felt as if the person I was then was gone.

Brace. I trusted him. How could he have lied to me about something so fundamental? How could no one know, not even Josian?

On top of this I also couldn't shed thoughts of Lucy. But until I saw her lifeless body with my

162

own eyes, I would never accept her death. I was stubborn and single-minded that way.

Eventually I pulled myself together somewhat, and the tears stopped flowing. There only so much 'pity party' I could throw without being very annoying. I knew, once I was free, I'd have ample opportunity to drown my sorrows, but until then I needed to get myself together.

I found the strength to open my eyes before lifting my head to once again see my surroundings. My earlier burst of temper had collapsed all four walls so I could see beyond. I was on a small island, surrounded by the large stone blocks that used to form my prison. The stone room must have been set up as a sole dwelling. The island was surrounded by large cavernous turrets and huge gulleys. The Walker had never planned on setting me free. No way could I have traversed this type of unforgiving terrain without the aid of a doorway.

I opened my mind then, dropping the energy encasing my thoughts. No way was I sitting here like this for all eternity. I was not a fan of crazy nut jobs. I'd spent enough time with Olden, the psychotic Earth compound leader, to know that could only end in tears, or near-fatal stabbings.

Josian, Dad ... I need help ... Can you hear me?

163

I knew it was a long shot, but if anyone could save me it was my father. Of course, I was only guessing, since I'd never bothered to learn the mind-speak thing.

Brace, I said tentatively, uncomfortable but willing to try the liar. I'd take rescue from anyone at this point.

"There is really no point in screaming quite so banshee-like. This is my realm, and no one can hear you." He appeared before me again, but this time I was too exhausted to react.

"I have finally figured out what bothers me about you, baby Walker." He paced a few steps before spinning around to face me. "You're not a Walker. Josian is slumming it with a First-World ape woman, and you called him father."

He shook his head. "But it's not possible. You cannot be a halfling. We were told it was a legend and that no one could bring Walkers to heel." He muttered like the crazy he had inside was spilling out.

I watched a myriad of emotions cross his face, and suddenly all I could see was fear. I could tell he was not happy about it. I held my breath, knowing this was about to get really bad for me.

He threw out a hand, and I screamed as the agony of a lightning bolt coursed through me. The pain burned, charring me from the inside out until my body was on fire.

I glanced down to see if my skin had been crisped from my bones. I gasped as I noticed small burn marks littering my arms. They almost looked like exit wounds. Strangely, none of these round, red burns marred the lace design. I was distracted from all thoughts as his assault continued. And no matter how hard I tried, I couldn't stop my screams. I hated giving him that satisfaction. The moments blended together. Minutes or hours, I could no longer tell one from the next. There was just pain.

"Tell me what you are. Give me an explanation that doesn't go against everything I've known." He lifted his hand, allowing me a small reprieve from the agony.

My entire body shook as it burned.

"Must be a trap." His mutters grew louder.

His tone wasn't exactly panicked, but for the first time some of his confidence wavered.

His hand shot out again, only this time I tensed. It did nothing to quell the agony. My screams echoed, bouncing off the acoustics of the surrounding landscape. Over and over he burnt me alive, peppering me with questions I would not answer. I would not set this psycho against my father or Brace. I would protect my remaining loved ones, if it was the last thing I did.

Eventually, my voice was barely a whisper, the screams faded to hoarse gasps. I knew if I looked down again I would see more of the burn marks scattered all over. But I didn't look.

"You're strong. I respect that, and I'll leave you for the moment. I don't want to break you before I enjoy you." He studied me, his violet eyes dark. "Try and remember, I can do this for all of eternity. It will be easier if you simply give me the answers. You don't have to suffer."

I didn't move as his presence disappeared from the small island. I gasped in small breaths, my aching throat protesting even the light presence of air through the raw space. Despite the fact I had no moisture left in my body to cry tears, I sobbed in my mind.

One face continued to appear before me. My body and soul were battered and bruised and they were screaming for Brace. I hadn't forgotten that he had deceived me, lied with every breath he took. But my soul didn't care. It ached for the comfort of its mate.

Brace.

The scream of a soul in agony was stronger than anything I could have ever imagined. There was no answer, and this time no blond psycho even appeared. I was well and truly alone. Shifting my aching shoulders, I could not move and find comfort. Slumping forward again, I closed my eyes. Again I drifted. For endless moments I was semi-conscious. I needed to pull myself together. I was stronger than this, and after I found Brace and killed him for his deception, I'd have to get used to being alone.

"Red."

I thought for a moment I was still dreaming. The familiar voice, the annoying nickname, it was too much to believe that he had found me.

"I will always find you, Abby. Always." When he answered, I realized I'd spoken my thoughts out loud, my voice rasping over each word.

The ropes binding me fell free, and if strong arms had not encased me I would have fallen forward to the floor. I found a sliver of strength to lift my heavy head. Brace's beautiful face was close to mine as he held me up. His eyes were black again, fury burning in their depths. But his features remained gentle as he pulled me even closer, his scent brushing across me as he let out a relieved sigh. And in that moment my soul began to sing.

"Shit – sorry, Abbs – I'm just ... not sure where to hold you." He shifted his arms in an attempt to avoid the obvious burns.

My entire skin blistered like it was still on fire. *Why weren't the marks healing?*

"Hang on, baby. I'll get you out of here. And then I have a Doreen to eliminate."

Fury crashed in around me, and I realized that Brace was just barely holding onto his self-control. His aura was pulsing blood red, and despite his gentle hold I could somehow feel his unrestrained rage.

His anger awoke my own, and as clarity returned I began to struggle in his arms.

"Get your hands off me, you big lying liar," I murmured past the rawness in my throat.

I pushed at his chest, which did not move him even one fraction of an inch. A flash of fear chased some of the heat from his eyes.

"Your voice, Red? What the hell happened to your voice?"

His concern brought tears to my eyes. I managed to stop them from spilling over. He pulled me closer.

"I need to know ... what did he do? He's already to be destroyed. But I haven't decided if I'll make it quick, or take my time."

"Don't ... just, just don't." Weariness spilled from me.

His lips brushed against my cheek, whether by accident or design, I wasn't sure. He inhaled deeply as he rested his face in my neck.

"I promise I'll explain everything to you. I don't know what the Doreen told you, but I have my own side to this. Swear to me you won't reject us until you hear the entire story."

I lifted my head slightly to examine him. His vulnerability appealed to me in a way I couldn't fight. I knew that Brace was an exceptionally strong man. He contained himself and his emotions, but his power was always apparent. Vulnerability was not something he generally displayed. But how could I trust his words again?

"Lucy?" I had to ask, even though I wasn't sure if I could handle the answer.

"She's fine. Sammy and Lucas as well."

My heart stopped. I clutched at him for the first time, pulling him closer.

"Swear to me that they're all fine. Where are they? How did you survive the city collapse?"

"I swear to you, Red. I would never lie to you about something so important."

I snorted.

He continued, although his expression held something ... shame maybe ... and pain. "I opened a doorway and pulled everyone through. They're on First World. Josian returned just after as well.

169

For some reason he knew you were in trouble. Right now I'm pretty sure he's out destroying worlds trying to find you."

"How did you find me?" I asked, my husky voice high with relief.

No one had died. I hadn't lost those few people who made my world complete.

"I don't know. I was going crazy, calling in every favor I've ever had to figure out who the Doreen was that took you."

I held up a hand to halt him.

"What is an Abernath and a Doreen? And don't even think about hesitating. When I ask a question about my life, I deserve to know the truth."

I'd had enough of being the last to know. That ended today.

"They're two of the Walker clans. You're a Doreen – red marks. I'm an Abernath; we have black."

"Like Talina?" I questioned.

He nodded once. His eyes locked on mine as he continued to hold me close. There wasn't one inch of space between us. And, despite my anger, and the pain of the burns scattering my skin, I couldn't find the strength to pull away.

Brace examined me closely. "I heard you – you were with me for a moment – in my mind. I felt you calling for me, and a doorway appeared. I didn't think twice, I just stepped through."

"Impossible!" The angry word echoed around us but with the acoustics here I couldn't tell where the blond Walker was. "How did you find her? I have this realm barred to all doorways."

My kidnapper strode out of a crevice to stand before us. Damn freak must just hang around in the caves.

Brace lowered me to the ground, but my legs refused to bear my weight and crumpled. Without a pause, he simply shifted his stance and brought me back up into his arms.

"Sorry, I think my arms and legs are asleep from being tied for so long." I had tingles through them now, but they felt like they weighed a ton.

"Don't apologize, Red. I can hold you up and rip his head off. No problem." His smile was confident.

I resisted the urge to touch his perfect white teeth. At least one thing was explained: his unnatural looks: he was Walker.

The ground began to shake beneath our feet. I turned my anxiety toward Brace. He smiled. A large crevice began to divide the space between us and the Doreen Walker.

Could Josian ex-communicate Walkers? Because this psycho needed to go.

171

"Your pathetic little power show does nothing but tire you," the Doreen said. "I have claimed the baby Walker. Leave now and I will forgive your intrusion."

I expected Brace to lose it then. Instead he threw back his head and laughed. With a twinkle in his eyes, the stormy black faded slightly, not quite back to his beautiful brown, but closer.

"How can you have spent any time with Red and not know that she's owned by no one? I only wish she knew how to use her powers. She'd have ended your sorry ass."

My lips turned up in a half-smile as I lay my head against his shoulder. Hearing him swear was a novelty; he usually didn't use much slang. Only what he'd picked up from me and Lucy.

Exhaustion was getting the better of me. I started to miss bits and pieces of their words. Whatever lightning thing he'd zapped me with earlier had really knocked me around.

"You cannot escape. Why would you start a clan war over a halfling?" The Doreen's words were interrupted by a bolt of energy smacking him straight in the face.

He was knocked backwards, off the island and into the endless abyss below.

"Shi – did you just kill him?" I struggled to sit up.

172

"Come on, Red. He's a Walker. That wouldn't have even scared him. I'm just looking to buy us some time until I figure out how to get out of here."

Okay, I felt a bit stupid, but it wasn't my fault I continued to forget that they weren't human. I wasn't raised to believe in Walkers.

As Brace strode us closer to the edge of the deep gulley, I could see his mind working away, trying to figure out how to save me.

Since I wasn't the type of person that generally waited for a knight to rescue me, I decided to see if I could access a doorway. Brace had said I'd brought him to me, so maybe I could send us home. I gathered some energy. It responded far quicker than the last time. My power was growing.

Picturing my bedroom back home, I was about to draw from my sticky taffy energy and create a doorway when I noticed something. Around the image of my room were these long, dangling and glittering threads, a bit like strings that anchored it to ... something. I hadn't noticed them before, but maybe I just hadn't been paying attention. Without much hesitation, with instinct guiding me, I latched on to one of the tethers and yanked hard.

"What the hell, Red? – "

My eyes were still closed, but they flew open at his exclamation. I was in his arms, but we were no longer on the island of crazy. Instead we were standing on my bed, in my room, on First World. In the exact spot the cord I pulled had been attached. Brace and I stared at each other for a moment. My eyes were so wide with shock I was sure they were about to fall out of my head.

"Did you just trac –?" His words were cut off as my bedroom door slammed open.

"Baby girl." Josian's words were strangled as he wrestled me from Brace and engulfed me in a bone-crushing hug.

I breathed in chunks of his flaming red hair as he held on. My skin screamed in protest, agony coursing through me. But I wouldn't have pulled back for anything.

"Josian, you're hurting her." Brace's words were flat, his anger simmering once more.

Immediately the bands surrounding me loosened and I could breathe again.

"How did you know I was back?" I asked him, still cradled in his arms and my feet dangling off the floor.

Walkers had this ability to make me feel small and dainty.

His molten eyes were bronze today, although they had a habit of changing color like the turning leaves in fall.

174

"I sensed the intrusion in your room. I didn't know it was you." His arms trembled slightly as he held on. "Who took you, baby girl? Who will answer to me and our clan's wrath?"

Brace, who'd just stepped off the bed, paused next to us. "He's of your clan, Josian. The man was a Doreen."

This statement was followed by a moment of silence and then an explosion of cursing. Josian placed me on the bed so that he could storm around the room. He alternated between languages, but I figured out the general tone.

Brace eventually interrupted him. "I know we have a lot to discuss, but I really need a few minutes with Abby." He was standing beside my bed, his entire demeanor hard, his expression borderline frosty.

Josian stomped over, getting right into Brace's face. He pointed his long finger in jerky motions as he spoke.

"If you do anything inappropriate for an unmated Walker I will rip you into little pieces, and then scatter them through the worlds. It will take you a long time to put yourself back together."

Brace nodded.

Josian kissed me on the cheek before leaving the room. The door closed loudly behind him, before slamming back open again.

"Leave the door open, Brace." Josian's words drifted in to us.

I stared up at Brace as he began to shake, his anger filling the room until I couldn't breathe.

"When he took you, Abby, I have never felt fear like that. I'm unused to this concept of worry. I don't know how to contain my rage. I find I don't like this feeling."

Did anyone?

"What did he do to you?" He closed his eyes. "Tell me he didn't touch you ... violate you." As he locked me in his gaze I could see the agony and fear that I'd been hurt.

"Would it make a difference to your feelings for me if he did?" I had to ask.

His anger swelled again. I found it hard to breathe.

"You haven't really grasped the concept of mate, have you, Abigail? The only difference would be the level of torture I would inflict before I killed him. My feelings for you will never be influenced or affected."

I decided to put his mind at ease. "No, Brace, it was more along the lines of torture, nothing sexual." For which I was more than thankful.

176

"I need to see that you're okay." He approached me, arms held up in a pose of calm. "Please, and then I'll leave, if that's what you want."

I doubted very much he would leave that easily. But, right now, I couldn't bring myself to be without him. I needed more energy than I currently possessed to hold on to my anger and push him away. Anger definitely takes energy. I nodded my permission.

He picked me up and strode into the bathroom. I noticed that the huge bath was half full, bubbles lining the surface and a sweet smell permeating the air.

I didn't question it; he'd probably used Walker powers.

He set me down gently. And for the first time I noticed my reflection in the large mirror. I couldn't help the small gasp that escaped. Stepping closer, I realized that the Spurn attire hid nothing. Instead, the tattered white wraps highlighted the red burns that covered my body. Although, strangely, there was still not one burn through my marks.

"Why are they not healing?" I said, biting back a whimper. The pain seemed to increase in that moment.

"It will take longer for you to heal from a Walker attack." Brace stepped closer to brush my tangled hair back.

My red curls were everywhere.

I continued to stare at my dirty and injured image, and suddenly the weakness erupted in my chest. I crumpled in on myself as the sobs began. Strong arms encased me.

"I didn't know how I would take the pain any longer," I sobbed, hating my weakness but needing it all the same.

"I will kill him."

Finally I pulled back. I couldn't believe it when I noticed a shine in Brace's eyes. Despite the hardness of his features, he looked to be fighting back tears of his own.

"Let's get you in the bath, Red. I'm sure you want to wash away the last couple of days."

I let him lead me across and I even let him strip the remaining mesh from my body. I couldn't find energy to be embarrassed. Besides, he'd seen me naked before, and he refused to leave, worried that I would slip getting into the bath.

I eased into the hot bubbles. I couldn't help the small whimpers that escaped as the water hit my burns.

Brace cursed, but his hands were still gentle.

"You have no idea the level of self-control required right now." His teasing helped to shift my attention from the pain. "And I think I hate bubbles."

I managed a smile. "You hate bubbles?"

"They're caressing every naked inch of your beautiful body, and that's really my job."

His words were the perfect distraction. My body was now flush with levels of want and need I was very much unaccustomed to. I almost reached out to pull him in with me. But before I could react, he reached behind me for some type of soft sponge and started to gently dab it over my shoulders.

He didn't go any lower, for which I was both grateful and disappointed. But I knew my wounds couldn't stand to be touched.

After a few sweeps from Brace, my panic took over, and, grabbing my own cloth, I started to scrub harder. I had to erase all moments in that prison. I dropped below the water for a moment to soak my hair. After many rinses, I finally felt as if I was clean.

Suddenly the water started to bubble. I could feel pulsing shoots of water from jets all around the tub.

"Close your eyes and relax, Red. I'll be here, and I promise not to let you drown."

Since I was safe, clean and warm, I dropped my heavy head back into the groove and, closing my eyes, drifted off.

Chapter 8

After awakening in my bath, I opened my eyes to see Brace leaning against the wall. It looked as if he hadn't taken his eyes off me the entire time. Striding forward, he touched my face gently.

"Find Lucy and Lalli. They're worrying themselves to death," he said, giving me one last nod before leaving.

I hurried to dress and make my way downstairs.

Descending to the next level, I looked around. The house seemed strangely silent. Where was everyone?

"Aribella," Lallielle exited the theatre room at a rapid pace, "thank god you're here safe and sound."

She gathered me gently into her arms, her sweet scent surrounding me. She ushered me into the room, where Lucy pounced on me. I found myself bundled up on the cinema room couch, its luxurious depths once again enfolding me in a loving embrace. I had Lucy snuggled up on one side and Lallielle on the other. A *Man vs Wild* episode was on the television.

Lucy was bringing out all my favorites, trying to distract me, but I couldn't concentrate. I didn't even care about the popcorn and chocolate, although I still ate them (I'd hate to waste that type of goodness). Thankfully my burns were finally starting to heal; I was barely in any pain now. Although their rapid scabbing over was itchy and a little annoying.

"Honestly," I said for the fiftieth time, "why the hell couldn't they just leave it alone?"

Apparently Brace and Josian had taken off to find the blond Doreen.

"I still can't believe he didn't tell you he was a Walker. That boy needs his ass kicked." Lucy was furious.

When I told her everything, including the possibility Brace was my mate, she'd exploded.

"I still don't understand how your father never sensed Walker energy from him. I was under the impression they could always tell one another," Lallielle fretted.

"I'm pretty sure Walkers don't know the ass end of a Walker from the ass end of a donkey," I said bluntly. "All their stories are useless. Not one of them has worked out yet." I crossed my arms, daring Lallielle to rebuke me for my language.

She wisely remained silent.

"I might be spitting mad at Lying McLiar," Lucy had started giving Brace a variety of nicknames, "but, Abbs, you should have seen him when you went missing. The moment he pulled us through the doorway he went nuts. The air around him was pulsing with energy, and he kept setting things on fire."

Lucy's anger had re-sparked my own. Despite Brace's sweetness when he had cared for me upstairs I was still upset. The betrayal was hard for me to get over. I didn't trust easy, and it felt like such a slap in the face since he was one of the very few people I had counted on. But I did know one thing. I owed Brace for the rest of my very long life for saving Lucy.

"But, let me tell you, the most shocking was Lucas," Lucy continued.

I spun around in my chair to face her directly.

"What do you mean? What happened with Lucas?" I hadn't seen him. He'd been called back to the palace, something about his father.

"Well, Abbs, he was almost as angry as your big giant Le-Liar. But he's like the opposite of Brace; he froze, wouldn't talk to anyone. When I walked past him, I swear, icicles attached to me."

"Well, those two have always reminded me of bookends, one fire and the other ice."

Lucy winked. "Pretty sure that's a dirty movie title, Abbs. Better get your schoolgirl outfit."

I blushed, the heat traveling all the way to the tips of my ears. I dropped my head, hoping I wouldn't catch my mother's eye. She didn't need to hear about the time when we were kids and accidentally discovered a pirated porn channel. In typical Earth fashion, even when almost no television shows existed, there was still pornography.

"I can't believe Talli didn't make it through the doorway." I hoped Lucy would accept the subject change for once.

And I was really worried about Talina. I hoped she'd made it out of the city collapse. We would have to go back soon and convince them to let her free. We needed her, and I couldn't leave her there for Gladriel to torment.

184

A jolt of power suddenly coursed through my body. Don't ask me how I knew, but a large energy source had just entered the house.

"Josian is back." Lallielle jumped to her feet.

But by this time the two men were already walking through the door.

"Dad!" I shrieked, running to him.

Lallielle was right behind.

We both threw ourselves into his arms.

"Did you find him?" I said, pulling back.

He shook his head, an arm around both of us. "No, we managed to figure out where his little floating rock was, but by the time we got there he'd vacated." He raised his head. "Brace made sure there was nothing left for him to come back to."

I looked behind me to see Brace standing in the doorway. Lucy gave him her squinty evil eyes, I think daring him to step any closer.

"Brace and I have had a conversation. And he has some explaining to do." Josian appeared to have gotten over the majority of his anger.

"Why should Abby ever trust a single word out of your lying mouth?" Lucy crossed her arms, moving a foot in quick hard taps.

"I know it's going to take time before you can trust me." He locked eyes with mine. "You deserve more than words, Abbs. You deserve actions, and I

185

plan on being that man. But I'll give you some words now, because there have been too many secrets between us."

I moved away from my parents to sit on the couch. Lucy sank in next to me.

"I'm listening." No matter how angry I was, I'd been dying to know his secrets since the first moment we locked eyes.

I had been too exhausted during the bath, but now I'd had plenty of time to process his lies. And if he didn't explain something I was putting my foot in his butt.

With a sigh, he moved further into the room, but didn't take a seat, just stood with his feet apart and arms rigid at his sides.

"I've been on First World for about fifteen years. My mission was to gather information."

I held up a hand. "What about Deralick? You said he was your father."

Brace shook his head. "No, he's not my father. I do some work for him. It allows me access to the royal forests. Deralick never even knew I broke you out that day. I've been around here for a long time, everyone knows me, but no one's ever bothered to find out who I am or where I'm from." He laughed without humor. "It was my mission to stay as undetected as possible."

The depth of his deception had my heart sinking. But my traitorous soul didn't care. Brace could have killed half the town and it would think he was awesome.

"Who were you gathering information for?" Lallielle had her hand tightly wrapped around Josian's.

"My father." Brace turned away. "I never questioned my orders. If you're an Abernath you do as you're told, especially if that command is from one more powerful than you."

"You were waiting for me?" I just knew that had been Brace's mission.

His stoic control broke for a moment, before he recovered. "Yes, I've been stationed here waiting for the moment you returned." He rubbed at his eyes in a tired manner. "I just never knew it was going to be you. The stunning redhead I'd escape with in my dreams. The one I knew was mine to find and protect."

"What does your father want with Abby?" Lucy leaned forward.

He laughed drily. "My father doesn't share his plans with me, but over the last few weeks I've been forming a theory."

We locked eyes.

"He might be the one releasing the Seventine, or at the very least he's involved. He knows about

187

the prophesy ... and he doesn't want anyone to stop it." His frustration rose. "I would have stopped him, but I've never questioned my orders. I was raised to accept him as the all knowing authority on everything, but I should have delved deeper."

"How could you keep lying even after you met me? You must have known then; you must have felt the connection." My voice broke.

Don't cry. I repeated it a few times to myself. *He's not worth your tears.*

"Of course I felt it, but I knew I had to keep you safe, and having this information would have been dangerous for you."

He rubbed his hands through his hair. "You have no idea how difficult it is to question my father. He is the Princeps, the supreme ruler of our clan. You accept your missions and never voice an opinion. I attempted to keep him satisfied with small useless pieces of information. And I stuck by your side to protect you."

I was on my feet now, tears forgotten as the anger flowed. I was afraid if I sat any longer, I'd be the one setting things on fire.

I turned to Josian. "Dad, how can you be fine with this? You should smite him where he stands or something."

Josian's lips turned up in a small smile. "My smiting skills are a little rusty, baby girl. And

188

unfortunately I understand Brace's position. Don't get me wrong –" he interrupted my unspoken words, "I'm not happy about what he's done, but Walkers do have a strong control system. There's not a lot of room to question the orders of those more powerful. And as Que is also Brace's father, he was in a tough position." He turned his head. "The fact that Abby's still here, still alive, and not in the hands of Abernath, tells me you've worked very hard to keep her safe."

"He's going to come for her now." Brace rubbed his chin. "He knows I haven't followed my mission. He won't rest until Abby is captured."

"He won't start a clan war over this; he's going to be sneaky about it." Josian didn't seem overly worried.

"I thought you'd be flipping out, Dad, locking me in my room until I'm thirty," I said, confused.

This didn't mesh with his personality; he was much too calm.

He laughed out loud, and I realized how much I'd missing that booming sound. It gave me a happy feeling deep down.

"Oh, I'm thinking about it, but since Brace believes you aren't exactly governed by the laws of Walkers, I doubt I could keep you anywhere you didn't want to be."

"Yes, Red, how did you get us off that island? I couldn't open a doorway. That Doreen had it barred with ancient stones. I didn't even know any of those still existed."

I faced him then, letting my eyes scream my anger. I felt betrayed at the basest level. I would never have deceived Brace. I don't think my soul would have let me.

"Don't call me Red," I said to him.

The rest I directed to my father.

"I didn't open a doorway. I was trying to picture my room like you showed me. Instead, there were all these glittery ties ... ropes tethered to the image. I was desperate enough to just grab on to one and yank hard. When I opened my eyes, we were on my bed."

"You ... you traced," his brow furrowed, "and not just yourself but another person. Aribella, that's astonishing and thoroughly impossible."

Of course it was.

"I thought she traced, but I couldn't believe it either. No Walker has been able to do that since ... well, the originals, right?" Brace's voice held the same contemplative wonder as Josian's.

He was still staring at me. I continued to ignore him.

Lallielle's face fell. "I'm so tired of hearing that my children have yet another thing to deal with, another trial they must overcome."

"No, Lalli, this is a gift. Aribella is one of the few Walkers not bound by the doorways," Josian said.

I was with Lallielle. All these new powers kind of stunk. Well, it wasn't that they were so terrible. It was not knowing how to use them, and what new one would pop up when I least expected it.

"And it's also instantaneous." Brace was close.

I could feel that heat he always generated.

"You don't have any time-delay, as there is to walk between the worlds using the doorways."

I sat up straighter. Could I actually have a skill that was beneficial and not just a pain in my butt?

"So what exactly is tracing? And don't ask me to do it again. I have no idea how I did it the first time." I spoke artlessly, but on the inside I was extremely interested.

Josian smiled.

Sneaky Walker could probably read my excitement.

"Every object, whether alive or inanimate, contains energy, which you already know. But what I haven't taught you is that they're all connected to each other and to the planet they inhabit. This is part of what allows Walkers to open doorways. Our energy isn't connected to any planets. We're not held down in ways that other races are.

"Those ropes you saw attached to your room are the energy tethers that allow this room to exist in this house and on this planet. If the energy wasn't tethered down, it would disperse and no longer exist in the manner in which you understand it … as a bedroom."

I held up a hand to interrupt. My Walker brain was having no problem keeping up, but my Earthling side was going: *What the hell?*

"So without these tethers nothing would exist? Well, not in the form our brains could see, process and understand."

Josian nodded. His deep voice rose in timbre. "Yes, it's quite a concept to wrap your mind around, but the sole reason that the planets exist, that things are formed as trees, lakes and all of that, is because of these tethers." He took a deep breath. "And that's why you also should not be possible."

He has such a way with words.

"I mean, how can something be tethered to a planet, and then not tethered to anything like the Walkers? Obviously, your dual nature has found a balance, as have the other halflings, but because of this it's as if all the general laws that govern energy don't apply to you."

I ignored that for the moment. I was a freak, not exactly a new concept.

"What are the planets tethered to?" I tried to picture them swinging off a star or something. Lallielle's lips lifted in a gentle smile as she answered.

"Well, you know all of the younglings are tethered to First World. And First World is tethered to the star system itself. The effect just continues to ricochet backwards."

I gasped, my hands covering my mouth in shock. "That's what the Seventine do, isn't it? They sever the tethers."

Josian looked impressed.

Geez, I must look slow.

"Yes, Aribella, that's exactly what they do. Their entire aim is to eliminate all existence except Walkers. And once this happens, all of that free, untethered energy is ours for the taking. Since we have no tethers, we cannot easily be undone, or reformed."

I wondered where that left me in the scheme of energy tethers and not existing. I pictured half of my body floating away.

"So, if First Worlders are tethered to their planets, how can they travel to other worlds?"

I thought of Lallielle going to Earth and ... what about Lucy? She'd been traipsing all over the place.

"Tethers are not bound by space, time or distance. As long as the object of tethering still exists, then so does everything tethered to it."

Brace groaned and ran his hand through his dark hair in a jagged manner. It fell messily across his forehead again.

I had to restrain myself from moving forward and pushing it off his face.

"My father is a purist. He's adamant that the Walker line is being polluted with the mortality of others." His words brought back my anger.

"Can I have a few minutes alone with Brace?" I asked the room, my eyes locked on his perfect Walker features.

I alternated between wanting to kiss him senseless and wanting to smash him one in the jaw.

Lallielle and Josian touched my arm briefly before they exited. They were so tall and graceful. I never had enough of watching the love and trust between my parents. But right now it felt a little bitter-sweet.

"I'm going to find Sammy." Lucy paused in front of me. "Follow your heart, Abbs. If it says not to trust him until he proves himself then go with that." She leaned in even closer. "I know he's hot, but so what? Lucas is also hot and he seems a damn sight more trustworthy. And the way he lost it when you were taken and all the questions he asked, well, Brace definitely has a little competition."

The mention of Lucas still gave me a strange jumping sensation. But honestly I was about ready to write men off completely. A low growl sounded from where Brace was standing, but a quick glance at him didn't reveal any obvious emotion.

Lucy turned then and, moving almost Walker-quick, was in Brace's face ... okay, more like his navel.

"If you hurt Abby again, Mr. Liarkins, you're going to have to answer to me. And trust me, I do not play nice. I can get down and dirty with the best of them, and you will eat every one of your lies."

I smiled. She was as tenacious as a pit-bull for those she loved.

Brace refrained from smiling, although his eyes were laughing. "I promise you, young warrior, Abby is my reason for existence. I will never knowingly hurt her again."

She stared at him for a few moments. Something in his words must have mollified her because she turned away. As she reached my side she stretched up to kiss my cheek and left the room.

Brace and I stared at each other from across the room. He'd straightened infinitely but didn't move closer. I liked that he didn't ask for forgiveness or beg. That would have just been pathetic. Words couldn't undo the hurt he'd caused me. They couldn't regrow the trust he'd damaged, and they sure as hell couldn't govern any forgiveness.

He seemed to read my thoughts.

"I won't apologize to you again, Abby. I know I effed up, as Lucy would put it." He looked so serious, his eyes almost black. "I want to show you ... no, I need to show you what you mean to me. You can't possibly understand. You've not grown up as a Walker. You've not spent hundreds of years searching. You're the light to my darkness." He finally took a step closer. "I never thought I would find you. I hoped, of course, but my life hasn't led me down the road of gracious gifts. And you ... with your beauty, your strength, you're the most gracious gift I could ever have hoped for."

Again, it was as if he had a direct link to my mind, as if he plucked out the most perfect words that anyone could hear. I wanted to bawl my damn eyes out or fall at his feet and beg him to love me forever. But the burning in my heart reminded me of one thing: I had responsibilities, big ones.

I'd continue to be hunted and hurt and would probably die in a huge fiery war at the end. And right now, with all my anger, I needed to step away from the intensity that was Brace. But I knew, without any doubt, that it was going to be agony to not have him close by. My soul felt him now, and it wanted him by its side forever. Maybe I just needed some time. Time to finish my mission, and deal with all the crap that was my life.

"I can't say I understand why you lied to me for so long. I really don't. Maybe I wasn't raised Walker, but I know the concept of right and wrong. And what you did was wrong."

I turned away from him then; I would never be able to get these words out while I continued to drown in his beautiful, depthless eyes.

"My soul tells me that we're mates. But my heart needs some time, Brace. I need some time to figure out who I am and to go on these missions. I have to find the halflings. There's no other option."

"I understand that. I would never ask you to stop being who you are, even though I want to wrap you up and never let anything touch you. Let me help you, Abby. We're partners, and we're stronger together."

I shook my head in short stuttering motions. My heart ached. I was so afraid that because of me Brace would be hurt or killed. Yeah, he was Walker, but he could still be destroyed.

"I need you to leave, Brace. I need time to think about everything."

I was surprised when a grin crossed his face. "I'll be gone for a brief moment. I have a certain family member to confront. But I'll be back. You can't get rid of me that easily. I won't leave you, Red. Not ever."

And then he was standing before me. Reaching out, he pulled me hard. I landed against firm muscles, and then his lips were on mine. The kiss was scorching, burning me to the depths of my soul. Brace kissed as if there was nothing else in the world but me, as if I was the very substance he needed to exist.

I felt it then, that moment of pure unadulterated joy between us. Something changed; the ties cemented between us. In the way that I saw pink circling Josian and Lallielle, strands of gold, shining the brightest I had ever seen, surrounded Brace and me.

"I'll leave you now, Red. But don't get too comfortable without me." He kissed me gently on the corners of my lips. "So soft and full, tempting me every day." His expression was stoic as he visibly devoured me, like he was memorizing every tiny detail. "You have lips built for sin."

Then, with another gentle caress, he walked out of the room.

I stood there for a moment, my finger tips touching the smoldering of my lips. I knew when his presence left the room, and then when he left First World.

My heart shattered, and my soul screamed. With a groan I dropped to my knees. The tears spilled over then. I wiped at them quickly, but they were flowing fast. I knew I'd done the right thing. Resting my face in my hands, I let the pain free. Barely holding back a scream, I sobbed out my heartache.

"Damn."

The softly spoken word broke through my hurt. I'd been crouched on the floor for so long that my legs protested as I straightened to face Lucas.

"I'm sorry to intrude." He looked uncomfortable. "It's just for some reason I felt your pain, and it's hard for me not to respond."

Rubbing a hand over my hot, swollen face, I took a step back. My head was heavy, and I felt a little slow.

"How did you ... What is our connection?" I demanded.

He shrugged, his eyes tight. "You're the chosen Empress of First World, Abby. I'm the chosen Emperor. We're connected and have been since birth."

My nose wrinkled as I attempted to digest his words. Was he still riding that gravy train?

"Lucas! I'm a Walker. I can't be the Empress."

"Abby!" He mimicked my tone. "You are half-Walker. Tell me why your First World side can't be the Empress?"

I stopped dead at those words. No ... oh, my fricken gods. Could my life be any more complicated?

"So you're telling me that my Walker half is Brace's mate, and my First-World half is the Empress connected to you?" My voice was almost hysterically high by the time I'd finished that sentence. A ridiculous sentence, which unfortunately explained a lot.

"I'm not sure about the Brace part, but you and me, that's a sure thing, gorgeous."

I rolled my eyes. Always with the sweet-talking.

"I find it difficult to take you seriously, Lucas. I'm not going to be your dalliance for this month. Not my style."

I couldn't even think of anything beside the ache deep down for Brace. I couldn't stand not knowing if he was okay. I straightened my shoulders. This was my choice. I had to get it together.

"Let's get this straight, gorgeous, you and I are cosmically connected." He leaned in closer, the light icy blue of his eyes darkening just slightly. "Not to say I don't enjoy the occasional dalliance, if that's where you want to take this."

Shaking my head, I gave him a shove. "Dream on, Lucas, you and I – never going to happen." I waved a hand dismissively. "You should probably attempt to think with the head on your shoulders. The other one is leading you astray."

He laughed. "Don't say that. You'll wound his humongous ... pride." He winked. "And I mean humongous."

I blushed. Of course I did, and of course he noticed.

"You know red is your color, gorgeous."

My next derisive comment was interrupted by Josian entering the room. He didn't acknowledge Lucas, just strode forward to stand before me.

"We have trouble, baby girl; you might want to head downstairs."

Chapter 9

I stared at Francesca, gobsmacked by her words.

"You're freaking kidding me, right?"

She shook her head, her demeanor apologetic, but the chill in her eye spoke of something different.

"I know before you left I said two of the Seventine were released, but apparently the second one wasn't quite free. Now it is. And the first tether has been severed."

"The Seventine are on the countdown to the final battle," she had told me the moment I stepped into the room, her creepy soothsayer voice washing over us.

And apparently we were now missing a few landmarks on Earth. The French population was probably stunned by the sudden disappearance of the Eiffel tower.

"And I have to leave straight away, to both collect Talina and move on to the other worlds?" My cup was running over with crap today.

"We're almost out of time, Aribella." She stood, her white eyes boring into me. "I know you're not stupid; I shouldn't have to explain this to you."

What the eff? I wasn't taking that from anyone, especially not a know-it-all soothsayer. I moved closer, getting in her face. I was taller than her by at least two inches.

"You better check that attitude, Francesca. I'm on my last sliver of patience, and it's been a long day. Which includes, but isn't limited to, me being kidnapped and tortured." I huffed in a few breaths. "So if you don't want to find yourself trekking to other worlds, dealing with the natives, and basically copping the crap we have, then be very careful about how you phrase your requests."

My power flew from me again, encasing the room. I recognized this energy. This was the dream thing I'd done before. When I looked around, I saw everyone was frozen to the spot. Josian shifted almost instantly. His eyes flew open in concern.

"What did you do to them, baby girl?" His brow was furrowed.

He moved toward Lallielle and gently nudged her.

"They're fine, Dad," I hurried to reassure him. "I did this once on Spurn. It appears to be a variation of Mom's power. I can project a dream out to people and they're virtually frozen in time whilst they relive moments of my life, or whatever I shoot at them. I don't know what they're seeing; I didn't mean to do it." I snorted. "Which pretty much sums up my energy."

Josian didn't leave Lallielle's side, his expression a combination of concern and a little pride. "Well, baby girl, I have to say Walkers don't possess the ability to freeze people or trap them in dream worlds. Once you grasp this power you'll be in control of something very useful and dangerous."

"Will you help me learn how to control it?" It was no use having a power if it only randomly sprang from me.

He nodded. "Of course. Like any ability or muscle, you just need to practice the projection, learn what triggers the release, and then you'll be able to dictate when it happens."

That sounded good to me, his words instilling a confidence that one day I'd be strong enough to control my half-Walker nature. I hoped we could start as soon as possible.

It took differing amounts of time, but eventually everyone started to stir. Anger poured off Francesca.

"I don't appreciate being included in your Walker energy show, Aribella." Her movements were stiff as she took a step away from me.

"Shouldn't you have seen that coming? You know, being an all knowing soothsayer." Sometimes smart comments just fall out of my mouth without my consent.

"Did you mean for us to see that, Aribella?" Lallielle interrupted Francesca's tirade by moving to my side.

I shook my head.

"I have no idea what you all saw. The power seems to adapt to whatever is annoying me at the time."

Lucy had slouched into Samuel's arms; he rubbed her back in soothing circles.

"Your torture, Abbs. We got to relive your torture by Captain Insano Walker."

I bit my lip, the memories a little too fresh. When I tasted blood I realized I'd clenched too hard. Setting my poor abused lip free, I looked for a distraction. Lucas was perched in the doorway, observing the room. Well, observing me, actually. I ignored the annoying tummy-jump; he was not the distraction I wanted.

"Sorry about that, Luce. Just remember, I'm half-Walker. I'm tougher than I look." No point clueing her in to how agonizing and debilitating that torture was.

She laughed into Samuel's shirt front. Before tipping her head back to face me.

"Don't lie to me, Abigail. I know you, and I've never seen you like that. Those screams were pure anguish."

I waved a hand to dismiss her worries. There was nothing she could do now, plus something she'd said reminded me of important information I was yet to share. My dismissal had fury flashing across Lucy features, but with a sigh she let me get away with it today.

"Dad, the Walker who kidnapped me, he said he was going to be the one to cleanse the worlds. He was starting with Spurn. I think that's where we'll find him." I couldn't let Walkers destroy their world; they deserved to be saved.

"He's probably responsible for that dragon creature," Lucy muttered, still looking annoyed.

I locked eyes with her, my emerald green and her baby blue clashing as we reached the same thought.

"Hell, yes. That makes sense. The Spurns can't fight that thing. A few more of them roaming the waters and they'll be wiped out." I looked at Josian. "I have to go back now."

"And this time I'll be going with her, Francesca." Josian glared at his sister-in-law.

She dropped her head into her hands, and even I could feel the worry bleeding out into the room. But as she lifted her face, the worry dispersed. She even smiled.

"You have gathered some Walkers, and I see that word of mouth is spreading as well. It should be okay for you to help them out this one time." Her white eyes continued to dart around, something that happened when she was 'seeing' the future.

"What is the big problem with Dad helping on the planets?" I had to ask.

She was really adamant about it. "You must learn, grow and develop your abilities, Aribella. If Josian helps too much and shoulders the bulk of your responsibilities, you won't be ready for the final battle."

I gulped audibly. "Have you seen anything about this battle?" I asked.

All I really wanted to do was scream. Who do we lose? Who will I lose?

Francesca rubbed her arm absentmindedly. "I can't tell anything yet. The future shifts and changes so rapidly. There are too many unanswered questions, too many choices that can change everything." She focused on me again, the freaky eyes giving me cold shivers. "But one thing is clear: if your abilities are not developed, we lose."

She coughed then, dropping to her knees, her head cradled in her arms.

"Go to Spurn now. You have to go ... Talina is in trouble." Her panicked words echoed around. "Go to the land again."

I turned to Josian. He already had a hand held out. I grabbed on.

"Everyone wait here. We'll be right back," he said as he opened a doorway.

Without hesitation we stepped through. In the last second Lucy yelled something at me. But I was gone before the words registered.

We arrived onto the golden beaches, right into the midst of chaos. Josian's bronze eyes flicked around as he tried to discern the most immediate threat.

I ducked instinctively as a mass of blue-hair dived at me. He was followed by another Baroon, who sailed over my head, courtesy of a cranky seven-foot Walker. Josian continued to throw around the tiny Spurns as they dived and attacked us.

"Aribella, baby girl, what the hell is going on here?" He lazily deflected an Earon this time. "We seem to have walked into a world of angry little people."

An emerald-haired woman had come quite close to landing a jab with one of their spears.

I spun around quickly, letting loose a roundhouse kick into the gut of a gray-haired – I couldn't remember their clan names. He flew through the air, crashing into three yellow-hairs, name unknown too.

"Get off me, you dirty Gerk," the yellow-haired snarled as he disentangled himself.

Right, gray was Gerk.

"There are four clans on Spurn," I yelled to Josian, but my explanation was cut off when I had to dodge a series of lightning-fast punches directed at me from a team of Baroons.

When one ducked in from the front, another came at my back. I elbowed the first one in the face, cracking his nose. A dark purple blood sprayed around violently. The other screamed in anger, diving onto my shoulders. I spun around fast enough that my own head spun, before running backwards and slamming into one of those tall trees. The groan from behind me indicated pain, but the weight didn't shift.

Josian was charging in my direction with at least twelve Spurns hanging off him. Suddenly, the weight on my back lifted. And I was free.

"What are they? Evil little munchkins?" Josian worked to dislodge all the Spurn barnacles he'd gathered.

They were so small and light compared to us that he could easily throw them a distance down the beach.

And for the first time we were alone, far enough from the main foray that we had a moment to prepare for the next onslaught.

"So there are four clans," I continued. "Blue is Baroon, emerald is Earon, yellow is ..." It took a minute for their names to come to me. "... Yertle and gray is Gerk." We were getting noticed again so I shuffled him behind a few trees. "None of them like the other clans. It's a constant battle, and they have the cold nature of their dual status. Think fish-people."

Josian looked like he was going to roll his eyes, but refrained. Like all Walkers, he carried a certain level of arrogance, especially to those less evolved species, amongst which I counted myself.

"Can you see your half-Walker anywhere?" He watched, quite interested in the bedlam on the beach.

I found the entire thing more comical than scary. At least half of the Spurns couldn't even walk properly on land. At one point they were actually taking themselves out.

I shook my head. "Her name is Talina. And, no, she's taller than almost all the Spurns: she should be easy to spot."

And then, as I scanned the running, fighting, wrestling mob … was that someone biting? I shook my head before noticing a large congregation down on the sand, in nearly the exact spot where we'd faced the creature before.

I gasped as the scene came into a clear and horrifying focus.

I took off at a sprint.

I could hear Josian hollering after me, but I didn't pause for a second; I wasn't sure we had an extra second.

It took no time to traverse the distance, thanks to my Walker genes. The horrifying scene I'd noticed from so far away came into focus. The Spurns had Talina, Raror and Gladriel strung up in some kind of rope contraption, suspended over a wooden platform. They were dangled out in the ocean. In the distance, two of the creatures were drifting closer.

"We sacrifice these Spurns so that you will leave us alone. They are the bringers of evil, so they will be eliminated for the greater good," a Baroon yelled, his lisping voice echoing over the ocean.

Where was Ladre? Wasn't he the spokes-Spurn around here?

Creature one and two were moving in. They'd been about a hundred yards offshore, but were closing that distance fast.

"Oi!" I yelled as I came up behind the jeering Spurns. "What the hell do you think you're doing?"

Pink faces spun in my direction.

I was so angry that both my fists were in the air. "Let them go, you dirty, rotten ... fish-people."

Opening my tight hands, I shot waves of light energy at them; this was one part of my powers that I could control.

But I also wasn't very strong or skilled.

My little stream just blew them around the beach. I didn't have to worry, though. I'd forgotten that Josian was right behind me, and he definitely knew what he was doing, blasting the group in all directions, throwing them far across the beachfront. Of course, this resulted in ropes being flung free, and the three captive Spurns plunging into the water.

"Dad, they're tied up; they can't swim," I yelled as he reached my side.

We were at the edge of the water.

Could they drown if they were bound? Did they need movement for their gills to work? So many questions I didn't have the answers to. I pointed out toward the fast-moving dragon-octopus animals.

"Those are the creatures, the ones Lucy and I think were modified by the Walker who kidnapped me."

"If I keep the big bugs occupied, can you rescue the Spurns?" He was already stepping out into the water.

"No, Dad ... I can't swim. Dad!"

But he wasn't listening any longer. He'd decided he was a cowboy and was already astride creature one, holding on to two of its tentacles.

Bloody Walkers.

With a deep panicked breath, I stepped into the water. Saltiness lapped around my shoulders as I continued further out into the cool waves. Suddenly, the ocean floor stopped its slow tapering and dropped away violently. I went under, spluttering the entire way. Luckily, I managed to close my airway, otherwise I'd have drowned immediately. Kicking my legs, and doggy-paddling my arms, I made it back to the surface. I pushed my heavy hair off my face, wishing I was wearing the light Spurn wraps instead of jeans and a t-shirt, which weighed a hundred tons.

After a few deep breaths, I ducked my head under, looking left and right. I was at a loss as to where Talina and her family were. The waters surrounding me were empty of all life forms – not surprising if those creatures were cruising around.

I continued my frantic search, my churning legs pushing me further from the shore. If I didn't find someone soon, I'd be the one in desperate need of rescue. Finally, I made it into the deeper water, close to where Josian was wrestling two giant octo-dragons. I shook my head, transfixed for a moment by the sight of such reckless stupidity. Walkers were awesome.

Ducking under again, I could still see almost to the ocean floor. I noticed some movement in the dark area to my right. Pulling my head out, I gulped in as much air as possible. Hoping half-Walkers didn't really need oxygen, I dived under and powered down. My muscles worked effortlessly; I enjoyed the mild burn as I churned through the water. I was relieved as the three Spurns came into sight.

It was their rolling movement that had caught my eye as they strived to free themselves from the ropes. Talina's eyes widened as I came into focus. My lungs weren't struggling yet. I wasn't

214

panicking, but I didn't want to push my luck. I knew if I got one of the three free, the rest would be okay. I was good with knots, but I didn't have to worry about that since I'd strapped a small knife into the side of my now ruined right boot. I don't like to leave the house unless I'm armed with at least one weapon.

Reaching down, I yanked it free, and started to swim around Talina. The clear lenses flickered up and down over her eyes, which honestly made me want to barf into the water. Luckily, I managed to control that impulse.

Once I was at her back, I lifted the knife; it was difficult moving against the water at this depth. Why the hell did the water feel heavy? Eventually I held the blade level with her bound hands. I sawed through the top section, groaning as I realized this was a double-layered vine-rope. I'd just cut into the second part when something that felt like steel bands gripped my ankles. I screamed, bubbles streaming from my mouth as I was dragged.

Pure panic gripped me as I was pulled at the speed of a bullet through the water, heading out in to the deep. I shifted my head to the side, trying to see what was taking me. Images of sharks and octo-dragons ran through my head. But as I finally glimpsed my captor I realized it was something much worse than an ocean creature.

Psycho-Walker was back.

I didn't have much time before I lost it, the lack of oxygen was starting to make itself known to my confused nervous system. My brain was pretty sure we needed oxygen to live, and it did not like going without.

In the back of my mind I knew we were eating up the miles, traversing away from the land. I clenched my fist and winced as something bit into my palm. I still had my knife. Somehow my pincher finger had clamped down on it. But how was I going to get into a position to hurt a Walker? It would have to be a near-fatal blow to slow him down. I would need to hit one of the major arteries. I quickly thought back to anatomy class, which at the compound was more a combination of first-aid and murder 101.

Sometimes you needed to know how the body was designed, so you knew the easiest way to kill a person. I wasn't generally the compound's perfect little soldier, but in that class I'd eagerly listened. I was always on the street and needed all the advantages I could find.

Considering how fast Walkers healed, I'd have to sever the artery, hitting it at a jagged angle to give myself the most time.

I had a few options.

One of my favorites was the femoral artery, easy to find, high on the inner thigh. It was a big artery, and if I hit it right he could bleed out in a minute. I had also been particularly proficient, during dummy practice, with the jugular vein and carotid artery. Although, considering how tall this Walker was, I'd be lucky to have enough reach for a clean shot into the side of his neck, which left, in the upper body, the brachial artery, though this small knife would have trouble severing the bicep muscle, and the axillary artery, which I could get to under the armpit.

I favored the axillary. It would be hard for him to reach and apply pressure to slow the bleeding. Therefore, it was my best hope that the healing would take long enough to give me a chance to escape.

I need a different life.

Probably a true thought, since I'd just spent thirty seconds of my remaining oxygen contemplating the best way to bleed out a Walker.

He was slowing in the water, and it was light around us now. As my head broke the surface I took a huge gasp of air. My lungs seized as I coughed in a rough manner.

"Hello, my precious baby Walker. I missed you, lovely." His caressing words washed over me.

I shuddered in revulsion. There was an obsessive stalker quality to not only his actions, but also now his words.

"The feeling is not mutual," I muttered, trying hard not to think of my last lot of torture at his hands.

Panic hovered much too close to the surface and I needed to stay in control a little longer.

His expression darkened. "I think maybe you just need to spend a little time with a real man. You will come to realize that we are a much better match than you and that Abernath."

I laughed, thinking he was kidding. The grip he suddenly had on my throat told me he was serious.

"No need to disrespect me. Do not forget your place. No matter the beauty I behold, you are still a half."

This was probably my best chance. He was holding me close, his eyes locked on mine. He wasn't looking down to see what my hands were doing. I didn't even care that I'd be left floating in the water. Anything was better than being in his presence.

With his arm gripping my throat, I had a perfect angle to hit the axillary. I tightened my grip on the smooth handle, preparing myself. I didn't shift my eyes, afraid to give away my intention.

Instead, I distracted him by moving my face closer to his. He didn't remove his hand, but he allowed me this.

"Tell me what you have to offer me. What am I missing out on?" I appealed to his massive ego.

Considering its size, I should have enough time to not only hit the artery, but probably dismember him too.

He smiled. His large white teeth reminded me of a shark about to devour its prey.

"Aribella, I shouldn't have to explain anything to you. You have experienced my power."

I bit my lip. I had absolutely no problem remembering the burn of his power. Psycho. I almost had the knife in position.

"You have witnessed my intellect and skills. My creatures are perfect; they have done the job I intended." He looked out over my shoulder, slight chuckles shaking his upper torso. "I have seen what no one else could. I scoff as they worship their so called gods and challenge them to be more omnipotent than me."

Out of the corner of my eye I could see the glint of steel, and my angle was perfect. Without hesitation I stabbed upwards, the shallow water offering almost no resistance to my Walker speed and dexterity. Despite my squeamishness, I never hesitated as it made contact with his skin. I continued to push until it was at its hilt.

I noticed once I pulled back that I had not only cut him with a knife, but had also depleted some of my power. It was bleeding from me in slow ebbs. As soon as I recognized this, I halted the flow. Shock registered on his face.

"Should have used your omnipotent powers to see that," I snarled as reached forward to twist the blade. "Maybe what you meant to say was impotent; it'd be more accurate."

He bellowed then, dropping me from his grip. Reaching around, he attempted to staunch the flow of blood before realizing the knife was still lodged. As he pulled it free, small spurts of blood erupted from the wound.

"What have you done to me, Aribella?" he spluttered as his blood gushed into the water, coloring it a dark red.

I kicked my feet, keeping my head above water and working my way backwards. He didn't follow me. Instead he went a deathly white color and started to sink into the depths of the water.

I lay back, floating like I'd practiced on First World, and began to kick my legs hard, powering in the direction I hoped was land. I stared up at the half-sun. Its weak light was my visual guide. I didn't think or worry about the creatures that much blood could bring. I just kicked.

It took me a long time to tire myself. I couldn't even say when I noticed the slowing of my kicks, the heaviness of my body. But eventually, when I couldn't kick any longer, I just floated. The sun disappeared.

The world shifted into shades of blue as the four moons spanned the sky. And for the first time I wondered if I would die out here, if my First-World side, which could drown, would prevent the immortality of my Walker genes. Finally, as my exhaustion reached its maximum, I let the few tears that had been threatening fall free.

Faces crossed through my mind. Lucy, Lallielle, Josian – my family would be devastated. And then lastly, Brace.

I wished that I'd told him how I felt, that although I hated that he'd lied to me, at the end of the day life is short and I didn't want to die out here and never know what being loved by Brace was like. That he was the one to get me through the tough, lonely nights on Earth, and that I'd wait for an eternity for the perfect kind of love that I thought we'd have.

I held his image close.

For some reason I could feel his warmth, and a renewed sense of energy flowed through me. With a deep breath, I kicked out again, determined not to give up. Despite the fact I loved the inbuilt protection half-Walkers had – that I could keep my thoughts private and that no one could sense my energy – right now it felt mighty inconvenient.

"This seems like a strange place to be having a swim, Abby."

I wondered for a moment if I was having one of those hallucinations-right-before-death. It spoke of my utter exhaustion that I barely even reacted as Talina hooked me under my arms, and pulled me close for a hug. I slumped into her, my head hanging heavily on her shoulder.

"I'm trying out for the next swim races, long distance," I slurred.

She just squeezed me tighter. "Thank you for saving us. Raror and Gladriel are also out looking for you. I can't believe I found you. We need to get you back before your father kills all Spurns for their stupidity, and then drains the ocean to figure out where you went."

I managed a chuckle. Her words were humorously accurate.

"Can you hold onto my back while I swim us to the Isle?" Her serious features regarded me in concern.

I must have looked a little worse for wear, but I managed a nod.

She helped me hook my arms, not too tightly, around her neck.

She started off slowly, probably to see if I could actually hold on, before her speed increased. Despite my greater height and weight, she seemed to have no problem dragging my butt through the water. I closed my eyes.

I must have drifted off because I was startled as Talina came to an abrupt halt. Shaking off my fatigue, my lids opened slowly. We weren't at the Isle yet. Water still surrounded us, but there was an obstacle in our path: an anemic-looking blond Walker.

"I would normally say give me the Walker and I won't kill you. But today I'm not feeling so generous." His fury ricocheted ripples through the water.

"Seriously, can't you take a hint? She doesn't like you, creep. Go back to your own planet and, like, invent a girlfriend. That's your best chance of locating someone who doesn't find you toxic."

Talina shocked me again, channeling her inner Lucy and challenging the crazy man. Beneath my hands I could feel her start to vibrate. Within a matter of seconds we were in the midst of a full storm. The water swirled in great arcs around us, large crashing waves and whirlpools utilizing massive volumes of water.

And then he was gone, swept up in a water spout.

The winds were out of control, strong enough to bundle up the Walker and drag him into the air. But we were safe in the center. Talina was burning hot to touch, I could feel the power as it erupted from her. I was afraid to move or speak, knowing I would disturb her focus.

Eventually, though, I had to help her reel it back in.

"Damn, Talli, you certainly pack some punch there. Tell me why you didn't destroy Gladriel and her petty words years ago?"

Her head whipped around, and I was staring into pure yellow eyes. For a moment there was nothing in there that resembled my friend, just a cold-blooded creature. I kept my expression calm, waiting, allowing her to examine me, and then slowly my friend bled back into her darkening eyes.

"Abby, did I hurt you?" Her voice was frantic as her once-again-brown eyes scanned me.

"Nope, girl, you saved me again." I had no idea where the Walker had disappeared to, but he was like a damn yoyo; he'd be back. "But let's book it out of here. I'm thinking once again we only have a temporary reprieve."

She nodded and, gripping my arms, threw me over her shoulder. We were off. I thought she'd been going fast before, but I realized I'd been deluded. Now her pace was so rapid we were almost skimming the water.

"So, that's some pretty amazing power you have there. You seem afraid of it, though." My tone was as casual as I could manage.

She shifted her shoulders under my arms, I couldn't tell if it was a shrug or just uncomfortable movement.

"I can't control them, Abbs. It's almost as if I black out and they take me over. I have no problem initiating the energy, but then I'm lost."

I snorted. "Tell me about it. That flow of energy is the most addictive thing I can ever imagine. You feel invincible, and it's so hard to shut it down. I'm always terrified that the next time I won't be able to."

She came to a screeching halt again. I frantically scanned my surroundings, looking for the next obstacle.

"What, Talina? What did you see?" I was tense enough to resemble a plank of wood.

She spun her head back to face me, there were tears streaming down her cheeks.

"You understand, Abby. For the first time in my life, someone actually understands what it's like to be me." She sobbed out loud.

My face softened as a flood of sympathy inundated me.

"You don't have to worry about being alone anymore. I promise that whatever happens we're a family ... half-Walkers have to stick together."

She smiled through her tears. And then she pulled herself together. It was amazing to see. One minute she was crying, her face full of emotions, and then it was gone, as if they'd never existed. It was unparalleled emotional control.

"Sorry about that, Abby," she said as she turned to face forward. We started swimming again. "I don't like to lose control; it's a shameful act to cry."

Lifting my tired arms, I managed to slap her shoulder. Not enough to hurt – I didn't have the strength for that – but she still noticed.

"Don't let me hear you say that again, Gladriel," I taunted her. "Your ability to feel and express that type of emotion is what separates you from the fish."

She actually laughed a little then, and I joined in.

"Plus we're females, Talli. We'll cry for no apparent reason. You don't have to explain or justify it. We get to claim that one just because we can."

"Not on Spurn," she said ruefully. "If you cry here it better be because something just ate your arm."

I shuddered at the mere thought.

Of course Olden hadn't encouraged crying on Earth either, but in a compound full of females, there'd been someone in tears at least once a day.

"How far are we from the Isle?" I glanced behind, just waiting for something to pounce on me.

"You should be able to see land soon," she said, moving again, her breath even and calm.

"How do you orientate yourself with the same ocean surrounding you on all sides?" I was major jealous. I'd have been lost at sea forever. Well, until I drowned.

"All Spurns are taught how to use the moons as guides. Each of them is slightly different, and we know the general direction to follow. The largest and most rounded is the Baroon's moon. Earon's is more yellow, and has a curve to the left." She pointed up as she talked, and I could see what she was saying. "I always know which direction to travel."

"No one back home would believe this place could exist," I said wistfully, enjoying the soothing sensation of water flowing over me, my exhaustion slightly abated.

"I thought First Worlders are taught of the youngling planets. Spurn shouldn't be a surprise to them," she said, sounding confused.

"Oh, yeah, I meant Earth. It's a force of habit to think of it as home. I guess, deep down, I'll always be an Earthling."

I had never been so relieved to see land as the trees that spanned parts of the Isle came into sight.

"Josian!" I screeched as we entered the shallows, unable to wait any longer.

Talina leapt out of the water, dumping me into the briny depths.

Probably should have warned her.

Strong hands fished me out, and I clung to the familiar scent of my father. I knew he'd have heard my shouts this close to land.

"Aribella, can you see gray hair?" was the first thing he said to me.

I pushed my masses of wet curls off my face and looked up over his sternly set features, all the way to his fiery blood-red hair. There wasn't an ounce of other color, especially gray.

"No Walkers in history have had gray hairs, and yet one teenage daughter has decided to prove us wrong again."

"Dad, it wasn't my fault. That stalker-Walker." Where was Lucy when I needed a high-five for rhyming. "He took me again and ... I can't get rid of the creep."

Josian blinked a few times, but he remained relatively calm.

"What happened to the creatures?" I couldn't see one ripple on the still water.

"Well, those two won't be bothering anyone again." Josian chuckled.

"What did you do to them?" I didn't want him to have killed them.

It wasn't their fault stalker-Walker wanted to play god.

"Had a bit of fun. They were quite temperamental, and then I figured out where the Walker manipulation came from and reversed it. They are now harmless." He chuckled. "Well, semi-harmless sea-dragons and octopuses."

So they had been some kind of mutant hybrid. How did he even do that?

"Don't get angry, baby girl," Josian changed the subject, "but there is someone on land who wants to talk to you."

He dragged me out of the water.

Talina kept easy pace with us.

I looked toward the land, wondering who was waiting there, though I had my suspicions. And then I could see him. In fact it was impossible to see anything but Brace as he stood bathed in the blue moonlights.

In the time we'd been apart, and yes, it wasn't that long, I'd forgotten how impressive he was. I couldn't read anything on his calm face. He didn't approach us as we made it to land. He just waited. I was more than aware of how waterlogged I was. I never seemed to look my best around Brace, but I really didn't care. He looked perfect enough for both of us.

Although my first few steps were shaky, I managed to gather strength and move up the beach. As I drew closer I could see that although his expression might be calm, his eyes were black.

"Hey, Red, I'm glad to see you didn't drown at sea," he said in a tight voice. "I would have helped search, but since you asked to be left alone ..." He shrugged.

Josian laughed loudly, head thrown back. His red hair already looked dry as it flew everywhere.

"Don't believe a word of it, Aribella. Brace here did more than his fair share of scouring Spurn for you." His laughter died down to random chuckles. "And he's quite the bossy taskmaster."

Brace's face shot up – Josian was one of the few people who topped him in height. He glared his annoyance.

Talina muttered. "All Walkers are domineering asses."

I imagined it hadn't been easy being around Brace or Josian while I was missing.

"Tall ... overbearing ... domineering asses," she continued.

"We can hear you, Talli," Brace said drily, a slight smile crossing his face.

Talina blushed then. This snarky attitude didn't seem to be her normal personality. It had been a stressful few days.

"So the monsters are pretty much gone?" I asked.

Josian's broad planes sobered. He nodded. "Yes, I've removed that energy, but if there are more out there they will need to be disabled." His bronze eyes narrowed. "And of course the Walker must be dealt with."

Out of the corner of my eye I could see Brace clenching his fists. It was one of the only signs of his anger and frustration. I was mesmerized by the continuous open ... close ... open ... close.

"I'm going to need Brace to stay around, to help me out," Josian continued.

His expression didn't change, but I noticed the gleam in his eye.

I glared at him. My father better not be playing cupid. Brace and I had enough problems without his clumsy attempt at mending bridges.

"I want to stay and help. My father is off on an unanticipated journey and will be busy for a while. Which should give us time to figure out what to do about him." Brace's eyes were locked on mine. "But I won't stay if you don't want me here."

His voice wasn't sappy with romance. It was just direct and to the point. And he was leaving the power with me.

"If Dad needs your help, then I would appreciate if you stayed," I said stiltedly.

His grin said everything. I wanted him to stay with me. It was as simple as that. I was so off-kilter when he was gone and stronger when we were together. I'd had my little hissy fit, kicking him out of my life for all of five minutes.

And in those five minutes, especially when I was near drowning, I realized something. I didn't care what Lucas said about me and destiny.

Brace was mine.

I could feel it in a tangible way when we were together, and if I survived this entire ordeal, he was my choice.

The connection between us was more than any prophesy, a true fate, not the illusion that Lucas was under.

Or should I say delusion.

I knew trust would take time to re-build, but I needed to give this a chance.

Chapter 10

"Has anyone seen Raror?" Talina's words interrupted my sudden burst of understanding.

She frowned, scanning the deserted beach.

No one had.

The beach was completely devoid of all life.

"Where did all the other Spurns go?" I asked.

"They went back to the ocean as soon as I dispatched the creatures," Josian said.

"What was all the fighting about in the first place?" I looked at Talina. "It was the Silver City, right?"

A single tear escaped from her simmering brown eyes. "Yes, everyone lost it when the city's bubble collapsed. Ladre hasn't been seen since. We don't know what happened, and everyone assumed it was caused by you 'aliens'. My family was chosen as a sacrifice."

That explained some of the chaos.

"Of course, not everyone could agree, and then the creatures were back," Talina continued. "They all went crazy. I couldn't use my powers. I was so stressed, nothing responded." She sniffed loudly.

"Yeah, you Walkers have a lot to answer for. These half-powers are not reliable at all." I lifted my brows in Josian's direction.

"Your mother filled me in on what happened, and we need to look closely at this. You can obviously utilize large portions of energy when you need, and then other times there is no response." He looked thoughtful. "It may just be about training and development, or possibly it's your half-sides warring with each other."

"Talina!" The words were screamed along the beach, and we all spun around.

Brace moved protectively to my side.

Gladriel was fifty feet from us, closer to the water edge. Where had she popped up from? Her wraps were black, emerald hair blowing free in a long stream behind her.

"There you are, daughter. I have a little surprise for you," she said.

I could clearly see her haughty smirk. She turned away from us to face the tree line to her left.

Two men stepped out from the rows. I clenched my fists. One was my stalker-Walker, and the other ... I was pretty sure was Walker too. He was tall, with pitch-black hair, so black there seemed to be no other color or depth. His face was arrogant – big surprise – and his striding walk confident. Their faces were eerily similar, although their hair color was different.

"Oh, shit," I blurted.

Josian laughed. "You're lucky your mother isn't here to hear that."

I snorted. "I don't know, something tells me she might have said something similar."

"I have no comment on that, baby girl."

The men paused on either side of Gladriel. The three just stood there staring at us.

"Do not make the first move," Josian muttered from the side of his mouth.

I was about to question his reasoning, but the slight movement of his face warned me to stay quiet.

It took fifteen minutes for us to find the limit of Gladriel's patience.

"Talina, you have asked me repeatedly about your father," she shouted again.

I noticed that as soon as she spoke twin looks of anger crossed the two Walker faces. They'd been playing the same dominance game as Josian, and were not happy to be on the losing end.

"Come and meet your father, Talina." She gestured up to the black-haired Walker. "Apparently, he, like your friends, has a great need for the special half."

Between the lisping and sarcasm, her words were almost indecipherable. But we got the main idea. Talina faltered for a moment. I laid my hand on her cool arm. I really didn't want her to go over there.

"Can it be true?" she said, her tone shaky.

"Well, he is Walker," Brace said, "and I'm pretty sure he is of our clan."

"Do not step away from us, Talina." Josian's voice was low and serious. "I will protect you, but I need you to stay close to my side." He glared down at me. "You too, baby girl. Lucy told me how you like to run off and play hero." His warning was clear: no one was to play hero today.

He turned from us to boom along the beach. "Identify yourselves and state your business."

Gladriel's group shifted uncomfortably as Josian's power bled from him.

The blond one stepped forward. "I am Traktin of Doreen, and I wish to officially challenge you, Josian of Doreen, for possession of the redhaired half that you have protected at your side."

Josian groaned low then. I turned questioning eyes in his direction, but he was still focused down the beach.

"I am Almastore of Abernath." The black-haired man stepped forward. His hair was shorter than I had originally thought. "And I wish to claim my daughter. She is Walker, and belongs with her clan."

"Give me a moment to confer with my associates, and I will respond to each claim." Josian's expression remained impassive, but I could almost see his cells vibrating.

I wasn't sure why.

He gathered us closer, his voice low and serious.

"I am sorry, both of you, but here is a crash course in Walker politics."

He looked at us, and I had no doubt something serious had just occurred. The waves of fury flowing from both Josian and Brace attested to that.

"Our female Walkers are rare, and in the last few millennia the unmated females have become almost non-existent." He put an arm around me, pulling me close. "If you have not been through the mating ceremony, any Walker can challenge for the right to mate with you."

I snorted then, pulling out from under his grip. "Are you kidding me? What, are women like possessions you just trade around?"

Talina nodded, but instead of showing anger like mine, her face was pale and drawn.

He shook his head vehemently. "No, you don't understand. We are a very old race, and we value our rare precious women like no other."

Brace sighed then, drawing our attention. "We have darkness inside. It grows as the years pass by. Loneliness is an emotion that destroys the best of us. Many of the very old Walkers are desperate to find their mates." He paused. "Desperate enough to either misjudge or not care that you are not their true mates, and now the Doreen has challenged Josian."

"Which means what exactly?" I demanded.

"It is an official challenge; if I do not accept then he will take you. If I accept and fail, he will take you. If I win, he will be dead," Josian said it all in a matter-of-fact way.

"No," I gasped, "no, you can't do this. I won't risk you. I'll go with him until you can figure out how to rescue me."

He laughed in his low husky tones. "Thank you, baby girl, for trying to protect me, but it is my job to protect you, and I will not fail."

"Besides, even if Josian did fall, which is practically impossible, I would claim you and he would have to face me." Brace's features were dark, his eyes black.

If this was going to be so easy, why were both of them disturbing the airwaves with their palpable anger?

"So say I just left with him now, because this is my choice to make – don't think it isn't – what would happen then?" I wanted to know all my options.

"He will perform the mating ceremony with you, whether you consent or not, and then we cannot touch you without risking retribution." Josian's eyes twinkled.

As if he had read my previous thought, his worry dissipated.

"Dad, you're not taking this seriously. He's going to hurt or kill you." I tried to contain my panic but it spilled out in my words.

I had felt this Walker's power. It was debilitating.

"Have some faith in me. I am not that easy to defeat."

"Your arrogance is going to be the death of you, Josian," I said, beaten.

I couldn't stop him accepting the challenge. But I was ... annoyed, yeah, let's go with that.

"What does the ... other Walker want with me?" Talina blurted out.

I could tell she'd been as patient as possible.

Josian faced her, his expression sympathetic. "Family can also claim females, as a manner of keeping them safe until they are mated. We don't own you." He looked at each of us. "We protect you. Women are precious, and without their seed of life nothing would exist or continue."

My eyes widened. *Over-share. Thanks, Dad*.

"In short, I am going to have to battle both of them to keep you." He faced Talina. "I know you probably want to go with your father, but until we are sure of his intentions and whether he is who he says he is, I would advise against it."

"I will battle for Abby." Brace spoke up. "You shouldn't have to battle for both of them, and I owe this Doreen for every single mark he placed on her."

"You can't, Brace. You know the challenge for Aribella has been issued directly to me; however, you can battle for Talina. She's of your clan, so it's acceptable. We might as well get them out of the way." His bronze eyes narrowed. "And I promise he will not be around to hurt her much longer."

My panic threatened to overwhelm me. This was what I'd wanted to avoid: people I loved in danger – especially because of me. Josian stepped away to take three long strides down the beach. My right arm lifted to grab him back, but he was too quick, and I knew I'd never be able to stop him.

"Neither of the females wish to leave with you, so we will accept both challenges. I, Josian of Doreen for Aribella of Doreen, and Brace of Abernath for Talina of Abernath, will convene here in ten minutes for the first challenge."

He was back at my side. "If by some chance we fail, I need you to trace to your room again, baby girl. They can't follow either of your energies so if you can stay hidden, you should be safe. I have contacted my brothers and they will protect you and Talina."

"It is against the rules to use a doorway to escape a challenge," Brace explained, "but there is nothing about tracing."

"Shit ..." I said again, softly this time.

But no one was listening to me anymore.

Brace and Josian were discussing tactics, and Talina had sat down on the sand, her head hanging between her legs as she took deep breaths.

I just stood there glaring down the beach at the two Walkers, and Gladriel more than any. She was evil. If looks could kill ...

"Where is Raror?" Talina's question caught my attention; her voice was unnaturally high and breathless.

I moved over to sit next to her. "I don't know, Talli."

"I'm so worried. He wouldn't have left me alone like this unless something was wrong."

"You can bet Gladriel knows; she's been planning this," I said tonelessly.

"I should have ended her maniacal tirade a long time ago." Talina's tone was hard and brittle.

She sounded as if a swift breeze would break her apart and she would drift away.

"You have two more minutes. Prepare yourself, Walker." Traktin, the stalker-Walker, had stepped away from the other two.

He stood in the space between our groups.

"I love you, baby girl." Josian pulled me to my feet.

I examined his features, relieved to see no nerves or fear. I had to trust my father knew what he was doing.

"Love you too, Dad. Just win," I said to him firmly, "or I'll be hunting down your free essence and kicking its ass."

I stood on tip-toes to kiss him. He leaned down so I could reach his cheek without a struggle. Breathing in his familiar scent, I blinked back my tears. I would stay strong. Josian was the toughest, most arrogant person I knew. That had to mean something.

He touched my face, and walked away to halt opposite Traktin. It was with a malicious joy that I noticed Josian was much taller and broader through the shoulders, and Traktin finally looked uneasy. A warm hand cupping my arm drew my attention. Brace smiled gently as he stared down into my face. My returning smile was a tad shaky.

"It will be okay, Red, I promise. Josian is tough and smart. You have nothing to worry about."

"What about you?" I said fiercely. "I have everything to lose here today."

He moved quickly.

I had no preparation as he pressed his lips firmly to mine. I opened my mouth, always needing more. He flicked his tongue out and, as I tasted that which was uniquely Brace, the rest of the world disappeared. All too soon he pulled away.

As reality returned I realized that the blond Walker was shouting. Josian held back Traktin as he attempted to charge down the beach.

"I'm not supposed to touch you until the challenge is complete. You belong to no one. The only reason that Traktin doesn't already have possession of you is because we were still inside our ten-minute window." Brace spoke low and fast. "But I cannot touch you again, Abby."

"Do you fight now as well?" I asked, still a little shaky from the kiss.

"No, we issue one challenge at a time. The rest of us stand as witness to the winner and ensure that procedure is followed."

I was starting to despair about these stupid Walker rules. They were unevolved Neanderthal children. No wonder there were limited Walker women; they probably drowned in all the testosterone.

"We aren't human, Red," Brace said, reading my expressions. "You cannot expect the same thought patterns or behavior. We are ancient creatures. The endless years have molded us."

For the first time I could see the gulfing gap between my experiences and Brace's.

"Don't die, Brace. I want to know about your years of experiences. I want to see if our marks line up. I need ..." I hesitated over the last words.

I needed him. It was as simple as that.

He breathed in deeply. "I've searched for you forever, Abby. I will not cease to exist now before I even have the chance to ... give you everything ... the world."

His hesitation was unusual. He seemed almost nervous.

I wanted to touch him. But a glance up the beach halted me. The blond Walker was staring in our direction, just waiting for us to break the rules again. I stepped back before my wandering hands moved.

"Well, in that case, go kick some butt. I'll wait right here." I crossed my arms over my chest.

He strode across the sand to Josian. They were joined by the black-haired Walker.

"We stand witness to these challenges and, as the original seven decreed, so shall we uphold."

We had no problem hearing as Talina's father spoke the formal sounding words.

They all nodded once and gripped hands in a strange type of handshake, crossed-arms thing before releasing their grip. And then the area was flooded with moonstale light as each of them produced a piece. I could see Josian flick open his flat ring.

I gasped, my nails digging into my cheeks, probably leaving crescent-shaped indents on my ivory skin. I was speechless. The sight of their marks left me shaking in awe, and something pressed me to step closer. I realized Talina was moving ahead of me. We stopped when we reached the edge of the sphere of moonstale light surrounding them. I couldn't take my eyes off Brace. His marks were black, tribal like Talina's, and amazing.

He wore a fitted black shirt so I could see them run down his neck and along his muscled bicep. Each mark wrapped around, hugging his skin, so detailed and bold. I wanted to run my fingers along them. I wanted to know their texture.

We stepped into the light. We couldn't stop ourselves. The moonstale drew us like moths to a flame. The four men locked us in their gaze. Brace's eyes narrowed. He shook his head, urging me back.

But our marks had other ideas.

The red of my marks began to dance along my skin. They glowed so brightly it was difficult to look at them. And then to my astonishment they started to bleed off me. Trailing away, they searched for something, and I knew exactly what it was.

They were going to connect with Brace.

I could see the edges of his marks along his forehead and down his cheek reach for my own. And then when the black collided with red, we connected.

I landed on my knees in the sand. I could feel him, everything about who he was. As our marks intertwined, so did our energy and souls. The mind

247

blocks we'd kept in place were negated, our thoughts and memories smashing together in a destructive and intimate fashion, as if they had been straining forever to reach each other. I recoiled from the alien nature of his thoughts, and at the same time sought desperately to understand.

Then his feelings flooded through me, and I gasped, my heart swelling. I could never understand the depth of emotion he felt for me, the hundreds of years he'd searched, growing weary, lonely. His love and emotional tie to me eclipsed every thought in his mind, like I was his very soul, ingrained in the essence of who he was.

And underlying that was the confusion about his father, his guilt over not questioning things, of being a good little soldier.

I'd just delved even deeper, immersing myself in all that was Brace, when he cut me off, slowing the flooding tide of emotions. He was gaining a little control, although he was moving toward me.

Josian intercepted him.

"Brace!" His shouted words were dull, though they did register in our minds. "You have to fight the melding. The challenge still stands. You cannot lose her now."

"How is this possible?" the blond Walker snarled.

My distracted mind almost missed the flash of the knife in his hand. He stabbed out at Josian then, so quickly I couldn't track the movement.

"We have not had a Walker melding in millennia." His fury echoed.

I almost protested as Brace took a step away from me. I could feel him gathering control, separating our minds. I shivered as the sensation of loneliness engulfed me, and yet I could also feel his unwavering presence through my entire essence.

At least now I felt separated enough to concentrate on my father's fight. In my distracted state I'd missed the weapon Josian had produced, also a dagger-shaped knife. Both men drew blood with their first slice. Traktin landed a large gash to Josian's left bicep, only to look down and realize he was bleeding profusely from a wound above his ribs. Josian hadn't missed his mark.

Talina and I were suddenly thrown backwards from the group. We ended up about ten feet away, and although I expected to hit the ground hard our landing was cushioned.

"What the hell just happened?" Talina clutched my arm as we scrambled to our feet.

"I have no idea, but don't let me go to Brace," I said.

I knew I might need help staying away from him.

It's okay, sweetheart. I'm always here now.

I jumped as words echoed in my mind.

What. Was. That?

We melded, the ultimate joining of mates. I haven't heard of it happening in hundreds of years.

His chuckle echoed around my brain.

But of course you are writing the book on bringing back the lost Walker traits.

I pulled my focus out of my head for a moment. Josian and Traktin were involved in some type of weird duel right now, and I wanted to pay close attention. I didn't give two shits about Walker rules. If I had to save my Dad I would.

Laughter echoed.

I think I am going to enjoy hearing your inner thoughts.

I groaned.

Get out of my mind. It's rude. I'm going to figure out how to block you.

More laughter.

I look forward to you trying.

And then he gave me some privacy – I could feel Brace still occupied a small section of my mind, but mostly he was gone. That was not fair; how did he do that?

I focused again on the fight. For some reason the men were still going head-to-head with small weapons. Sweat flung off Josian as he sliced Traktin across his chest. It was high on the left side, but deep enough to shoot off small arcs of blood. The beach where they were dancing was decorated in large patches of red. I'd had enough fight classes to see true skills before me. I'm guessing these men had learned to fight with weapons ... well, at the dawn of weapons. Actually, for all I knew, they were the inventors of weapons.

I could never battle a Walker. There was no way to compete with that amount of knowledge.

I gasped as Josian dodged an obvious jab, only to find himself struck hard in the chest. In a sly move Traktin had pulled out another knife with his left hand, and Josian now had a deep stab wound above his heart.

My heart stuttered as he faltered, just a slight stumble. I stifled my scream of warning as Traktin took advantage of this weakness to go for Josian's throat, his hand whipping around so quickly that all I could track was the glint of silver blade as it headed for my father. But before the blade could hit its target, Josian fell to his knees.

The kill-shot sliced through empty air. Then Josian dived sideways, brought his knife up from underneath, slicing through the light clothing that Traktin wore and eviscerating him. As his super-sharp blade sliced the man from navel to throat, Josian ended up in a shower of blood.

It had been a ploy: Josian had pretended to be hurt to gain advantage.

I'd have to kick him later for that added heart attack.

Talina and I clutched each other. She looked very pale, but although I felt a little uneasy watching the scene before me, I wasn't as freaked as I thought. Plus, it wasn't over yet. Evisceration wasn't enough to kill a Walker.

Traktin fell to his knees, his face a display of disbelief as the blood drained from him for the second time that day. He slumped forward, landing face first. Josian staggered to his feet but didn't turn away. I couldn't see the front of my father, but all of a sudden his shoulders shifted uncomfortably.

"What's he doing?" I asked Talina. She had a better angle to see.

"It looks like he is mixing up a sandstorm," she said.

I nodded, noticing the swirling sand before him.

"No, not just sand, energy," I said in awe. "Josian is gathering energy."

The swirl continued to grow until we could see it clear across the distance. He took a step back, dropping his hand and releasing the energy. It didn't rush away, but slowly descended to encase the slumped Walker.

He was lifted into the air. The silence was all encompassing.

I don't think I breathed the entire time.

The energy began to glow and swirl faster. At no point did Josian's expression change, and I wondered if he still controlled that energy or if it had been let free to do its job.

Spheres of lights echoed off it, arcing in all directions. Blindingly bright, it became impossible to stare at it directly. The closest my eyes could observe were the flickers over the water. I was unprepared for a sudden outward ricochet of force, and for the second time in ten minutes we were flung backwards. Talina and I landed in a pile of tangled limbs and hair. I coughed up a few mouthfuls of inhaled sand.

"Well, that went well," Talina said drily as we extricated ourselves and stood.

"Where did he go?" My gaze flicked around, trying to find the Walker.

Josian still stood there, his head thrown back, staring up at ... something.

"I can't see him, and something strange is going on with your dad."

Talina was right.

Josian always glowed; his skin was luminous. But now swirls of light shone in red slithers along his bared skin. Standing tall, and so stonelike, it was not hard to understand how Walkers were mistaken for gods. I felt awed and intimidated and he was my father.

"Aribella, can you come to my side now." His words echoed, deep and low.

He even sounded different, but I didn't hesitate. I wanted a closer look. Tugging Talina along for the ride, I sprinted to Josian. Within seconds, I was staring up into his blood spattered face.

I gasped. "Dad ...?" My face fell as I stared into his eyes. The striking bronze had been replaced by swirling whirlpools of red. "Your eyes are fre-a-ky," I said, attempting to lighten the mood.

His expression didn't change.

I didn't even realize I was holding my breath and silently praying. Maybe death wasn't the only way I could lose him.

It's the absorption of power, Red. He will be fine. It's an adjustment, but Josian is too old and wily to let the power control him.

Apparently, Brace was back in my head.

I can't ignore your distress. It makes me want to slay dragons and kill spiders.

I got a mental wink. I smiled. I couldn't help myself. There was something delightfully enticing about this new Brace.

"I'd say your weird smile is kind of creepy, but I recognize mind-talking," Talina said, examining me. "Are you speaking to Josian? Is he okay?" Her voice held concern.

I shook my head. "No, Brace has decided to mind-stalk me. I can't get rid of him."

Liar, you don't want to get rid of me.

I ignored him for the moment. Josian still hadn't answered me.

"Dad!" I said it more forcefully this time. "Pull yourself together. We don't have time for this." I raised my arm high so I could snap my fingers in front of his face.

Slowly, with deliberate movements, he stared down at me from his lofty heights. I gulped audibly as I copped the full force of his red eyes.

Rocking the vampire, I thought to myself.

Never really been a fan. How is an unnaturally pale bloodsucker attractive?

I was surprised Brace had understood the reference, and I'd had enough of this one-sided conversation.

I reached out in an attempt to connect with him. Before I knew it, he'd sucked me in to the warm foreign depths of his thoughts. I laughed out loud. I couldn't help it; he'd created a mental picture of Josian as an emaciated old vampire.

I was distracted by the real Josian as he reached down and took my chin, capturing my attention and forcing me from Brace's mind.

"We need to let Brace concentrate now; it is his turn to battle." His voice echoed, sounding disconnected.

But I saw a sliver of bronze blending into the red of his eyes. He was gaining control.

"What did you do to Traktin?" I asked. "And is Brace's battle the same type of thing?"

Talina interrupted us. "I really don't want my father to be absorbed or whatever you did. We aren't sure if he's a bad guy yet."

"I chose to end the energy that was Traktin. He kidnapped and threatened my daughter, and I could see he would never stop. His obsession was intolerable." He gestured to where Brace and Almastore silently faced each other. "Brace simply has to best him in battle. He will not make the same choice."

Josian was trying to reassure us, but his current scary aura wasn't really helping.

"Do we need to move closer?" I said, already walking in Brace's direction. I was too far away for my comfort.

Red, you stay out of this. Promise me. I need to concentrate, and as always half my attention is on you. I need to make sure the other half stays on this moron.

He was in my mind, but to look at him you'd never know it. His gaze didn't waver, not even a flicker from his eyes.

I'm not promising anything. But if you don't get your butt kicked, I'll stay over here.

I lowered my 'mind voice' in warning.

So don't lose.

His laughter echoed through me, warming, comforting. It was so familiar, and yet it gave me chills. Bumps broke out across my skin as though a swift breeze had startled every hair on my body and they were now standing up on end. But the weather was warm and calm. Nope, that was all Brace.

"It is about to start," Josian said.

Shivers crossed my skin again. I couldn't watch and yet my eyes refused to shift.

Almastore bowed formally, which Brace reciprocated. The animosity that had been between Josian and Traktin was missing from this fight. However, I wasn't reassured.

They started without any fuss.

Brace dived to the side as the first of a series of energy balls shot in his direction. He continued to play defensive as Almastore moved in a circular pattern, shooting off one flame after another. The flashes of energy were all different colors and I wondered if each one did something special.

"Why isn't Brace fighting back?" I whispered, worried about distracting him.

"He is testing the Abernath, assessing his skills and abilities. It's clever, especially if you're quick and skilled enough to avoid the attacks." Josian was engrossed in the fight. "He will strike soon. Brace is fast and lethal. Don't you worry, baby girl."

I wasn't worried. Sure my nails had just about drawn blood in the pads of my hands, but I was cool. My eyes closed as Brace just missed copping two full – were they lightning bolts? – to the chest. That was way too close.

Keep your eyes shut. I'll be finished in a minute. You don't have to stress.

Of course the moment he issued his 'order' my eyes flew open. I snorted out loud as I glared at my bossy mate.

I love when you call me mate.

His caressing words distracted me, along with a stroking sensation down my body. I jumped two

258

foot in the air. I found it supremely unfair that he already knew these tricks.

Narrowing my focus, I ran my eyes slowly, deliberately over his entire body. I started at the silky strands of his black hair, which fell messily across his forehead, before making my way down all six and a half foot of muscles and tanned skin. My experiment was starting to backfire.

The chemistry between us had me sweaty and a little annoyed. I was possibly going to self-combust soon. During my mental assault he stumbled once, and a burst of light from Almastore glanced off his shoulder.

Oops.

Red, he said in warning.

I stopped messing with him. I did want him back in one piece.

"What are you doing?" Almastore said. He appeared to have had enough of this dodge-and-retreat from Brace. "Fight me. I don't have all day for you to show me that you are weak and afraid."

As he poked at Brace's ego, I was pleasantly surprised to see that Brace didn't rise to the bait. I had always assumed that the male ego was fragile.

Brace just grinned and nodded once. With a deep breath he stood straight and then he moved.

I'd likened Brace's fighting style to a ninja once, and it had never appeared truer than now. He flowed from one movement to the next. There was no energy or throwing of light. He got in close and personal, and began to land heavy blows on the other Walker.

A serious of kicks, followed by a well-placed elbow to his face, drew the first blood. Almastore attempted to stem the flow, but the thick red fluid continued to pour freely.

Brace moved again.

Using a judo throwing style, he smashed Almastore into the ground, before he really started to fight dirty.

I heard a distinctive crack.

He'd twisted Almastore's arm behind his back, snapping it without effort. The other Walker let out a yelp, but made it back to his feet, his left arm hanging uselessly at his side.

"You can concede to me at any point," Brace said carelessly.

He hadn't broken a sweat. His breathing was even; he looked like he hadn't moved at all.

"You don't understand: I need my daughter." Almastore's reply was quiet, but we could still hear what he said.

I was concentrating so hard on his words that I accidentally tapped into Brace's thoughts again.

I'll just bet you do.

I agreed with him; this Walker was up to something.

Try and find out what he wants her for, I thought to Brace, hoping he'd hear.

He flicked his eyes toward me and nodded.

"So, maybe if you tell me why you want Talina, I will leave her in your capable hands." His tone was perfect, not too interested, with just the right amount of push.

"There is another of our kind whose son is interested in a mate exchange. I promised my ... uh, daughter, and I think that would be best for her."

Talina snorted. She pawed at the ground, her bare feet digging trenches under where she stood.

I patted her arm. "Yep, Walkers are big, not so hairy, unevolved apes."

Josian laughed, as did Brace in my mind.

He's lying, Red. I get deception at its finest. A few more beatings and he will concede.

Yes, we need to know his true intentions so we can prepare, and Talina needs to understand.

I'll find out.

And he did.

It took a while. He beat on him over and over, asking the same questions. Almastore suffered through another broken arm, I would guess quite a few broken ribs and what looked like a fractured jaw.

Brace did his job smoothly, with a methodical intensity that would have freaked me out except I could see into his mind. And he wasn't enjoying this task. But he had a protective streak a mile long and would not stop until he was satisfied with the answers.

I enjoyed digging around in his mind; there were just so many layers to explore.

"No more," Almastore finally said.

He was on his hands and knees before Brace, his face and hair streaked with blood, one of his arms still broken, though the other looked to be healed.

"You have demonstrated your ability to outclass me in every fight style." His head fell forward to rest on his chest. He couldn't lift it again. "It's Que. Your father wants Talina and he is going to kill me if I come back without her."

"Are you even Talina's father?"

The man nodded, but before he could speak Gladriel interrupted.

"Of course he is."

We turned to stare at her. I wasn't sure about everyone else, but I'd forgotten she was even there.

Talina gasped out loud, her hand flying to cover her mouth. Gladriel was holding an unconscious Raror, her hand wrapped around his throat as she propped him up.

"Raror!" Talina screamed and started running toward them.

The seawater swirled around Gladriel. A sudden storm had blown up. Or, judging by Talina's fixed expression, she was brewing one.

"Stop, my pathetic little half," Gladriel ordered, one hand held up in warning, the other tightening on Raror's throat. "Do not come any closer, and halt your powers or he will be destroyed."

"You would not destroy your own son," Talina said, although she did pause about ten feet from Gladriel. "He is all you have, next in line to rule Earon." Her voice was tinged with desperation.

An evil smile spread across Gladriel's face, followed soon by manic chuckling.

I had a sick feeling that very bad news was coming for Talina. And Gladriel did not disappoint.

"He is not mine, Talina. He was abandoned years ago, and since I could not have children I decided he was better than nothing." She glanced at the Walker Brace had bested without even breaking a sweat. "Of course, that was before I fell pregnant with you." She gestured away. "I told you your father was weak and spineless. Look at him."

Almastore groaned from where he lay face down in the sand. I assumed each Walker had different abilities to heal, because he was still hurting.

"Brace is Que's son." He groaned again, attempting to shift onto his back. "I could never have bested him. He's been training since birth to take over all Walkers as leader." His words were mumbled.

He lifted his head and we all noticed the myriad of darkening bruises on his face. His lips were puffed and split open, although the leaking blood had slowed.

"However, I cannot disobey Que. I had no choice."

Walker leader? I questioned Brace.

He bristled slightly at my incredulous tone.

Don't sound so surprised, Abigail. Even though I am reasonably young for a Walker, I am strong and powerful. Don't doubt my ability as your mate.

I realized that my careless words had wounded his pride. I was reminded again how stupid pride could be.

I look after myself, Brace. I've never needed anyone and I'm not about to start now.

His arrogance was a sting to my own pri ... no, not pride ... independence. Something I had always been protective of. I didn't like this whole 'need a mate' thing. In fact, every time I felt as if I couldn't take one more breath without Brace's kiss or my arms ached to hold and be held – it made me want to break things, send out energy bolts and go a little nuts.

Damn, I'm the guy in this relationship.

I was the commitment phobic, the one rebelling against this feeling of ownership.

Trust me, sweetheart, you are definitely not the guy in this relationship.

What was with this sweetheart all of a sudden? Yeah, I kind of liked it, but still.

His eyes ran over me, slowly, provocatively ... I knew he did it deliberately, but in that moment I was my usual raging mass of teenage hormones and didn't really care. I worked hard to calm my breathing, slow my heart rate. I had to think about something else, anything. I really didn't want to self-combust in front of my father. Instead I focused on how disconcerting it felt to have my inner reflections heard. Most of the time my thoughts were random and stupid. They'd had no filter applied, no checking of their permissibility to be spoken out loud.

I worried a little that Brace would think I was young and unintelligent. His mind felt ancient, despite the fact he sounded twenty when he spoke. In the layers of his mind he had lived through more than I could have imagined.

You're perfect. I could not have asked for a better match. You make me feel young, less weighed down by the burdens I've witnessed. Your passion, humor and fiery personality. You're perfect for me, Abigail.

"No!" Talina's screams drew me from my head.

I realized I'd missed most of her conversation with Gladriel.

"Please, don't hurt him anymore," Talina begged, apparently afraid to step closer, but still unable to stop from moving toward her brother.

Gladriel had gashed Raror across his face, and it slowly dripped blood.

"I warned you, Talina. If you do not go with your father then I will kill him." Her voice was cold.

She didn't even look down at the Spurn she'd raised as a son.

I realized Raror's eyes were open now, just slightly, but he looked dazed. Whatever they'd done had really hurt him.

"I will go with him. Just promise you won't hurt Raror anymore. You have to let him come over here." Talina waved her arms in the air.

The storm and ocean were still in tumult behind Gladriel, but Talina seemed to be in control.

"What is in this for you, Gladriel?" I asked.

Why was she working with Walkers? It just seemed out of character for her.

She turned her yellow eyes in my direction. She spoke immediately, as if she'd been waiting for someone to ask.

"Traktin approached me with a plan. He promised to take out Ladre. He said that if I made sure you all went to Silver City then he'd guarantee that I became the ruler of all of Spurn. I want the power. I hate to be dictated to by anyone."

"Traktin is gone now," I said, "so what's the point of continuing this?"

She gestured to Almastore. "He promised me the same thing if I made sure Talina would go without drama. I will not stop until I achieve my deserved crown. The Baroons should not rule over me simply because they are Baroons. I am the most powerful."

She turned from me again. "Now, dear daughter, since I know you value none above your

267

brother, it was easy to figure out the way to assure your cooperation."

"And you have my full cooperation, bitc ... witch." Talina stuttered over her attempt at a curse before finishing with a word she was more comfortable saying.

I smiled as she took her chance to finally insult Gladriel.

"So let Raror go. You have made your point. He is already hurt."

"Talli." Raror coughed then. His words rasped. "Do not go with him. Do not sacrifice yourself."

He attempted to move away, but Gladriel still held him tightly around his neck and he was just too injured to fight her.

"Save your energy and breath, son." Gladriel squeezed tighter. "Talina will do as she is told; she'd do anything to save you."

"Dad, do something?" I turned to Josian. "Blast her."

Talina shook her head. "No, Gladriel is a master at shielding herself. She is protected at the moment. Unless we can move closer, there is no way to hurt her."

That must be why Talina's ferocious weather wasn't touching them. I'd thought she'd developed some type of awesome self-control, but no ... Gladriel had a shield up.

"Go to your father, Talina, and I'll leave Raror with your friends." Gladriel was getting impatient.

"No, I don't trust you. You need to leave him there. Step away, far away. I'll go to Almastore, and then you can leave."

"I have all the power, you ungrateful half. Now move, or I rip his throat out."

Talina stared at her mother for a minute, but I knew she would never risk Raror. Turning without another word, she marched over to where Almastore had pulled himself to a half-sitting position.

He shook his head, his expression serious. "I can't just take her, Gladriel. Don't you understand? Brace beat me in a challenge. He is Talina's guardian now, and he is the one who has to release her." His voice was dull. He didn't really seem that interested anymore.

Wasn't he afraid of Que? Shouldn't he be trying to save his ass and get Talina to go with him?

"It would be in his best interest to release her into your care," Gladriel said, her yellow eyes focusing on Brace.

He laughed out loud. "And why should I do that? You hold no leverage over me, and I am afraid Talina is important to us as well."

"Brace," Talina said urgently. She stood at his side now. "Please release me. I need my brother to be okay."

He shook his head. "You cannot trust her. This Walker is going to take you through a doorway, and then there is nothing to stop Gladriel."

They argued for a few minutes. She clutched Brace's arm, and I could feel his wavering. Despite the fact this might cost us the battle with the Seventine, he was going to release her. Stupid as it was, that spoke to me of his true nature, and I liked it a lot.

Josian was just stepping forward to intercede when a roar had us spinning to the ocean. One of Traktin's creatures had risen from the water behind Gladriel and Raror.

Chapter 11

We'd been distracted watching Brace and Talina argue. No one was looking at the water, not even Gladriel. She was in the worst position with her back facing the briny depths. My warning screams fell into the roaring wind as the creature reared up behind the pair. Gladriel shifted, but she was a second too late. With a sharp screech the animal projected one of its many tentacles, and the straight sharp movement pierced Gladriel through her back, impaling her.

She was still holding Raror, so the spike also entered his body. I could see him arch up as the tip became visible in the front of his abdomen. Josian ran at Walker speed to the water line. On the way he gathered energy between his parted hands and blasted the creature. It shimmered for a moment as his projected power encased it and it screamed in agony, sending a shiver down my spine. It fell apart into two smaller creatures, which flapped helplessly for a few moments.

Josian caught Raror in his arms and dragged him up the beach. Gladriel was thrown to the ground behind them, but I didn't spare her a second glance. Talina and I reached them at the same time. Her face was white and I realized I'd seen dead people with more color than she currently had.

"Raror ...?" Her voice broke.

"Gladriel's dead," Brace said.

He must have checked her before moving back up the beach to us. Talina didn't look up from Raror or acknowledge Brace in any way.

"Hey, little mermaid sister," Raror rasped. Small bubbles of dark blood blossomed from the corner of his lips. "You are far too brave. You should never have tried to save me ... it's my job to save you." His yellow eyes were warm.

Talina pressed her hand tight against the injury on his stomach. But the blood continued a slow ebbing from his wound.

Her brown eyes filled with tears, overflowing and running in rivulets down her cheeks.

"Raror ... no ... you need to listen to me. You promised, so you can't leave me. You have to hold on. We can get you help." Her desperate features sought Josian. "Can you do something? Help him?"

Josian hesitated, his strong facial planes wracked in sorrow. I just knew he didn't have good news.

"Talina, I don't have any ability to heal; I could try and repair the outer damage that I can see, but there is too much internal." He looked up at Brace, who was standing protectively behind us. "Do you have any healing abilities?"

Brace stepped forward before kneeling beside Raror.

"I have some small ability, but I think he might be too injured."

Too far gone.

His thoughts were somber as he laid both hands across Raror's abdomen. I couldn't see anything happening, but I felt a gathering of energy and then warmth seemed to surround us.

"You stay with Abby." Raror coughed again. He had not taken his eyes from Talina once. "She will look after you."

A dull light reflected in the yellow of his eyes. I felt Brace's desperation. I placed my hand gently on his back, where he was crouched on the sand, sending him my warmth and support.

273

I can't heal this, Red. The limb pierced a major vein of the heart, the vena cava, I think. He is bleeding out.

Tears filled my eyes. I liked Raror and the scene between the siblings was just devastating.

This is going to kill Talina. But if you can't save him, then just step back and let them have this moment.

I knew he'd try until all hope was gone, but it would be better for Talina to say goodbye. After a few more futile moments he took my advice, straightening to stand next to me.

"I'm sorry, Talina. There is just too much damage. I did everything I could." His voice wavered. "You should say your goodbyes."

"No ..." she said. "No, you can't stop. He can be saved." Her voice rose in desperation.

"Talli, he is right." Raror's quiet words captured her attention again.

Her face crumpled even as she continued to shake her head in denial.

Raror finally tore his eyes from her.

"Look after Talina," he said to me. He didn't wait for my reply, turning back to her immediately.

"I love you, Talina of Earon. You save the world. You find your destiny."

Despite the alien nature of Raror's features, I found his face lovely in that moment. Talina sobbed once, and I could see from the corner of my eye that she was leaning against him.

"I don't think I can do this without you," she whispered in a broken voice. "You are my rock."

"No, you have always been my rock. I am a far better Spurn because of you. Do not mourn this. I will wait for you in the fade." He lifted one hand and wiped her tears.

This seemed to be the last of his energy. His arm fell back down and his eyes shuttered, as if about to close.

I turned away then, staring into the endless beauty of the ocean, searching for comfort. Brace placed a hand on my cheek before leaning down to rest his forehead on mine. I let the tears free. The salty river of pain flowed in an endless torrent. Brace wiped them away without saying a word; he let me have my pain, giving only his comforting touch.

I heard Raror's stuttered breath, and then there was no more. Talina started to wail, loud shrieking mourning wails. The wind went crazy around us. Brace dragged me backwards, just in time to avoid a tidal wave. From where we'd fallen into the sand I struggled to reach Talina. I couldn't hear that pain any longer and not attempt to comfort her. But the wind held me motionless. At least, from what I could see through the sand, Talina looked to be safe in the center of her storm. She'd gathered Raror's body up in her arms, and was rocking back and forth. Her wails increased. I couldn't say how many endless moments we waited, watching her as she begged, prayed and cursed to whichever god the Spurns worshipped.

"We have to get to her, Brace. How long can she do this?" I turned to face him.

He sat behind me, one of his large, warm hands rubbing gentle circles along my spine.

"She could mourn like this forever, Red. Raror was her everything. The grief for that knows no limits or boundaries," he said with a quiet sadness, and I wondered who he'd lost,

I swallowed audibly. "That's how I felt when Lucy was kidnapped, but even then I had no definite proof she was dead. I refused to even consider it."

His face hardened. "I can't forget the look on your face that day – that dead look." He took my chin in his hand. "I vowed I would never see that again. But it was there again when you found out about me, when you asked me to leave you alone. It was there and I was the cause." He growled. "If anyone else had caused you to feel pain like that I'd have ended them where they stood. But it was me, and there is nothing I can do but make it up to you forever."

He pressed a gentle kiss to my cheek, his lips lingering. It was odd to have him kiss me so casually, and yet it felt as if we'd been joined together for years.

I decided to change the subject. We still had a lot to work through – including his little episode of hiding the truth from me – but right now that was too heavy.

My eyes filled with tears. I couldn't help it. The scene with Raror's face in those final moments continued to play through my mind.

"Baby, please don't do that. Don't let it linger in your mind. You have to release the pain, or it will dig in deep and take hold."

I gulped in a couple of breaths, raising my eyes up trying to stem the flow of tears. Brace placed his hands on my cheeks, using his thumbs to gently wipe at my overflow of pain.

"I … just … it was so quick." My words stumbled as I tried to express the pain.

"Life is one of those things that can be over in an instant, even for those of us long-lived. We must embrace every moment."

I lowered my eyes to stare at him. The tears continued, letting free some of weight on my heavy heart.

"Want to know about my dreams?" Brace said his voice tinged with desperation. He didn't like me crying. Luckily, his attempt at distraction worked. My pulse race, I'd been dying to know what his dreams were.

I nodded briskly, and with his hands still resting on either side of my face, he leaned in close and touched his lips to my forehead. I was about to protest when I realized I was no longer seeing the Spurn beach but a scene of pure unending love. I was in Brace's mind.

I couldn't see the faces clearly, but I knew it was us. As his dream progressed the images came into focus. We were running through the forest of First World. No ... that wasn't right, not running, Brace was chasing me. But I looked like I was gliding above the foliaged ground. My red Walker marks were on display. I laughed freely and occasionally shrieked as his long arms almost captured me. I could tell he wasn't putting much effort into catching me. His expression was joyful; he was enjoying the chase. And even though I'm pretty competitive, I was just waiting to be caught.

Suddenly the laughter ceased and darkness flooded the sunlit trees. As an observer I couldn't do anything, but the Abby of the dream spun around, her ... my ... features alight with surprise. Brace was nowhere to be seen. She looked panicked as she pushed through the fog, the trees whipping around in a cruel wind.

"Brace!" she screamed out, falling to her knees.

The wind howled, blowing her red curls everywhere. I silently urged her to get back up, to run from the darkness.

Then he burst through the gloom, glowing, in the same way Josian always did – light surrounding him on all sides – and he was levitating off the ground. I expected dream Abby to run straight to him, but she hesitated. Standing slowly, she actually started to back away.

"Brace?" she questioned, and I suddenly understood.

His eyes were a swirling mass of gold. And the darkness that flooded the forest and was turning my blood to ice poured from his outstretched hands. He moved too fast, capturing her face in both hands. Leaning down, he was about to press his lips to hers, and that was when I noticed the darkness was inside his mouth also; he was going to flood her with darkness. I screamed my own warning. Which I knew was useless. The scene faded out at this point.

Back on the beach I yanked myself free from Brace. Safe to say, I'd been suitably distracted from my grief.

"What the hell was that?" My heart raced. The adrenalin flooding my system didn't understand that was just a dream.

He gave me a half-smile.

"I don't know, Red, which is why I haven't told you about it." He stared out into space. "That damn dream's been haunting me for years." He shook his head. "But one thing was always clear. I had a mate, a beautiful, sarcastic, funny mate. And despite the nature of the dream, I looked forward to it every night."

"Yeah, but now I have to worry about you doing that freaky gold-eye, evil-smoggy-hands thing." My words stumbled over each other in my haste.

He laughed. "I promise I've never gone freaky gold-eye before. You know most dreams are more metaphoric than literal."

He might not be worried, but I couldn't shake my unease.

Around us the winds slowly faded. We were still confined behind a wall of sand, but Talina's howls no longer filled the air. Instead, it looked as if she was speaking quietly to Raror. She lay next to him, staring down into his face. She held onto him, preventing the lapping water from stealing him away. The lump returned to my throat. Swallowing audibly, I turned back to Brace.

"So why do you call me Abby?" I said.

He'd been staring down, gathering large handfuls of sand, and then letting them flow out through his open fingers. But at my question he raised his head, his velvet eyes pinning me to the spot.

"That's your name," he said. His expression lightened.

I snorted under my breath. "You know what I mean. Why don't you call me Aribella like everyone else from First World?"

It was so hard to read him. He was very good at concealing his emotions, and right now I wasn't picking up anything important from our bond. He shook his head. He almost seemed sad.

"Aribella doesn't belong to me. I have always known that. She's Sammy's sister and Lucas' Empress and the First-World girl I was going to destroy for my father. But Abigail, well, she's been mine since we collided in the forest. Well, much before that actually, but it's since the forest I've known she was mine – you're mine." He flashed me a gorgeous grin, all blinding white teeth.

"That's a pretty good answer," I said, feeling the warmth of his words spread through me.

Leaning over, I threw my arms around his neck, hugging him tight. I was his, and he was mine, and there was no other he ever needed to worry about. We sat like that until the wind had completely died around us.

"Should we check on Talina?" I said, pulling back. My worry for her had not abated at all.

"Yes, we should deal with this before all the crazy Spurns return from wherever they disappeared," Josian said as he popped up behind us.

I barely prevented a shriek from escaping. I swore instead.

"I need to invent a collared bell for you Walkers," I said.

They were too quiet and sneaky. Josian snorted, looking amused.

I jumped up smoothly, marvelling at how flexible and athletic I was becoming.

"I have no idea what to say to her," I whispered as we closed the distance.

The bright blue moonlights reflected off the calm of the water. There was no evidence a storm had even passed. As usual, the men had no useful advice.

"Talli?" I said, dropping down. I knew instinctively not to touch her.

She didn't look at me.

"What do you need us to do?"

"I have to bury him, a proper Spurn burial," she said, her face resting against his neck. She was still rocking back and forth. "I promised him I'd see him home to the fade."

I figured the fade was their afterlife.

"Yes, we'll give Raror his final journey before we leave," I said, "but do we need to keep an eye out for the rest of the Spurns? Are they going to try and finish you off as well?"

"No, that will not happen." Lisped words came from behind.

Brace and Josian fell into a defensive pose, blocking our vulnerable position on the ground.

Looking around their legs, I could see an emerald-haired Spurn. She was stiff, and looked as if she wished she was anywhere else.

"We were all overtaken by some type of fervor. I could see what I was doing, but didn't care or understand why," she tried to explain.

Her hands were clutched across her stomach as she stared past us toward Talina and Raror.

"Earon want to mourn Raror. We need to prepare the fade ceremony," she finally croaked out.

There was no mention of Gladriel. Talina didn't move or lift her head, but she spoke strongly.

"Do not come any closer," she said to the other Earon. "I know you were Raror's mating partner this season. But I will not share the honor of sending him off. He was my brother for all seasons."

She spoke with such dignity, and for the first time raised her face to stare at us directly. Her lovely brown eyes were swollen, ringed in heavy red. Her features were grave, a sadness that could never be resolved. She wore her loss in such a profound manner that again I found my eyes filling with tears.

"I understand, Talina. I will let the others know of your wishes. The pontoon is being prepared. We will leave as soon as you are aboard."

The Spurn walked away.

"We need to go to sea for the ceremony?" I asked, even though I knew on Spurn there would be no other way.

"Yes, I will carry Raror, and release him back to the ocean from which we are born." She stood then, and with a deceptive strength gathered her brother into her arms.

She began her journey along the beach. Every step she took weighed her footprints into the damp sand, but she never faltered. She bore her burden with poise and a sense of purpose that would have made Raror proud. As we walked, I finally let my eyes rest on the fallen Spurn. His eyes were closed and he looked peaceful, despite the myriad of cuts and bruises littering his features.

I had seen my share of dead bodies on Earth, but not anyone that I really cared about. My thoughts were heavy as we followed Talina. She never showed the burden of his weight. The only time she stumbled was the moment the Earon pontoon came into view. It was the only break in the horizon line. Emerald-green flags flew from every level. Talina fell to her knees, but didn't drop her precious parcel. She sobbed tearlessly into his chest.

"I am sorry, my brother. The flags should have flown for me first. It was never supposed to be you."

She continued to talk to him as she rose again and stepped out into the water. We watched from the beach. It took her no time to reach the pontoon, even dragging Raror with her. Many Earon hands helped pull them aboard. There were many sorrowful faces with so much grief pouring from them.

Talina stood on deck to wave us over.

"I wondered if we were invited," Brace said as we paused at the edge of the water. "Do you need help, Abby?"

I shook my head. "No, I've spent enough time in the water recently. I think I'm getting the hang of this swimming thing. Just don't let any creatures eat me," I added when we were standing waist deep.

They both laughed, which was in no way reassuring.

Keeping my head above the water, I paddled out at a reasonably fast pace. I wished again that I hadn't worn jeans. They were not the most comfortable swimming attire. Brace stayed close to me. By the time we reached the pontoon, there was no sign of Talina. Other Earons helped us aboard and directed us upstairs to wait as the pontoon started to move off swiftly as if a hundred seahorses pulled it.

"I wonder where they go for this ceremony," I said as the land disappeared behind us.

"Someplace sacred to them," Josian said.

Every culture, race and religion practices different traditions for birth and death. On Earth, we'd been taught of the elaborate funerals that were performed to mourn the dead. I didn't understand the entirety of the event, having never witnessed any myself, but it seemed quite abundant. But that was before the downfall.

In my lifetime it was common practice to burn our dead. There were just too many bodies and not enough burial ground. When the spread of disease peaked around the early twenty-first century, it just became more practical. So this Spurnian death ceremony was something very new for me.

We learned that the Spurns look at birth and death as opposite sides of the same coin. They took Raror back to the waters from which they are born. An eeriness filled the air as thirty Earons entered the water. We stayed on the edge of the pontoon; we could see but were not too close. It felt very mystical here, situated directly under one of the moons. The ceremony started the moment the moons reached their highest peak. It was at this point I gasped, but quietly enough not to disturb anyone.

A luminescence of some type spread along the surface of the water surrounding them. It was like the most beautiful oil slick, shiny and filled with intermingled greens and golds. It wasn't thick and filmy; instead it flowed.

At this point the Earons began a chorus of lilting song. There were no words, just a heart-wrenching keening that formed a melody. Talina appeared on the side of the pontoon, away from where we stood. She carried Raror, although he was now completely wrapped in white, even covering over his face. She descended slowly into the water, pushing her floating brother before her. Her brethren continued their song of mourning.

For what felt like the fiftieth time that day, tears gathered in my eyes, spilling over. I didn't wipe them. The magic kept me immobile. There were no words spoken, no goodbyes or memories of Raror shared. Instead, they swam in a circle, keening their song, and letting the glow surround them.

Finally their music reached a crescendo. Talina paused with Raror in the center. She held him slightly aloft, as though he were an offering to the gods. And then she released him. I expected him to sink beneath the briny depths, but that wasn't the case.

Talina moved away, and left Raror floating in the middle of a large circle of Earons. They continued to sing, although it was quieter now, coming to what felt like its conclusion.

Then slowly the luminescence moved across to surround Raror, shifting and growing over the top of his shrouded form. I wanted to rub my eyes, not quite able to believe what I was seeing, but my heavy arms still wouldn't move.

Then he disappeared into that glowing slick.

The moment this happened the waters cleared, the moon moved from the peak of the sky and the glow, along with Raror, was gone.

None of the Earons moved. Raror's body had been long departed before they broke the circle, making their way back to the pontoon. I raised my hands to wipe away the last traces of tears. The spell was broken. I realized that during the entire ceremony none of the Earons had cried. In fact, except for Talina's tears, I hadn't seen one shed. And yet the pain was clear on their faces.

"I am ready to leave with you now." Talina interrupted my thoughts, her words were flat.

She stood there looking the same, just with red and swollen eyes, but she was also different, as if something inside her had died along with Raror.

"Are you sure?" I asked. "We can stay a little longer."

That may not have actually been true. I didn't know how urgent it was that we returned home.

"No! Raror is in the fade with our ancestors. I have no reason to stay on Spurn." Strands of her emerald hair fell across her face, and for once she didn't shift them away.

"We need you to stay and rule Earon." The female from earlier was standing before us.

The rest had disappeared inside the pontoon. We were still on the lower decking.

"And ... I need you to stay. I am pregnant with Raror's young."

For the first time since her brother's death an emotion besides devastation crossed Talina's features.

"You have no idea how happy it makes me to know that my brother's essence will live on. But I cannot stay here. I have never been welcome on Spurn, and this is not going to change. If anything, Raror's ... death ..." She hesitated over the word. "His death is only going to make things harder for me."

She moved closer to the smaller Spurn. "It is your responsibility to rule now. You are carrying the only true heir to Earon."

And with those words she turned away and held out a hand to me. Her message was clear: get me away now.

Chapter 12

We'd been back on First World for two days. And for the first time since discovering my home planet the skies were cast in low dark clouds. Heavy shattering rain trapped us inside my parents' massive house. The weather was almost a direct reflection of the darkness Talina was living in. She barely left her room, and refused to speak with anyone while she struggled with Raror's death.

The first morning I'd found her standing out on her balcony, letting the pouring rain wash over her.

"I wish Raror could have seen this," she said as I leaned in close to her.

I couldn't tell if it was tears or rain that washed down her cheeks in a rhythmic manner. I didn't know what to say, so I reached out and held her hand.

The rest of her time was spent in the ocean, or trying to adjust to First World: she hated the clothes and the food. In fact, most of First World's food made her sick; it was far too rich and fatty compared to what she had survived on previously. Although Josian assured her she should eventually be able to eat anything, right now I think she was basically eating quant, the sweet pink fruit I loved. Its juice was the closest thing she could find to Spurn's cucreamer.

On the third morning I made my way down the hall. Pausing at her door, I rapped my knuckles lightly against the wood. I wasn't surprised that once again there was no answer. I understood her need to mourn, but I was at a loss about the correct etiquette. Should I leave her alone or offer comfort?

"Hey, Abbs, trying to find Talli?" I turned to see Lucy sauntering out of her room, which was ten feet from Talina's.

"Yeah, but as usual she isn't answering me," I said.

As I examined Lucy, I wondered what was up with her uncharacteristically disheveled appearance. Her blond curls were everywhere, and

I was pretty sure her shirt was buttoned up wrong, which was very unlike my fashionable friend.

"I saw her just before, out my window. She was making her way to the ocean." She had started running her hands through her hair in an attempt to tame it.

"What've you been doing?" I had to ask.

"What do you mean?" Lucy said, guarded.

"You don't keep secrets from me, Luce. Aren't you the one that says 'life is for sharing'?"

She laughed a little, but it didn't quite reach her eyes.

"I'm not secretive, Abigail. I'm just trying to be a good guest and allow everyone to settle in before indulging my need to share," she said.

And then suddenly all was explained as Samuel strode out of her room.

"Aribella." He looked uncomfortable as he squeezed past.

I waited until he'd almost cleared the hall before I faced Lucy. Her smug expression told me everything, and I really should have guessed.

"So I'm guessing the underwear plan worked."

I felt kind of annoyed and couldn't figure out why. Maybe it was that Lucy seemed to be moving so fast. I didn't want my friend to change too much before me.

Chuckling, she watched Samuel's broad shoulders until he was no longer visible. "Actually, no, he's staying adamant that we be properly mated before that."

I hadn't expected that answer.

"So, I assume you're planning to hold the ceremony tomorrow?"

Lucy's lack of patience was as legendary as my own.

"Word, Abbs." She winked. "But ... actually I am enjoying the practice and prelude more than you can imagine. Samuel's skills are numerous." She trailed off.

I covered my ears and hummed, before sighing as I dropped my arms back down. "I knew I'd regret asking. Oh, and your shirt is buttoned wrong."

"I've missed you." She linked her arm through mine, not even bothering to glance down.

Must be love. No way would she be this disheveled in public otherwise. I gave her a squeeze. I'd missed her too. We had gone from spending most of our time together on Earth to being so busy we regularly had to make time to catch up on each other's lives.

"Where's Brace?" she asked as we made our way downstairs to the main living area and slouched into the soft couches.

I slanted my right brow in her direction. Her tone was mildly sarcastic.

She smirked. "It's just odd not seeing him attached to you."

I bristled. "I'm still my own person."

She held a hand up in mock surrender. "I didn't mean anything. And it's not like I can talk. I understand this mating bond thing. You have no idea." She looked curious now. "And Sammy explained that it will be a hundred times stronger for you two being Walkers."

It had been coming for days. Her words acted like a catalyst and all of my suppressed emotions suddenly burst free. But instead of words all that emerged was this crazy kind of screech. A long, loud scream that stole the breath from my lungs. Lucy jumped at least a foot off the chair, her face a picture of astonishment. And then the words started to spew from my mouth in a manner usually reserved for lunatics and ... Lucy.

"I cannot breathe without him. He's off now, something to do with leading his father astray, so he's too busy to search for me. And I literally ache." I stared at my hands. "This isn't what I wanted. It's too much, too big. He's slowly becoming my everything. I don't have the type of life that's gentle with someone's everything."

I fought against the unease that was always present when Brace wasn't close. And at this distance our bond was sporadic, kicking in sometimes while at other times I felt all alone.

"You shouldn't feel like that, Aribella," Lallielle said.

My concerned mother had just walked through the door, which wasn't a surprise; her daughter had just finished screaming like a banshee. "Your bond with Brace is the strength that will allow you to conquer all."

Josian followed looking relaxed, as usual he displayed no sign of worry. He lifted us both together into a bone-crushing hug. Despite the pain, I sank into their warmth and comfort.

"I'm sorry, baby girl, that you feel your independence has been taken. I understand Earthlings are raised to be strong and able to survive alone. You don't trust easily." He set us free then, allowing me a few deep breaths. "But that's the reason you should cherish this gift you've been given. Walkers are designed as two halves of a whole. We have a genetic predisposition to never betray our true mate."

I nodded then, in a quick bob. "I understand that Brace is a gift. He's amazing. But what happens if I lose him? How do you survive?"

"There's no point living a half-life to prevent hurt. I would rather one day with your mother, than an eternity never knowing the joy she has brought me. It just wouldn't be a life."

Lallielle's eyes sparkled, although I couldn't see any tears.

"I feel the same way," she said.

The pink aura surrounding them was again visible as their bond tightened and flexed.

Josian smiled. "You only feel so bereft because he's not close. You get used to the sensation, but I remember how uncomfortable it was in the beginning, being away from your mother, as if a sense had been cut off."

Josian was right. Brace better get his butt back soon. If he was going to meld with me, then he better stick around so my brain didn't go insane thinking he was dead.

"I wish the rain would stop so we could explore the town," Lucy said. "That would be a great distraction."

She'd told me earlier that it had been pouring for a week before we returned.

"Ah, we have rain so seldom. I'm really enjoying this cool and soothing weather." Lallielle stared out of the window. The ocean was a stormy gray color, matching the sky above. "Perfect weather to snuggle up and watch a movie."

297

"Speaking of which, Frannie has me leaving on another mission tomorrow, so we are off to enjoy a movie," Josian said.

He swept Lallielle up over his shoulder, and stormed off, caveman style. She gave me a resigned smile behind his back, but didn't protest.

"I'm not sure I believed Jos' story, but his plan is a good one. We could actually catch up on some flicks." Lucy was sprawled back in the chair. She looked almost asleep.

"I don't think you're going to make it through a movie." I laughed.

She opened one eye a little wider.

"Tell me about it. I seriously need to start getting sleep, but the nightmares are putting a dent in that plan."

"You're still having nightmares?" I hadn't realized. "Why didn't you tell me? What're they about?"

She snuggled down further into the white couch, her face partially covered.

"There're a few different ones that visit me. And they're as real and detailed as that dream I had before I was kidnapped. I sometimes wonder if I'm actually there, and it's not really a dream."

"They sound almost like premonitions."

She wiggled around, shifting her feet so they were further apart. "I know, but when I was kidnapped facets of my dream were there, although mostly it was very different."

"You need to ask Frannie about them," I said.

She met my eyes. "I don't trust her, Abbs, and these dreams ... they aren't good. We seriously do not want them to come true."

"Give me some details." She looked really freaked out.

She flipped over, her discomfort obvious. On her back, she stared up at the high white ceilings. "The first dream starts on First World. We're searching for something, but no one will ever tell me what it is."

"Who is we?" I interrupted her.

"All of us that went to Spurn, plus your parents and Frannie." She glared at me. "And stop interrupting if you want me to have a chance at getting through this."

I mimed the motion of zipping my lips. She smirked before continuing.

"So, we're searching for something, and then suddenly we're standing at the base of these black mountains ... which I assume are those Brace described to us." Her voice lowered. "Even in the dream I get this urge to shower. I have the creepiest sensation up my spine the entire time we're standing there. Suddenly, this hole opens up and an army emerges. But they're like zombies,

Abbs. Disgusting, stinking, rotted, half-human things. And they attack us."

She gulped then. "It's not pretty."

"I've dreamed of the mountain too, and as crazy as it sounds, I think we need to explore there." I knew it held an important clue or information.

Lucy dropped her gaze to glare at me, but before she could reply we were interrupted.

"You must finish gathering the halflings. That's the most important job."

Francesca stood in the doorway. Her white eyes looked ... somewhere. It was hard to tell.

"Dammit, woman! How long were you standing there?" Lucy was sitting up now, looking more awake. "Don't pop up in the middle of a scary story."

"I sensed a divergence from the plan, and needed to make sure things stayed in place."

"You're weirding me out, Frannie. Maybe you should back off with all this prophesy stuff," I said, standing.

Just being in the same room as her set off my inner alarm. Lucy was right: something was off with her, and I couldn't quite put my finger on it. I could never tell if it was her gift that gave me chills or if there was more.

"We're taking your word for lots of things without an ounce of evidence." I stepped closer to her. "How about you give me a quick glimpse inside your mind."

She smiled, but it wasn't nice, and it did nothing to reassure me. "You know I can't let you do that. People shouldn't know too much of their future. You may alter something that is fundamental to survival."

I wondered if she meant her survival or mine. She swung around to leave the room. I still couldn't understand why my Walker abilities couldn't break her mind-block. But Josian said he couldn't either.

"We need to keep an eye on her." Lucy stood next to me. "Suspect is an understatement."

"Word," I said darkly.

Late that night I lay curled up under my fluffy covers. I was enjoying the sound of heavy rain, but if it continued like this we were going to need a boat. Talina would be fine at least. A shock of electrical spark suddenly flooded me. My heart jumped in joy, and the melancholy that had been plaguing me lifted. Brace was back.

"I'm more than back, Red." His words came out of the darkness from the rear of my room. "I'm waiting patiently to kiss my beautiful mate."

Jumping out of bed, I tripped over before throwing myself into his arms.

"Where the hell have you been?" I demanded, my fear and anger clipping the words short.

"I missed you too," he said, sounding happier than usual, "and thank you for wearing such outstanding attire."

I blushed, wishing Walkers didn't have such good night vision. I was in a little singlet and matching shortie shorts. No bra, of course, just the inbuilt one already in the top. Pulling back, I crossed my arms over my chest.

"What happened with your father?" I asked.

"I don't want to talk about that." He took a step closer, devouring me with his eyes.

I shivered.

He smiled in a slow curve. I suddenly noticed where we were standing and a thought burst free.

"You remember that day you ran into me, when I'd just ... uh, gotten out of the shower?"

A low rumble emanated from his chest. "It's indelibly imprinted on my mind."

I snorted. "Indelibly imprinted ... seriously?"

He usually had a handle on sounding young, but occasionally his age shone through. He ignored my mocking and raised his eyebrow.

"What were you doing in my room?" I blurted out.

He didn't answer immediately. I could almost feel him weighing and judging what to say. Finally he met my gaze.

"I don't know how to answer; I'm not actually sure what happened. I was heading in the opposite direction, to grab some plans from Josian's study, when I found my legs moving." He shook his head. "Before I knew it, I was standing in your room."

I blushed and chuckled. "I'll bet you didn't expect that exact situation."

He refrained from laughing, although his eyes sparkled. "Oh, it far outweighed any expectations I could ever have had." He leaned in very close to me; I could feel the hairs on my entire body prickle as bumps crossed my skin. "Next time I get you naked, though, I won't leave ... You have no idea how hard it was the first time."

"Uh, you had me naked in the bath just the other day."

He shook his head. "That doesn't count, sweetheart. You needed care and love. As your mate, I will always be what you need."

"Sometimes it sucks, you know," I blurted again.

He stilled, waiting for my next unfiltered gem of wisdom.

"You want me because of some pre-destined mating bond. It wouldn't matter what I looked like or if I was shallow and mean. You would still want me."

His expression alternated between frustration and resignation.

"Red, I know you don't see yourself clearly, and that's okay. I see more than you could imagine." His eyes captured me. "We would always have had this attraction and bond. It's the way mating works; you wouldn't be my other half unless we had the foundation of a perfection bond." His eyes darkened. "But let's get something straight. I would want you no matter what. You are powerful and smart, and unusual enough that you would have always caught my attention. You intrigue me, entice me and, damn it, Abigail – you are hot. I mean so hot that any man would be insane not to want you."

His eyes trailed over me, slowly. My knees buckled slightly. But I caught myself.

I managed to take a shuddering breath, and then decided what the hell; you only live once. With a running jump I again threw myself at Brace, wrapping my legs around him. Lucky he was a big man. He caught me no problem and without pause we were kissing. Long, dragging, soul-burning kisses. If his expression earlier had been devouring, he now kissed me as if he needed to consume every part of my soul. With a gasp of breath I pulled back from his mouth. I closed my eyes as he started to press gentle little butterfly kisses all over my face. I could feel his adoration in every touch, every light caress.

Through our bond he glowed, our golden auras flickering brightly. Opening my eyes, I reached down to press the clasp on my necklace, needing to see his marks, needing them joined to mine. He pulled back at that point, halting my hand.

"Not here, sweetheart. We don't know what will happen, and your father will be in your room killing me quicker than you know."

As I dropped my hand his lips found mine again. I opened my mouth, taking his tongue boldly, drinking in everything that was Brace. I threaded my fingers through the silky strands of hair at the back of his head. Never lifting his face from mine he directed us toward my bed. As my legs dropped down, the back of my knees hit the edge. He lowered me, pausing to stare as I lay disheveled on my covers.

There was this endless depth of emotion in his eyes. I wanted desperately to seek his thoughts, but I refrained. Instead, I scooted along the cool surface until my back hit the headboard, my eyes staying locked on his face. I would never have enough of his soul-stealing beauty; he was pure perfection.

I almost lost my breath as he pulled his shirt over his head, leaving just his black pants on. I was sensually assaulted by expanses of tanned skin stretched tightly over muscles. He crawled onto the end of the bed like a stalking panther, moving on all fours until he reached me. I shuddered in some air. Just watching him approach was enough to have ripples spreading through my body.

Lifting one hand, he cupped my face. I lay back and he followed over the top of me. But instead of it making me feel claustrophobic, crowded by his huge body, I felt small and feminine. I reached up to wrap my hands around his muscled arms, pulling him down so I could cushion his weight. I loved the feel of his body pressed against my own, but for some reason I couldn't keep still. My lower body continued to shift and move over the bed. There were just too many sensations.

"You are going to kill me," he said, pulling back slightly.

Our heavy breathing intermingled.

"You seem awfully confident in my self-control. Don't test me too much; we're still under your father's roof."

"What he doesn't know won't hurt him," I said, running my hands along his strong back. I needed him closer.

"Red," he held himself up so he could stare into my face, "no matter what happens over the next few months, finding you has been the best part of my very long life."

His melted chocolate eyes were serious. He'd stopped kissing me; he wanted me to focus. I attempted to pry more information from his mind, but he had the bond shut down.

"You aren't going anywhere," I finally said – the only scenario I would allow to cross my mind. "I've made the decision to keep you. So you're just going to have to stick around."

"You've decided to keep me." He grinned. "I like that."

He pressed his lips to mine again, our kisses more intense than before. I groaned as unfelt sensations shot through me. Why had I wasted so much time not kissing him? I continued to run my hands over his soft skin. I couldn't stop myself from touching him; it was addictive. I paused briefly as I noticed some slight puckering ridges along his chest; I'd never seen any scars.

He distracted me by shifting his hand to rest on my stomach. My muscles jumped under the sensation, the rough texture creating the most exquisite feeling. He moved slowly, so slow it was surely registered as a form of torture, running his hand up my back until he gripped the nape of my neck. He then shifted his other hand over my stomach, moving upwards until he rested at the underside of my inbuilt bra. His fingers skimmed along the edges.

Someone needed to open a window. It was getting hot in here. Brace's hand froze at the sound of a loud knock. Who the hell was knocking on my door in the middle of the night?

"Are you going to answer that, Red?" Brace's voice was strained.

I shifted against him. His legs were plastered to mine, and I was having trouble concentrating.

"Um ... if ... I ig ..." I lost concentration for a minute. His hand was doing delicious things under my shirt. "If I ignore it, will they go away?" I ended breathlessly.

"No, Aribella, you and Brace need to get downstairs now." Josian's voice was clear through my door.

"Nothing wrong with his hearing," I muttered.

In that moment I was too hot and bothered to even feel embarrassed at being busted.

Neither of us moved. Even if I'd wanted to move, my muscles wouldn't respond.

"How dangerous is he; you know, if we ignore that request and stay here?" I would have no problem taking on my father to stay in Brace's arms, close enough to see every facet of brown in his eyes.

He gave a short laugh. "We need to get downstairs."

I sighed as we untangled ourselves. I had a sneaking suspicion that this interrupting was going to be a common occurrence.

Brace rolled over before groaning.

"What?" I said, facing him.

"You really need to discuss our situation with your laluna. I'm starting to feel like the third wheel." He reached behind his head to pull free my blue stone.

It was quite humorous how many times the laluna appeared in my room, on my pillows generally, no matter where I took it for safe-keeping. Josian seemed to think we were cosmically connected, and that it would always come for me.

"Leave it alone. It's my little friend, and I've grown fond of its blue beauty."

Brace stood, smiling down at me.

"I can't blame the laluna ... you are quite lovable, Abigail."

Tears flicked at my eyes as his words hit my heart, close to that small place inside that always felt alone and abandoned. I changed the subject before I said something stupid and sentimental.

"You should go down now. I'll throw on some appropriate clothes." I cleared my throat as I attempted to straighten myself.

He picked up his shirt from the floor, and shrugged it over his head. It was definitely a shame to cover all that. Then with one last look that was hot enough to melt bones, he left the room.

I stepped into my bathroom to splash some water on my overheated face. Staring into the mirror, I could see I looked a little off. My emerald eyes were wide and shiny, cheeks flushed, red curls tousled around in a wild manner. My full red lips looked even more swollen. Everyone was going to know immediately; I looked like someone who'd just had some good loving.

I changed into jeans and a plain black shirt.

"Abigail Swish." I spun around at Lucy's incredulous tone.

She was standing next to my bed, staring down at the sheets.

"What have you been up to?" Her tone brimmed with unshed laughter.

She was dressed in jeans as well, except she wore a low-cut red cotton shirt, which definitely made the most of her awesome boobs.

"Do you have a sex radar or something?" I said, staring around the room.

There wasn't anything that should have tipped her off.

Her blue eyes widened. "Like a sex-dar." She laughed. "So, are you saying that you and Brace sexed it all up?"

"You look a little worried – think I beat you to the final gate?" I teased.

She raised her brows, high enough to almost hit her blond hairline.

"Don't leave me hanging; if I have to torture you for the information, I will." She wasn't kidding.

Rolling my eyes, I gestured for her to move through the door first.

"Nope, Brace and I were interrupted before anything crazy could happen." My disappointment was apparent in my voice.

"How far would you have gone?" She sounded genuinely curious as we hurried downstairs.

I knew Josian wouldn't wait long. Something serious was up if he had summoned everyone in the middle of the night.

"I don't know. I'd like to think I'd wait until we'd spent more time with each other. But our chemistry just knocks all rational thought from my mind." My cheeks flushed again just thinking about it. "He kisses like he's trying to consume me, Luce," I said quietly, and she sighed, a small reflective smile crossing her lips.

"Don't you want to be married first?" Her words took me a little by surprise.

I shook my head. "Nah, you know I don't believe a piece of paper is a commitment. And what Brace and I have, being melded mates, well, I can't think of a more definitive promise."

"I know what you're saying is right." She looked wistful ... or just sad.

Why did I have a strange feeling that she was hiding something from me?

"I already feel like I'm losing myself to Sammy. I worry that if we take that last step I won't even know who I am anymore."

"What does Samuel say?"

She laughed without humor. "He wants to wait for a mating ceremony. On First World, even for those who aren't 'true mates', they still hold this ceremonial ritual. It's not a contract; it can be dissolved; but Sammy says that rarely happens. Unlike on Earth, they're all pretty loyal to their families."

312

"I would guess they break this bond in the rare events they find their true mates?"

She nodded. "Yes, that seems to be one of the only reasons. And it's understood and socially accepted."

I stopped her just before we reached the downstairs room. I leaned in and spoke quietly. "Are you okay, Lucy? Has something happened? Don't you want to be mated to Samuel?"

It was clear that she hadn't expected my question. A few tears sprinkled the blue of her eyes.

"Abbs, I don't know what to do. I'm not sure what's going on with Sammy. Our connection was so immediate and all encompassing that I never questioned him when he said we were destined mates. I figured I wouldn't know, being from Earth." She sighed. "But now I'm having some doubts. Things just aren't adding up." The last part was said so quietly I almost missed it, even though I was standing right next to her.

My mouth fell open. I spoke wordlessly, unable to coherently respond.

"I don't ... understand." Yeah, that was kind of what I was thinking.

They had been inseparable since the moment we'd rescued them from Earth.

"Never mind, Abbs. I'm probably being silly, and Sammy and I've had a few arguments lately, so I'm emotional."

I hugged her, hating to hear the desolate nature of her tone.

"You don't have to jump in without any thought. We know better than that, Luce. Think about back home; we didn't trust anyone."

She pulled away. "But he's your brother. We have no reason not to trust him."

"Lucy," I said aghast, "that's one of the stupidest things you've ever said. We don't know him and he was held captive for a year. He's damaged; that's been established."

"I know him, though, and he's a good person. He's made me happier than I ever thought I would be."

I stared at her before shrugging. "Well, just let me know if you need my help. I'm always here."

I dropped it because I could see she was done with this discussion that night. But it was going to be revisited later. Something was up, and I was going to figure it out.

"I'm going to die, Abby." Her words took me by surprise, and I couldn't stop the gasp that escaped me.

"What?" My immediate thoughts were dark.

Lucy smiled at me. "Calm down. I don't mean today, but I do have a shelf-life, unlike the rest of you. Sammy said there's some type of procedure here which can kickstart my cells' ability to regenerate, thereby halting the aging."

Finally we were addressing one of my primary concerns: Lucy's mortality.

"But it has risks, Abbs, and sometimes I think I'd prefer a hundred years with everyone, than die during this medical procedure because my body rejects it."

"I'll speak with Dad and Brace; maybe Walkers know of something less risky."

Lucy shrugged. "Honestly, Sammy and I have been arguing about it so much, let's just wait and worry about this once we've put those Seventine back in their cage. We may all die anyway, so no need to stress."

I shook my head. "Only you would think there was no need to stress about our demise."

"The dead don't worry; that's reserved for the living," was her final reply.

I guess she had a point; there would be plenty of time after all of this saving-the-world to figure it out. If we lived that long, of course.

Without another word we stepped away from the stairs and crossed the hall into the front room, which should be re-named 'the meeting room'.

315

Josian stood in front of the large windows. It was still very dark outside, but my Walker vision could see out to the crashing waves. Lallielle was curled up in a single-seat chair. Brace, Lucas (who just seemed to appear at important moments), Francesca and Samuel were squished into the long white couch, leaving two other chairs.

My face broke out in a huge smile when I saw Quarn filling one of them. I ran over to my old guardian. I hadn't seen him in forever. He'd told us that he was going away to catch up with family and old acquaintances. I wasn't sure if that was the entire story.

"Quarn!" I exclaimed as he stood to hug me. "I've missed you."

I don't know at what point our bond had formed so strongly, but he was such a dear person to me.

"I've missed you too, *miqueriona*." The rumble of his familiar accent flooded me with joy. I pulled back to look at him properly.

It amazed me that he was the only person who actively used the old language. No one else spoke like him.

"Ralph ... you look great." Lucy came from behind to hug him too.

"I have missed your unique sense of humor, Lucy Laurel," Quarn said drily.

"You do look good. Relaxed. Where have you been? What did you do?" I interrupted, peppering him with questions.

He just smiled that grin, the one that said he wasn't going to tell me anything I didn't need to know.

"You're so annoying." I gave him a gentle shove. "Keep your secrets, old man."

I followed Lucy over to the last chair, squishing in next to her. Josian straightened from where he'd been slumped against the sill.

"I'm sorry to drag you all from sleep." He hesitated over the last word.

I couldn't quite meet his bronze eyes. At least he didn't sound too angry.

"But I have received some urgent news. We must act on this immediately."

The window behind him opened. Josian spun around, and the rest of us watched dumfounded as a naked Talina stepped inside. Her long emerald hair covered most of her as she dripped water all over the ground.

"Sorry I'm late. I heard you all and figured something had happened," she said carelessly.

"Guess the question of whether they look the same as us under their wraps has just been answered," Lucy stated in a deadpan voice, breaking the tension.

317

Most of those in the room attempted to hide their grins.

Lallielle jumped up and dashed from the room. She was back in a moment with a white, corded robe, which she draped over Talina's lithe frame.

"I don't want you to catch a chill, sweetie," she said in a kind tone.

Talina looked confused as she threaded her arms through the sleeves. "I'm not sure what a chill is, but thank you for the covers."

She moved then, sitting on the floor between Lucy and me. Josian shut the window, preventing more rain from pouring in, before turning back.

"I have invited some of my brothers here to guard the house."

We were definitely unprepared for the flood of tall redhaired Walkers that drifted in through the open doorway, as though they'd just been waiting for an introduction.

I had never seen so many shades of red in my life, ranging from the brightest forest fire to dark auburn. Their heights started at low six feet tall all the way up to almost seven feet. Suddenly the room felt very small and crowded.

"I won't introduce them individually. You'll never remember their names," Josian continued.

Ten. I counted ten Walkers in addition to him. Brace had stood the moment they entered the room and was now behind my chair. I looked up at him. He was glaring at each of the Walkers. One by one he locked them in his stare. I sighed.

"Are you going to pee on me, Brace?" I could practically see the challenge he was issuing to the other men in the room, marking his territory.

"I don't know why I would do that, but if it helps these Walkers keep their hands to themselves, I will gladly comply." He never looked down, but a small smile softened his features.

"Brothers," Josian said, distracting everyone from whatever man-game they were playing. "Take note of Brace. He is an Abernath, and my daughter's mate. He will destroy any one of you that looks sideways at Aribella."

His blunt words did nothing except increase the interest I could see their array of dazzling eyes.

What's their fascination?

I couldn't help the thought, and as usual Brace picked it up.

Half-Walkers are myth in our world; you have your marks on display, and are uncommonly beautiful. You are like our version of a unicorn.

I groaned softly. Great, just what I needed, to be some type of Walker fantasy creature.

"Aribella and Talina are both halflings. They must be protected at all costs," Josian said.

I spoke up.

"I have to leave, Dad. You know I can't stay around here. I have to gather the other half-Walkers."

He nodded. "Yes, you will be gathering them, but at all times you will have at least one of my brothers as a guard. I might not be able to accompany you, but they will."

"But Francesca said – "

"I do not care. This is non-negotiable." His features were strained.

I'd never seen him so rattled.

"What's happened, Josian?" Brace said, with some impatience.

There was an uncomfortable pause. I almost stood to demand answers, but he finally spoke.

"They have found the bodies of two Walkers. Dead. And their essence was wiped clean. They no longer exist."

The room was silent.

"That's not possible," I finally stuttered out.

Walkers could not completely die. That's what Josian had said.

"I don't know what to tell you, baby girl. The release of the Seventine is bringing about changes that have never been spoken of. We have no choice now but to adapt."

Chapter 13

The next few days I had a tall redhaired Walker up my butt at all times. I'd started having extra long showers just to get some alone time. One positive had emerged from all the worry and lack of privacy. Josian was grudgingly allowing Brace to stay with me at night.

He seemed to understand that Brace would not be away from me when danger was close. We still had a Walker stationed outside the door. But since Josian had warned me that they had even better hearing than I did, I was pretty sure it was just to deter any untoward activities.

Apparently, he didn't approve of his daughter fooling around in his house, and so far Brace was complying, limiting us to some heavy-duty make-out sessions. I went to sleep most nights hot and bothered, and woke the same way.

First World had reached what I thought was the equivalent of spring. The rain had stopped, and the land bloomed in shades of green and multi-hued flowers. Technically, I wasn't allowed to roam or explore, but the few times I managed to escape with Lucy I fell more in love with the natural beauty here.

Lucy still wouldn't talk to me about her other issues with Samuel, and her subdued personality was starting to worry me. But with so many events in the works, there wasn't much time for our personal lives, especially since the vast majority of my time was spent with Josian and Brace.

They were trying to help Talina and I harness our Walker powers, though both found the limitations and unknown of our half-nature frustrating.

"I need a breather," I said to Brace, flopping into the soft sand.

Early that morning he'd started me forming energy balls to blast an old crate. Hours later I still hadn't improved.

"You have five minutes, Red."

Brace was either an ass or a dictator – probably both – but I could tell I was learning from a highly trained expert, so I couldn't whine too much.

We watched as Josian guided Talina. They stood calf-deep in the water.

"Great job, Talli," he said with a smile, "you are finally learning to stay in control of the power, and not let it control you."

Talina gave a rare grin, just the corners of her mouth lifting. "Yes, I didn't black out this time."

She was creating whirlpools and sending them off into different directions.

"Anticipating the energy allows me to fight against the corruptive nature of it," she said, shooting off another few geysers.

"You must never underestimate power. Like anything, it can be addictive. Always respect it, and fight to stay true, and you'll always be in charge. The moment the power controls you, it's too late."

"Alright, your rest time is up, Red." Brace jumped effortlessly to his feet. "We need to figure out if you can take back control."

"What do you mean?" I said, pulling myself up. I was definitely feeling the backlash of too much energy release.

"I think your powers are testing you, making you work for each and every skill. You must show it who is in charge."

I figured he was referring to the fact that every time I tried to blast the crate my energy fizzled out halfway.

"It scares me," I admitted, forming the golden sphere in my hand.

Unlike Brace's two-color ball, mine was pure shining gold.

The power always seemed to be outside my control, doing exactly what it wanted, and I was afraid to explore too deeply. It felt as if something was down there that I could not handle.

"It's like wolves. If you don't step up and be the pack leader, the rest will never follow or respect you. Take your power, Abbs; be the alpha."

I nodded, determination flooding me. I gathered the wisps, and shaped my sphere. As usual, the energy tried to escape. When I refused to let it, it started to form something else, but again I held concentration, determined to be in control. It still took me numerous attempts, but finally the last one held long enough to explode the wooden crate.

Brace, who was standing with his arms crossed, watching intently, gave me a nod of approval.

"Much better, but you have to keep working on it. Don't let the fear dictate your life. Your energy will control you, and a Walker who loses control is dangerous."

Maybe that was what I feared: losing control to the power.

Later that night, I lay wrapped in Brace's arms, his warm voice washing over me. He was all business when it came to training, but in bed he was different. It amazed me how he could be so varied, compartmentalizing and staying in control.

"Now that you've found your family, and discovered who you are, tell me another thing that you always wished to have but still don't."

He'd been quizzing me on all aspects of my life, dissecting each answer. The way his mind worked was beyond anything I was capable of following. I'd never felt stupid, and I still didn't, but he certainly had me thinking in entirely new directions. I guess it never hurts to broaden my knowledge.

"You mean besides Bear Grylls personally escorting me around New York?" I joked, wincing as Brace playfully tightened his arms. "Kidding, kidding."

Brace had not seemed that impressed when we sat through a few *Man vs Wild* episodes. Apparently, there was nothing exceptional about this man's abilities. Of course not, if you're a Walker.

"I guess I've always wanted a pet. A puppy or kitten. As a child, reading about the love and loyalty pets showed their owners, I craved a relationship like that."

All children loved animals, but when I was six, and learned how rare they were, it had really hit me hard. I was pretty sure I cried for a week.

"Animals are not pets on First World. They don't have owners; they have friends and companions."

"I like that," I said, smiling. "Animals are smart and beautiful. Many humans treated them abysmally, and I never understood how they could."

"They wouldn't have done that in my presence. Most animals I've known are far superior to any humanoids, no matter what year or world." He softly stroked my arm, lulling me to sleep and sending shivers throughout my entire body.

I eventually fell asleep listening to Brace describe the animals he had known throughout the years. They varied depending on which planet and time he was occupying at the time, but I could tell he loved each and every one of them.

326

The days blended into each other, training and exploring, and being followed around by the red Walker gang. That morning after a restless night's sleep, I opened my eyes slowly; it felt really early. I wondered what had woken me. I gasped as a strong arm reached around, pulling me back into a warm embrace.

It was still a shock to wake next to Brace. For someone who had always slept alone, I figured that it would feel smothering. Instead, I fell asleep at night snuggled into his broad chest, and woke each morning in his arms. It was pure heaven. Brace could go from asleep to alert in a matter of seconds, but I liked those first few moments when he was soft and drowsy. And no matter what position we were in when we went to sleep he always ended up curled around me.

Protective.

I wasn't sure if he was aware he did this or if some type of mate instinct guided him. Whatever the reason I was starting to think I'd never sleep again without his warmth surrounding me. The possessive way he held me, the sound of his breathing so calming whenever sleep was elusive. I was starting to think I could not live without him. I wiggled against him, wanting to be closer. He groaned into my hair.

"What have I told you about trying to kill me this early in the morning?"

His throaty words washed over me. I could feel his desire, and it brought out the worst kind of temptress in me. But I always pulled back. Despite my need, I wasn't ready to lose my big V with my father's Walkers outside the door.

"So did you find out anything in your clan?" I said.

The day before, he'd disappeared, and hadn't been back by the time I went to bed. He must have slipped in during the night. He shook his head, burying his face into my red curls.

"No, everyone just seems to be distressed and preparing for the worst. But no one has any answers. Even my father seemed unusually upset." His voice was low and muffled, thick with sleep.

I shivered. He was so close that every breath tickled the back of my neck.

"Any of the reds hit on you while I was gone?" His voice was carefully calm, for once.

"If you're referring to them making polite conversation with me, then yes, red one, four and nine were on duty yesterday and they all spoke with me."

I was slowly learning their names, but until then we had to make do with numbers.

"I think four is the worst. He stares like you're the last moonstale rock in the galaxy."

I laughed. But I knew it was a miracle that no fighting had broken out yet. I think it was by Josian's pure will alone that we weren't living in a war zone. In my opinion Walkers had an over-abundance of testosterone and apparently didn't tolerate their mates around other unmated Walkers unless some type of ceremony had been performed. Something Brace and I hadn't had time for. Our 'mythical merging' hadn't convinced the reds to keep their flirting to themselves, so we needed to do this binding ceremony soon, before Brace started killing them off.

"We don't like our mates around any other Walker males. Period. We know what they're thinking, and it drives our protective instincts crazy." He was so much better at picking up my thoughts.

I only got his on occasion. I ignored his chauvinistic male comment to ask a more pertinent question.

"What exactly is this Walker mating ceremony?"

He chuckled into my neck. I shivered as his breath fanned my skin.

"We journey to the birthplace of Walkers. There, we're mated before seven witnesses." He paused briefly, playing with the curls along my cheek. I waited for the rest.

"There are certain words exchanged and a blood ritual."

My stomach jumped. I still hated blood, and anything involving blood generally involved pain.

"But don't worry. It's not the right time now, no matter how badly my inner Walker is demanding that we claim you."

That wasn't the first time I'd heard Walkers refer to themselves as having an inner demon they needed to placate.

"What changes after the ceremony? How will everyone know we're mated?"

"You can see auras, Abbs, and although that's not a common Walker ability, after the mating ceremony anyone will be able to see our entwined aura. It's the first thing unmated male Walkers search for when meeting females of our kind."

"But I already see the gold surrounding us."

"That's from the merging. Gold is a sacred color, a powerful merge, but the others can't see this until we're officially bound. The color of the merge and binding will intertwine."

I wondered whether our other color would be the same pink that surrounded my parents. I closed my eyes, enjoying the sensation of my hair being gently dragged through Brace's fingers. I decided to stress about my loss of independence later. Of course, he picked up that errant thought.

"You and I couldn't be more tied to each other, Red. This just makes it official for everyone else."

He made a good point. But still I wasn't always rational, and strong independent women did not tie themselves for life to one man. It was supposedly going to be a very long life and, despite my growing feelings, I'd only known him in the flesh for a matter of weeks.

"Stop thinking of yourself as human. You're not human, Abby, and your body knows this. It's just over-thinking that causes to you to doubt such strong feelings."

"I know ... but it's easy to say something and another –"

He cut me off by pressing his lips to mine, silencing my doubts, at least for the moment. I opened my mouth, wanting more, never having enough of his taste, scent and presence. He slept in a shirt and a pair of soft dark-blue shorts. I think the shirt was to help with the no-sex rule. But I still had plenty of access under the thin cotton.

Things were just starting to get very hot. His breathing was heavy as I moaned into his mouth. My hands moved of their own accord, under the edge of his shirt so I could trail lower along his stomach, following the soft hair. I'd just decided that I didn't care about listening Walker guards when a fissure of energy split the room.

We pulled apart.

Brace pushed me back behind him as he moved forward in the bed. I leaned around him, expecting to see Josian standing there, energy ball or baseball bat in hand. But it wasn't him. Another Walker was at the end of our bed.

"Shit," was all Brace said before he threw up a shimmery barrier between us and the dark-haired man, who looked strangely familiar.

"Who is that?" I said, trying to move around to see better, but he wouldn't let me shift.

"Don't move, Red. It's Que." His tone was flat.

Shit, I mentally restated.

Brace's dad was one big bad-looking dude, and now I knew why he looked familiar. He looked like his beautiful son, only harder, more harshly put together, where Brace was all long lines and perfect features. Que had cruel craggy planes and a long scar running down one cheek. He wasn't as tall as Brace, nor as broad, but his energy felt strong.

"Well, it seems as if my little spy was right; my son is bedding the enemy." His cold eyes were blue, nothing like the melting warmth of Brace's dark brown.

He had the exact same hair, but Que's was military short. Brace liked to leave a little length on top to fall across his forehead.

"Leave now, Que, and nothing more will come of this. I owe you that much, but not anymore. And if you harm Abby, I will figure out a way to kill you."

Brace appeared calm, but I was close enough to feel the vibrations running through him. I mentally shouted for Josian. Where was the red brigade when you needed them? Any other day they were a damn recurring virus.

I really hoped Que had not hurt them.

"Bracelional, I hope this is some type of undercover game you are playing. I really don't want to kill you and the half. I have grown reasonably fond of you over the years."

Brace smiled – more of a grimace really. "You have such a way with words, Que."

"Bracelional." I couldn't contain my small spring of humor.

Brace glanced back at me and shook his head. "Not great timing, Red."

I still had to chuckle a few times.

"Get Josian," Brace murmured back to me.

How the hell was I supposed to do that? Brace had me trapped between him and the headboard of my bed.

Trace, he reminded my slow brain.

Right.

I closed my eyes and pictured the doorway to my parents' room. The same as before, I could see tethers floating off in different sections. Some were long, others very short. I reached out and grasped one of the major ones. It was thicker and longer than any other on the door. I pulled hard. The only awareness I had that anything had occurred was a slight dipping in my stomach. A gasp had my eyes flying open. Reds six and nine were stationed in this hallway, and when I appeared from nowhere I think I almost eliminated another two Walkers via heart attack.

"Josian!" I dodged around the two to bang on his door. "Dad, get up."

The door flew open, and he was framed in the massive doorway, wearing just a pair of long pants.

"Baby girl?" He didn't look as if he'd just woken.

He was calm and alert. Almost seven foot of towering muscles and fiery red hair. Walkers were too much; I swear they were carved from stone or something.

"Que is in my room. Brace was kind of holding him there. Why did no one feel him enter the house?" I was just shy of shrieking.

He left me hanging, of course, disappearing from the door. He was back and dressed in about thirty seconds.

"A question I'll be asking, with persuasion. Stay here with your mother." He took off then, followed by the other reds.

I hesitated outside the door. I knew I should follow his advice. I'd be a distraction neither of them needed. But I couldn't. I couldn't stay here and not know what was happening to my father and Brace. I ran without pause through the hallways and down one set of stairs, jumping every second step.

Reaching the children's wing of the house, I dashed past Samuel, Lucy and Talina's rooms. I finally slowed outside my own door. I couldn't hear anything inside. I ordered my door to open slowly. My room was particularly connected to me, so I had no problem with control. I stepped through, my eyes darting everywhere. The room was empty.

Brace ... where the hell are you?

I tried to connect with his mind. It was difficult as panic started to consume me. I had a really bad feeling about Que, and his reasons for invading a house full of Walkers. I could hear a faint sound. It took me a moment to realize it was coming from outside. I flung open my balcony doors before moving into the shadow of my eaves, eyes straining to see.

And my bad feeling was starting to make sense.

It was the reds versus the blacks. Walkers were gathered in large masses in our front yard. Moonstale light flooded the early-morning darkness. Que had not arrived here alone. Behind him stood at least thirty Walkers, covered in the black marks of Abernath. Josian, with the reds at his back, stood his ground.

"I only wanted the Doreen half, but since you have forced my hand like this, Bracelional, I want both halflings now. Send them to me, and I will not harm anyone." Que's voice rang out in the darkness.

"It's not going to happen," Josian said, sounding calm.

"Geez, is it non-stop drama in your house or what?" Lucy skidded to a stop beside me on the balcony. "Now we're having a break-dance Walker-style."

I grimaced. "More like a gun-shoot-out-at-dawn style."

"If you can hear me, half-Walkers, come to my side now or I will remove from existence every person you love. And if you think I am not capable of killing Walkers, think again."

"So either he knows about the dead Walkers, and is claiming credit to scare people –" Lucy started.

"Or he was the one who killed them." I finished her sentence.

She gripped my arm tightly. "Don't even think about going to him, Abby. If he's telling the truth then he's going to kill them anyway; you know he can't leave witnesses, especially not ones as powerful as other Walkers."

She knew me well and, while I saw the sense in her words, I wasn't sure I could just stand here and do nothing.

"If you take one step off that balcony, Red, I am going to kick your ass." Brace, who was standing between the two groups, almost in the center of the battle, turned in my direction.

We were about a hundred feet apart but I could see his expression clearly. And he was furious. His jaw was doing that tick-tick-tick thing that meant he was about to lose it.

"Do not in any circumstances listen to him. He coined the original saying of a forked tongue. His lies are legendary."

"Yes, my son, I may bend the truth to fit my plans, but whilst my lies are legendary so are my promises. Any punishment I have promised is always meted out ... ten-fold."

"I remember, Que," Brace said darkly.

Could this be reference to all those ridges I often felt along Brace's skin? What the hell could mark a Walker like that and not heal clean?

All of a sudden I was furious. Que was going down. No one threatened my family and hurt my Brace.

My balcony got a little more crowded then as Samuel stepped up to my other side, followed by Lallielle. Talina, who usually wouldn't have bothered leaving her room, had also made her way to the other side of Lucy. I did take a moment to glance in confusion between Lucy and Samuel. They never stood apart from each other. What was happening here?

"So I hear someone else wants a piece of rare half-Walker," Talina said with a sliver of her gentle humor.

I laughed, the words breaking some of the tension. "Yep, we're a hot commodity in this battle-for-the-end-of-the-world."

"I'll say it again." Lucy linked her arms through ours. "Quite happy to be a little old Earthling."

I was about to reply when the Walkers moved, distracting me.

"Issue an official challenge for Aribella, or leave now, Que. You have no power to demand anything." Josian's bored tone focused my attention again.

"You Doreens are always in a rush. I was simply enjoying this little visit, but if you insist, I call for a team challenge. The winners will take control of both half-Walkers."

"Two First-World weeks from now, in a to-be-disclosed location." Josian stepped forward to meet Que.

They grasped hands in that unique Walker handshake that I'd seen on the beach. Then the Abernath Walkers left through a doorway.

"I don't understand."I looked at Lallielle. "Why is Josian so calm, and why aren't they fighting now?"

"The one to whom the challenge is issued gets to decide the time and location. It is designed as a balance since they cannot really turn down the challenge." Her green eyes were wide; she clearly didn't feel any of the confidence Josian displayed.

And I knew why: Walkers could die.

I wanted the next two weeks to go slowly. I dreaded this stupid battle, and my mood was borderline psychotic as I stomped around the house. But the days were moving in fast-forward. I barely saw my dad or Brace. They were holed up talking strategy and something this and power that. The mood was tense in the Frayre household, to put it mildly. Talina and I had no chance of escaping our Walker guards, since we were under house arrest.

It took lots of badgering and maybe a threat or two, but Josian did explain some of the battle situation to me in a terse, distracted tone.

"Three Walkers are on each team. I will announce my choice on the day."

"What if they don't want to fight?"

He shook his head. "If you're present at the challenge, you can't refuse. The only exception is for women and children. Besides, none would shame their clan like that."

I asked a few more questions, but that was as much information as I was getting.

I fell into bed very late that night, exhaustion shadowing every thought and action. I had a bone-deep weariness that came from days of worry and nervous pacing. Josian and Brace were confident that I could trace away if they lost, so for them there was no real concern. Plus, they were arrogant enough to assume Que would play fair, and in a fair fight he wouldn't stand a chance, especially not with Brace on our side.

But I knew Que had something devious planned. I couldn't shake the sneaky premonition. And speaking of premonitions, Francesca had disappeared again, right when we could have used her foresight.

Despite my weariness, I jumped out of bed. The moment I actually laid my head on the pillow my mind went crazy. Brace hadn't stayed with me all week, and my head was starting to ache. I knew I could lose him in this battle, and he was so busy trying to keep me safe he was wasting these last moments we had together.

"You know it drives me insane when you bite your lip like that, Red." I spun around from where I was pacing in front of my windows.

The object of my thoughts was standing at the foot of my bed.

"God-damn insane," he said in a low deep rumble.

My poor abused lips had copped it the last few stressful weeks, along with my nails. A low rumble emanated from his chest, a sound that sent shivers down my spine and had my legs moving toward him. That was the sound of arousal, and I wanted him right then more than I ever thought I could want anyone. I hit his rock-hard body, and anticipating the move he caught me and spun around until we landed on my bed.

"Missed me?" His tone was teasing as I inhaled his scent and allowed my body to relax for the first time in what felt like forever.

"Nope," I said.

"Liar." He kissed me gently. Before pulling back and threading both hands into my free red curls. "I've missed you."

I snuggled into his chest, trying to get as close as I could. Sometimes I freaked myself out with this need I had for Brace.

"I can't lose you, Brace. Please don't fight. It's bad enough that Dad has no choice."

"I know my father, Red. And if I don't participate then there's no telling which way the fight will go. I definitely tip the scales in our direction."

"Yeah, but don't you think Que has anticipated this, and will counteract with something you haven't planned for?"

I was probably pointing out the obvious, but their over-confidence was very annoying. At least if they showed a little more worry and concern I would think they were taking it seriously.

"I have anticipated everything. He won't take us by surprise. He thinks he knows my weaknesses. But he's never paid close enough attention to me. He doesn't know me at all."

I couldn't help it; I'd been trying to keep them at bay all night, that burning in my throat, but my despair was not to be denied any longer. Thankfully my head was still buried in his shirt so he didn't notice the silent tears that tracked down my cheeks. Or so I thought.

"Sweetheart ... no ... please, you're killing me." His voice was strained as he attempted to lift my face. His hands moved from my hair to my cheeks. "I have to keep you safe. It's inbuilt in who I am."

I resisted, wanting to hide until I had these tears under control. But he was stronger than I was. Finally I faced his stricken features.

"Don't cry," he caught a tear, wiping it off my cheek, "I hate it when you cry, and if I'm the cause and can't kill the person who has upset you, well, that's unacceptable."

"I've missed you," I finally said softly.

"I knew it." His cocky smile was back as he stared into my face. "Wanna make out?"

I laughed. Lucy was certainly adding a new dimension to his language skills.

Brace dried the last of my tears, before kissing me gently on each cheek.

"Can I ask you something?" I'd been thinking a lot these last few days, and I didn't want to wait any longer.

"Anything." He pulled me closer.

"You've had sex, right?" I didn't hesitate.

I would never get the words out if I thought too hard about the questions.

He stilled beside me. I almost wanted to laugh at the comical freaking out his features were doing. The bond was shut down, but I didn't need it to know what he was feeling.

Finally he spoke. "I'm not sure if that was a question or statement."

I nudged him. "You know what I mean. Have you had sex?"

"Yes."

I waited for an elaboration, but there was none forthcoming.

"Okay, so a lot? With many different women?" My voice rose slightly.

I'd been preparing myself for these answers. I knew Brace was old, and that he was male and there must have been girls before we found each other. But that didn't prevent a dark jealousy coursing through me. I wanted to find every female who knew him intimately, knew him in a way I didn't, and ... I took a deep breath.

"Why do you want to know these things, Red?"

"I just think it's something I need to know before I ask my final question."

He shook his head.

"I have had sex with women, more than one, but there have been none in your lifetime. From the moment you were born, the last eighteen years, I have been searching for my mate. Somehow, I knew your essence was here."

My heart stilled, and some of the darkness inside dissipated. That made my decision even easier.

"How old are you, Brace?"

He grinned.

I knew he was old, but he'd never said exactly.

"I'm five hundred and sixty years old, give or take. You stop counting closely after the first hundred or so years."

My mouth fell open. He was old. Older than dirt.

He laughed into my neck.

"Well, despite the fact I shouldn't be mated to such an old man," I joked to ease my nerves. "I think we should have sex before you go into this final battle."

I needed to know him that way. I needed those memories, even if they were all I had.

Brace groaned. "You drive me insane, Abigail."

I wasn't surprised since I drove myself insane.

He cupped my cheeks so I couldn't turn away. His velvety eyes were soft. "We will not have sex. We will make love, because that's what we are. We are love."

We are love.

What did he mean by that? Was he saying he loved me, or just that true mates represent love? Either way my heart was beating fast, my pulse racing under his shifting fingers.

"And I don't want you to rush into this just because you think that this is the end for us. It's not the end. I will always come back for you. There are a million lifetimes for us to make love."

"I'm ready, Brace."

He shook his head. "If you were ready, Red, you wouldn't have asked the question. You would have just taken control. And trust me, I'm lost to you. I wouldn't have been able to resist."

I knew I should have gone with Lucy's sexy underwear plan. I dropped my head slightly. I tried hard not to let insecurities control me. This Brace being a gentleman; it wasn't a rejection. Maybe if I repeated that enough my poor confused heart would believe me.

"Abigail Swish." His tone was strangled.

My head shot up. I'd never heard him say my name that way.

"How could you even think that?"

And then he was kissing me, in a way that left no doubt about his feelings and attraction to me. I could feel every hard line of his body as he held me close. Eventually, when we had to breathe, he pulled back. We were both panting heavily.

"Sometimes, Abigail, I want you so badly I actually have to leave the room because sleeping next to you is the worst torture I've felt in five hundred years. You are stunning and sexy and even when you sleep you're the cutest damn thing. You make these little noises, almost talking, more like a mumble. And you wear these damn little shirts." He fisted a handful of my white tank top, exposing the higher planes of my breasts. "I swear, mate, you have no worries about my father finishing me off. I think it was you who was sent here to destroy every last semblance of my sanity."

He groaned again. "And stop staring at me with those witch eyes."

I blinked once then, slowly. I had never thought for a second that I affected him in the same way he affected me. I worried at my lips again before remembering his words and releasing them.

"I know my lack of experience must be frustrating. And honestly when we're together my hormones do most of the thinking and talking. But, Brace, your power and beauty stun me. You're just too gorgeous, tall, perfect. Before I knew you were Walker, I wondered if you could be real."

He shook his head, his expression amused. "Abbs, men aren't beautiful. You are beautiful. And I love your lack of experience; in fact, I'd be obligated to kill any man who'd touched you before, so it's probably for the best." He cupped my face again, pulling me closer. "Don't ever doubt your gifts."

It took me a moment to make sure I wasn't going to cry again.

"So you wanna make out?" he said.

I laughed through my tears.

"Yes, I definitely do."

The next morning when my storming around the house had reached its maximum annoyance level, I found myself in the basement with Brace. Downstairs was set up as a gym and fight-training area. I was pretty excited to work off some of my frustration.

"Okay, Red, let's see what you've got." Brace stood before me, relaxed, wearing just a pair of loose-fitting lightweight shorts.

It wasn't really fair; he had the advantage of muscles to distract me. Although, as I pulled off my shirt to reveal the black sports bra which matched my long fitted pants, his expression heated, his eyes liquid chocolate.

"Your distraction techniques are not going to stop me from kicking your butt, Abigail," he reiterated my initial thoughts.

"So there are no rules, and no specific technique?" I confirmed. "Just the first to yield?"

Brace nodded and stepped closer, sinking into the thick mat we stood on. I was never going to yield. I hoped he knew that.

I started to move then, dancing lightly on my feet. I had to constantly be in motion during a fight; it kept my reflexes sharp. I was waiting for him to give me an opening, let his guard down or something. He didn't shift as he observed me, the slightest glimmer of humor on his features.

"I didn't realize this was dance class, Red. You going to fight or ask me to waltz?"

I ducked in quickly then, feinting toward his left side, before sending out a kick with my right. With the slightest twist of his body, he shifted just out of my reach, and tapped me hard on the butt. Damn, I'd forgotten how fast and ninja he was. Usually, my speed was my greatest asset, but I'd have to be smart to even have a chance of making contact with Brace.

"You have to think, always assume your opponent is better at fighting than you, and you need to outsmart them. Observe, watch how they move, and formulate a plan."

Brace was playing with me. I attacked a few more times. Each resulted in me ending up flat on the floor. I pulled myself up again.

"Your moves are good, but you lack the ability to plan ahead. You simply react to what I'm doing. Make me do the reacting." He continued to lecture me.

I let out a short breath, my eyes narrowing. He was just trying to help, but I hated it when I wasn't good at things. It had never been a problem on Earth, although I guess there I had an unfair advantage. Not that I'd known it, but being half-Walker definitely gave me added skills.

I stopped attacking him for a moment, staying back as we circled each other. Moving slowly I remembered an old fight-move I'd seen on television – which I'd thought at the time was pathetic – I considered whether it would work.

Brace had his arms held up to the side, expecting my usual striking attack, but it was time to try something else. I started forward in the same manner, both hands held up defensively to protect

350

my face, but just before I reached him I faked a stumble, dropping to one knee.

I groaned.

He was at my side in an instant, but before he could help me up I spun around, my other leg extended, smashing into his lower legs. Brace landed flat on his back next to me.

"Hell, yeah!" I shouted, bouncing to my feet.

Of course I should have remembered his long arms as he reached out and yanked me down to land next to him. He pulled me close, our skins flushed as we lay in a tangle.

"That was a cheap trick, Red."

I laughed. "You told me to plan and use your weaknesses. I think I achieved both admirably."

Jumping to his feet, he leaned down to gather me in his arms, cradling me close. "You did well, sweetheart, but don't think the same thing is going to work on others."

And with those words he let go, dumping me straight onto the padded floor.

Ass.

And the torture began. He spent hours forcing me to learn techniques and skills I'd never dreamed possible. He was a machine, highly trained and dangerous. Four hours later I was finally free to hobble upstairs for a shower.

"Remind me to watch a movie next time I'm bored," I groaned as I passed Lucy in the hall.

"You look like half-beaten crap, Abbs." She laughed at me.

"Brace better sleep with one eye open tonight is all I can say."

"I sleep with both eyes open, Red. No one gets the drop on me." He'd followed me up the stairs.

I glared at him, my aching muscles protesting as I marched past, Lucy and Brace's laughter following me.

"I hate you both," I called over my shoulder, wincing the entire way to my room.

The night before the battle Lallielle insisted on a family dinner. The last thing I felt like doing was forcing down food all the while trying to ignore my panic and worry. But she insisted. The reds were stationed around the house, so we were reasonably safe for the moment. The conversation was stilted as we attempted small talk.

Francesca was still missing, but Quarn was here. He felt so much like part of the family that I would have been sad not to see him all the time. And the tension that existed between Josian and Quarn had started to disappear. Even Quarn couldn't ignore the love and devotion between

Josian and Lallielle, and he was finally forgiving him for leaving her.

"You listen here, woman –" Josian was a brave man arguing with Lallielle.

"Call me woman one more time, and you'll be listening to my fist in your teeth." She cut off the rest of his speech.

Josian grabbed her clenched fist, opening it gently before kissing her knuckles. Their interaction at least worked to ease some of the strain in the room.

Lucy and Samuel were sitting side by side tonight, but I could feel the chill between them. Something definitely wasn't right there.

"So who are you going to call for the battle?" I faced Josian.

I wasn't interested in small talk, and if I didn't ask the question, no one would. Silence descended over the room. Josian smiled at me. I glared back. I'd already asked earlier, but everyone was too busy to speak with me.

"I'll call Brace and Grantham of Relli."

My brow furrowed.

"He's the leader of another Walker clan, and one of my very oldest friends. His people will stand with us tomorrow."

"Do the ass-hole power-hungry morons in the Abernath clan ...?" I glanced at Brace, who was sitting across the table from me. "No offence."

A grin spread across his face. I almost forgot what I was going to say in the face of his blinding smile. Josian cleared his throat. I tore my gaze from Brace, my face flushed and breathing slightly erratic.

"Sorry, so the Abernaths, do they have any powerful allies?"

I should have asked about the specifics of the seven clans of Walkers a long time before.

"The Abernaths have always considered themselves to be above the rest of the clans. For some reason our members are powerful, strong and ambitious. We have no ties to other clans," Brace answered.

I hoped he was right. I blew him a little kiss.

His hard features softened.

I liked that it was something that only happened around me.

You look way too sexy tonight, Red. What on First World possessed you to wear that top? I've stabbed myself in the chin five times instead of getting the food in my mouth.

He locked me in his gaze, something he was so talented at. I wiggled on my chair. His words caused physical responses that were far too inappropriate for the dinner table. I might just have to attempt the underwear plan tonight. I needed some relief from the hormones.

"Is there a reason for all the questions, Aribella?" Josian interrupted my steamy thoughts. "I get the distinct impression you don't believe we're prepared."

I shrugged casually, all the while thanking whatever gods there were that no one else could read my mind.

"I just think maybe all Walkers are a tad arrogant, and it doesn't hurt to think of every possible scenario before just assuming you're stronger and therefore will be the winner." I swallowed as all eyes turned in my direction. "On Earth I often outsmarted much bigger and stronger men, even when I was outnumbered," I smiled down the table at Quarn, "although I know on more than one occasion I had assistance. But my point is ... they never thought for one second I was a threat; they underestimated me."

"You're Walker, baby girl. You're the biggest threat they will ever meet."

I sighed. Josian was missing my point ... on purpose, I think.

"Just be careful tomorrow, father. Remember Mom's threat about the fist in your mouth."

"Yes, remember that, dear," Lallielle said.

Josian flinched.

"Can you explain the Walker clans and hierarchy to us?" The question came from Lucy.

Josian nodded. "This is long overdue information for Aribella and Talina. There just never seems to be time to fit everything in."

He wasn't kidding.

"There are seven clans. On paper we're even in status, each descended from one of the seven original Walkers."

"On paper," Brace reiterated, his tone sardonic.

Josian grinned. "Yes. Unfortunately, as with all powerful, long-lived creatures, we tend to create our own drama and power plays." He paused briefly. "So, in very basic form the seven clans are Abernath, Doreen, Relli, Kaos, Gai, Laos, and Whar."

He said the names fast, flicking them off one by one.

"Dad! You're going to have to slow down or write them out for us." I sighed.

Lallielle stood and handed me a piece of paper. As usual, she'd thought ahead. I looked down at the stark white sheet. In my hand it had a smooth texture, more so than anything I'd felt on Earth. For a moment I wondered what they made their paper from, before shelving the random thoughts and forcing myself to focus.

Lucy leaned over my shoulder to read the list out loud. Talina even moved closer so she could see the paper.

"Abernath – (black tribal), Doreen – (red lace), Relli – (gray swirls), Kaos – (brown stripes), Gai – (white spots), Laos – (golden sunbeam), Whar – (indigo patterned)."

She stumbled over a few of the words but no one corrected her.

"I just gave a very brief idea of the colors and differences in their patterns." Lallielle smiled. "None of the clans have marks that are the same."

Josian kissed her on the cheek. "You're a genius, lady."

"Golden sunbeams?" I asked, wondering how that was a pattern.

"You'll understand when you see it." Brace nudged me under the table.

It must have been the fiftieth time he'd done that that night. I stomped down hard where his foot had been, but he was quick enough to move it in time.

"Kind of like a sun starting in their center and then beams shooting off over their bodies."

"They sound amazing." I glanced down at the list again, trying to picture each one.

"So, I am an Abernath?" Talina sounded unsure, "and Que, the ultimate evil Walker, is my leader?"

Brace's expression softened. "That's true, Talli, but since he cannot sense your energy, it's in our best interest to keep that information from him."

"Could he make me go with him? Like some type of leader mind-control?" Talina's eyes widened, fear flashing in their brown depths.

Brace snorted. "God, he would love that skill. No, Talli, your mind is yours to manage alone."

Josian interrupted then.

"Lalli has listed the clans in the undefined order of power," he said. "We have no real governing body. We basically self-govern our own clans. Order and control is carried out by the most powerful, the Princeps."

I assumed that was like the king or ruler, and apparently that was Brace's father.

"Can I borrow that writing tool?" I held out my hand to Lallielle.

She smiled and passed it down via Lucy. I examined the instrument for a moment, before deciding to ignore the strangeness of this semi-transparent, miniature object. I just pressed the pointed end to the paper and a dark blue mark appeared. Excellent.

"Okay, so who is the Princeps of each clan?"

I prepared to write.

Brace was the one who went through the list this time. I wrote as he spelled each name out for me. My scribble almost illegible compared to the lovely swirls of Lallielle's script. This was my finished list.

Abernath – (black tribal) – Princeps: Que
Doreen – (red lace) – Princeps: Josian
Relli – (gray swirls) – Princeps: Grantham
Kaos – (latte stripes) – Princeps: Krahn
Gai – (white dots) – Princeps: Jedi
Laos – (golden sunbeam) – Princeps: Tatiana
Whar – (indigo patterned) – Princeps: Nos

I studied it carefully.

"Since you have clan two and three's Princeps, technically you should be at an advantage." I looked up. "So why would Que risk it then? He must know something we don't."

"He believes that he's more powerful than all of the other Princeps combined," Brace said, his voice was amused. "I've told him many times that his arrogance will be the end of him."

"And we have clans one, two and three's most powerful, baby girl." Josian spoke softly. "Brace supersedes his father in power."

That would make him ... the most powerful Walker in existence.

Brace chuckled. "That's not technically true. I've never been tested against Que."

I stared into his perfect features.

"That's really ... damn hot," I blurted without thought.

The table erupted into laughter. Heat spread across my cheeks, and I knew I was bright red. Lallielle and Josian refrained from laughing, but did sport large smiles.

I had wonderful parents.

"Abby's starting to sound like me. I think I like it," Lucy said as she continued to shovel the roast meat into her mouth. "A little sex-crazed is the way to be."

I sank lower in my chair, trying to disappear. Josian cleared his throat then, before taking a huge drink out of his silver urn.

You're lucky we're in a room full of people, Abigail.

Brace's eyes devoured me. He looked as if he was two seconds from caveman-styling me over his shoulder and departing the room.

More like two milliseconds.

Lucy leaned in close. "He's eye-effing the crap out of you right now."

I was thankful she managed to keep her tone low this time.

"You should hear what's going on in my head," I whispered back.

She patted my shoulder. "That's my girl."

Chapter 14

I attempted to concentrate on my meal, but I honestly tasted none of the flavors. I might as well have been eating the gunk that passed for food on Earth. Small beads of sweat ran down my temple, and it wasn't overly warm in the house. I felt trapped, enclosed in this Walker situation. When I couldn't take the food any longer, I stood.

"I just need a few minutes," I told the surprised faces, before I ran out the door.

The moment the fresh clean air hit my lungs I breathed in a few deep breaths. Kicking my shoes off, I strode across the sand to the water's edge, ignoring the urge to step out into the cooling water. I needed to start jogging again. Nothing else cleared my mind. Of course, I'd have to ditch my red Walker babysitters first.

"You should swim," Talina said, startling me. "It's amazing how clear one's mind is while diving through the waves."

I attempted a smile, which at best amounted to a painful grimace.

"I would love to flee from my constant mental worry, but somehow I know it's still going to be here when I return."

"What will become of us, Abby? Eventually someone is going to figure out how to stop this. Bad people will do anything to assure their plans are a success. If Que or someone else wants to free the Seventine, how can seven half-Walkers stand in their way?"

I knew right then she was thinking of Gladriel. Her bitchiness hadn't been a surprise, but her plan, especially the part including Raror, had been unexpected. I took her hand, giving it a quick squeeze. She let our skins touch for a few moments before pulling away. It was the first real contact she'd allowed since Raror's death, and I was going to take it as a positive step. There was a semblance of calm in her eyes as she stared out into the darkness. I pushed my hair off my face. The wind was light but annoying.

"I wish I had some answers," I said. "I guess we just keep going with the plan, and hope that our luck holds out long enough."

My words weren't reassuring to cither of us.

I couldn't say how long Talina and I stood there, watching the play of lights over the ocean. Eventually the rest of my friends and family joined us. Brace stepped in close. His presence, as always, blocked everything else. I moved back until I was pressed firmly against him, soaking in his warmth and comfort.

"You okay, Red?" I could hear the uncertainty in his voice.

Sometimes it amazed me that he could be unsure of me ... of us.

I guess a lot of the time my random decisions were confusing to him. Walkers were slower but surer with their actions. I arched my head back, so I could stare up into his face. He lowered from the great height he existed at and kissed my lips ever so softly. I decided right then to stop some of the worry; I wasn't ready to miss these moments right in front of me.

"I can't believe I pushed you away in fear of losing you. I wouldn't give up this time we've had for anything," I whispered.

My extended neck was starting to hurt but I couldn't pull my eyes away.

"Don't forget I was a lying McLiar." He grinned.

"Who could forget every word that fell from your lying mouth?" Lucy piped up. She was sitting on the sand, Samuel next to her.

I snorted. "Privacy means nothing to you people, does it?"

Eventually, I couldn't hold that pose any longer and had to straighten my neck. I plonked onto the sand, pulling Brace down to sit next to me, which lasted all of ten seconds. Reaching over, he picked me up and placed me squarely between his legs. As I sank into him, I had a brief thought that all of us as couples may be making Talina uncomfortable. But when I looked over she was being thoroughly entertained by Quarn. I squinted, noticing that he was spilling stories about my life in New York.

"... covered head to toe in slime from the pond in the park, she's running flat out trying to escape some Gangers ..."

It was definitely an Abby story. I groaned.

"Want me to shut him up?" Brace leaned in close to my ear. "Or provide some entertaining distractions?"

I smiled before shaking my head.

"Nah, I guess I can put up with embarrassing stories if they make her smile."

"I'm certainly enjoying tales of your youth."

Would I have time to learn any of the countless things Brace had seen and done?

"We have forever if that's what you want."

"Let's just get through tomorrow, and then we can worry about forever," I said, closing my eyes and resting against his warmth.

I must have fallen asleep on the beach, enclosed in Brace's arms. When I woke early the next morning, I was a tad surprised to find myself snuggled into my soft bed. I was alone, but I could hear movement, and as I rolled over Brace walked out of my bathroom. I eye-devoured his huge expanses of exposed golden skin, lingering on the band of his sweat pants. He was heading out for a jog. I knew he ran when he was stressed, something I could relate to.

"Do you want to come for a run with me, Red?"

I sat up, pushing my curls back from where they were trying to strangle me.

"Yes!" I said, excited. "Give me a minute to get ready."

I didn't care if we had to sneak out. I'd been dying for a run.

I dashed through the bathroom and brushed my teeth before throwing on some sweats and joggers.

366

I met him outside. Apparently he had cleared this with everyone, and we were on our own. The sun was just starting to rise in the dark purple of the sky. It was cool but already looked like a perfect First-World day. I felt like a kid whose Christmas was being held at Disneyland. We warmed up; it felt so good to stretch my tight muscles.

"Hope you can keep up with me, Red," Brace taunted as we took off along the path.

I ignored him, but my eyes flashed in challenge. Our rules were that we had to stick to Angelisian. But the town was large enough that we would have a decent jog. I matched his pace for the first mile, running in silence. After that my muscles, which I had been neglecting, started to protest the exercise.

Gritting my teeth, I pushed through. It seemed to take longer than usual, but finally I reached that magic place. Every person who runs knows what I'm talking about. It's on the other side of the pain, where suddenly you're in the zone and could run forever.

Brace slowed a little, allowing me to step in front. Of course I didn't know the town very well, but I just followed the path we'd been on. It seemed to be winding along the outsides of the buildings, between them and the shielded boundary. Looking over my shoulder, I saw something that brought me to a halt. Brace stopped next to me, his breathing even, just a few small beads of sweat at his temple, unlike myself, who had really started to puff.

"You let me pass so you could stare at my butt." I gave him a shove.

He didn't even bother to deny it as a large grin crossed his face. "Red, you have a truly spectacular ass. I'm only human, you know."

I shoved him again, shaking my head. "You aren't human, but clearly there isn't that much difference between men on any planet."

He shrugged as we started running again. I was still in front, and the entire time I could feel his eyes on me as we made it back to the house. I left Brace to shower downstairs; I didn't trust either of us alone at the moment.

Back in my room, I shed my clothes into the laundry chute before stepping in for a long hot shower.

Once I was clean, I wandered aimlessly through the huge expanse of my wardrobe, wondering what one wore to a Walker battle. I decided to dress to impress. Sometimes clothes were as good as armor, and I needed to look more confident than I felt right now. The weather was neither hot nor cold yet, so I could get away with anything except deep summer or winter fashion.

I selected a fitted dark purple silk shirt. The color complemented my ivory skin. It had three-quarter sleeves and was cut deep in the neckline, which gave the illusion of an impressive bust line. Yeah, okay, the padded bra helped with that also.

I teamed it with my standard dark skinny jeans, finishing with my favorite selection: shoes. A pair of gorgeous black suede boots. They went over the jeans, and as I zipped them up they ended just above my knees. The best part was their impressive heel; it added a good three inches to my five foot ten height and yet felt as if I was walking on flats. I needed something I could move about in easily, but I wanted the height. Damn Walkers were too tall for their own good.

Stepping back into my bathroom, I checked my reflection. I had no need for cosmetics anymore. My Walker genes gave me a sheen that could not be replicated. My lashes were darker than ever, giving the illusion of kohl lining. My hair was working for me, and looked even longer, falling past my mid-back in red flecked with black curls. The enlightenment had certainly helped speed up my morning preparations. I walked out, leaving the comfort of my room.

Everyone was gathered in the white room, of course. It was the meeting place. As I stepped inside, all eyes turned in my direction. The reds were along one wall, their hair standing out starkly against the white. As usual, when we were all in the same room Brace was at my side in an instant. I was happy to see that my head just reached his shoulders. I wouldn't feel quite so short today. His low growls started over my head as he guided me to the couch, his hand resting in the small of my back. He was sending out a warning to the other men. Ignoring their posturing, I sank into the free seat.

"You look hot, Abby." Lucy leaned over Samuel to speak with me. "I want that exact outfit, except I need it in short, not giant."

I grinned. We'd had to have all of Lucy's clothes tailored. She was tiny on First World, and everyone was fascinated by her delicate stature – until she opened her mouth, of course. Then they were amazed that the outside didn't even come close to matching her inner smart mouth.

"I've decided that we will stage the battle in the hills behind Angelisian. They are secluded: I don't want any innocents hurt." Josian started without preamble. "Brace will send the message to Que and his people. We'll leave immediately. I would ask any of you that don't need to be at the

370

battle to stay here." He chuckled then, without humor. "But I know I'd be wasting my breath, so everyone get your things and wait for me outside."

"Whoa, that was lucky. I thought I might have to stow away in Abby's handbag. But then I remembered the girl's never carried one of those in her life," Lucy said, falling into step next to me.

I was too tall now; we couldn't comfortably link arms.

We gathered out the front. The reds' numbers had doubled: there were twenty, each as diverse looking and god-like as the next. They were silent, and just stood there channeling statues.

"Look, Abbs, it's the red wall of China."

I stifled my laughter. Lucy's comment nailed it; they did look like an impenetrable wall.

"What's China?" Brace and Samuel said together, stepping in front of us.

They were attempting to block us from the reds' scrutiny.

I waved a hand. "Just a country on Earth. It had this massive stone wall that ran through it."

"What was the point of this wall?" Samuel said, with an actual expression of interest on his normally stoic features.

"Protection," Lucy said. "China was protecting its borders from the surrounding countries."

"It's gone," Josian said, standing near us.

"What?" I said, shocked. "Where did it go?" *Did a hundred-year-old wall just get up and walk away?*

"It was one of the tethers lost during the last release of the Seventine."

"Is Earth the only world losing tethers?" I was having trouble picturing a four-thousand-mile structure just disappearing.

"No, Aribella, all of the worlds have suffered losses. Some significant, others smaller, but it's only going to keep escalating. Long before the last Seventine is released the worlds will rapidly lose their tethers." Josian's face echoed my own horror.

"We have to stop them. You have to kill Que," I whispered, knowing I was probably hurting Brace.

Que was his father, after all.

"I can't kill him." Josian words were terse and clipped. "What I did on Spurn can only happen if one Walker is immensely more powerful than another. It's rare, since most of the less powerful never issue challenges, and the more powerful, for the most part, don't absorb other Walkers. You never know when you could lose control of the influx of energy."

The only good thing in that information was the realization that Que shouldn't be able to absorb Brace or my father either.

Once everyone was gathered, Josian opened a large doorway and we all filed through. Unlike other times, this was almost a direct step from one side to the other. I suppose because the destination was so close. Everyone made it through and managed to stay on their feet.

I looked around. In normal circumstances I'd love it here. We were standing on the edge of a stunning lime-green field, at least four miles in diameter, bordered on all sides by rocky mountains reaching high into the clouds. Some were so tall I couldn't even see their peaks.

Josian was correct: this was large and isolated, and the mountains should contain any noise of battle. The field was flat, dotted through with tiny white flowers that almost gave the lime-green grass a silver sheen. With the sun shining, I had an urge to lie in the field and watch the world drift by. I couldn't believe a place of such beauty was to be the grounds for something as destructive as a battle.

My boot heels were wide enough that I didn't sink into the soft ground as I stepped forward. Of course I didn't have to worry as my feet were swept out from under me and Brace threw me over his shoulder. He sprinted across the field until we were standing right in the center. Despite the jostling – his shoulder wasn't exactly comfortable

– I loved the speed. Leaning over, I kissed his cheek, letting my lips linger on the semi-smooth skin there. Brace never let his facial hair grow, just a fine stubble I barely even noticed.

"Thank you," he said, his voice soft.

He set me down, without releasing me. I stayed plastered to his front.

"What for?" I said, confused.

"For being you. For being here. For making this a better day despite Que's attempt to destroy everything."

I clutched at his shirt as my heart melted. Pretty soon it wouldn't even be an organ anymore, just a love slush pile in my chest.

"You're turning me into a sucker for your words, Brace. You better not go and die today, taking them away from me." My tone was light but I meant every word.

"I second that, and add your ass into the equation. It's just too perfect for me to live without." Brace slapped one of his huge hands on my butt.

It was gentle enough that I barely felt it, but I couldn't let that slide. Without pause I swung around and landed a closed fist into his delicate lower ribs.

With a slight wince, he clutched my hand before I could smack him again. His little half-smile came out to play.

"There you are, Red. I wondered where my hard-ass girl was hiding. I need you to be tough today. Que loves weakness, and will exploit any and all of them."

His words had their desired effect. I was feeling decidedly less sappy and romantic and more annoyed and ready to kick him in the jewels.

I wasn't pouting, I decided, as I turned my back on him and watched everyone else cross the field at a slower pace. My head spun around as he chuckled.

"You're a funny girl, Red." He watched the same thing as me.

"Do you have any friends, Brace?"

He looked at me strangely. Yeah, the question was a little left-field, but I'd been wondering for a while. He always seemed so strong but a little removed from everyone else.

"Not really. Never had any time. My life was training and battle, and I've been stationed here for the past decade." His eyes held a weariness I didn't like. "Samuel was a very good friend to me over the years, but I always had to remember it was never more than a mission." He muttered something else but I missed it. He took my hand.

"I had one true friend, a Walker. We were the same age, and both of us were part of the training program. He's the only one I would trust with my life."

"Would you trust him with my life?" I joked.

He turned hard eyes in my direction and stepped closer.

I forced myself not to back away.

"I wouldn't trust the gods themselves with you, Abigail. My hands are the only ones that will ever keep you safe."

"Arrogant Walker." I shook my head, ignoring that secret part of me that loved it when he went all caveman.

A distraction appeared then in the form of a Walker doorway. It was about fifty yards from us. I'd never seen one from this angle; it was strange to see the Walkers start small and slowly get larger as they moved from one side of the doorway to the end.

"Are they the Abernaths?" I attempted to hide my unease.

"No," Josian said, "that's the Relli clan. Grantham's leading them through."

These were our allies. With my Walker vision I could see every detail of their leader perfectly. He was tall, as were all Walkers, but not quite as tall as Brace or Josian. His hair was a strange

376

shade of dark yellow. His features were not as hard as most Walkers. In fact, he almost looked jovial, with his plump red cheeks. All of the Relli clan had their marks proudly on display. They started in a small swirl of dark gray, almost a gunmetal color, and the swirls extended out in large arching waves. Still predominantly on one side of their body, some of the swirls ended abruptly, as if they were missing parts. I wondered if those were to be filled by their mates.

They exited the doorway smoothly, before continuing on to cross the distance separating us, their demeanor exuding confidence. So far I still hadn't seen a Walker woman.

"Josian. My old friend," Grantham said with enthusiasm before he'd even reached our side.

His deep voice, which was heavily accented in what sounded a lot like thick Russian, boomed around the field. His happy features creased in pure joy. I could see his eyes now. They were a pure green, much lighter than my own, and more grass-green rather than emerald. In fact, they were like big cat's eyes. Grantham was a strange-looking Walker.

"You don't have to break him down piece by piece, Red." Brace nudged me. "I'd hate to think of what my analysis was on first meeting."

I nodded in all seriousness. "Oh, yeah. It's lucky you weren't in my head then. It wasn't pleasant." I worked to keep my face straight.

"Liar. You wanted me," he said, before turning back to our new guests.

"We really need to work on your lack of confidence," I said. "It's starting to become an issue."

He hugged me closer, muttering what sounded a lot like 'smart-ass'.

Josian met the Rellis halfway across the distance. I expected them to hug it out in typical Walker fashion, but they didn't. Instead, they performed a complicated handshake, half-hug thing. The two of them leaned in for a few moments. I could see mouths moving rapidly, and lots of head nods but couldn't make out any more than that.

"Are they discussing the battle?" I asked Brace. His hearing was superior to mine.

He laughed. "Uh, no. More like a quick catch-up on the last time they did a little galaxy-hopping together. I get the distinct impression that before Josian met Lallielle ... he was adventurous."

"Probably a good thing I can't hear them," I muttered.

"I know many of your father's stories and, trust me, once you hear some of them, you cannot un-hear them," Brace said.

Lallielle's head spun around. She was sitting near Samuel, Lucy and Talina. The four had sprawled on the ground as soon as they made it to the center of the field.

"Isn't that the truth, Brace? No matter how hard you try," she finished with a smile.

The men were making their way back. Grantham came straight at me. I took a step back, but that was no deterrent. I found myself scooped up in an embrace by the big yellow-haired Walker. The low growls from beside me did nothing to halt him as he squeezed me tight.

"That's enough, Grantham. Give me my mate back."

I could see Brace's hand resting on Grantham's arm.

"Calm yourself, Walker. Even a blind man can see you are mated." He was referring to the way our visible marks blended into each other. "I'm simply greeting my best friend's daughter. I have already missed too much of her life. She's going to love her Uncle Grantham."

I patted his arm a few times, and finally he released me, stepping away. For some reason I did already like him. He was so warm and open, without that untouchable god-like arrogance most Walkers held. Brace swept me up, his heartrate calming as soon as I was back in his arms.

"Hi," I smiled at my father's old friend, "this is Brace, my mate; Lucy, my best friend; and Talina from Spurn." I pointed out only the three people he may not know.

He scooped Lucy up in her own Walker hug. Samuel didn't move or flinch. Usually he'd be growling his own tune like Brace. Later, I promised, later we would deal with that. The future held high hopes that Samuel was about to get ripped a new one.

"You're one big friendly dude." In his arms Lucy looked like a doll, blond curls lightly lifting in the breeze. "It's nice to meet a Walker who doesn't have a stick permanently up their butts. Always so serious."

Throats were cleared and quite a few smiles hidden as the Walkers in the vicinity tried to figure out if they should be insulted by this tiny gorgeous human. I laughed out loud. Lucy really had no filter between her brain and mouth, and it was mostly entertaining. I gave her a metaphorical high-five across the space.

"Would you like to come and live in my household, little one?" Grantham's large green eyes twinkled. "You are perfect."

This time Samuel did take a step forward and, wrapping a hand around Lucy's wrist, he tugged her back toward him. She almost lost her footing; he was unnecessarily rough.

"Watch yourself." Grantham's voice held a hint of steel for the first time, giving us a glimpse of the reason he was Josian's choice to call into battle. "We don't treat precious gems in such a manner."

Lucy must have agreed. She stomped down hard on Samuel's foot before wrenching herself free and marching away. She stopped next to me.

"Your brother is about to get his ass beat down," she said, her tone low, "and then I'm going to give him over to the Walkers for their chance."

I reached over to take her hand and give it a tight squeeze. She was right; Samuel was in for the smackdown of his life.

"I'll hold his arms for you." Brace nodded once.

"Don't underestimate her. She might be small, but she makes up for that in pure evil and imagination," I said, knowing Lucy didn't need anyone's help.

She could hold her own against Samuel. One thing the compound had taught us was to battle opponents larger than ourselves.

I watched the rest of the Walkers interact across the field. This mostly included blowing up things and roughhousing. Moonstale shone as almost everyone had their jewelry open and glowing, although it was hard to tell in the bright sunlight. At least I didn't have to keep explaining my permanent marks. All were on display at the moment, and I fit right in. While I was used to my own marks, I still had a moment every time I saw the sexy black tribal design on Brace's skin.

With effort I pulled my eyes from my mate as a new doorway opened. Unless this was an uninvited guest, the Abernaths were on their way. Brace tensed beside me, and he wasn't the only one; the field fell silent as we waited.

"And so it begins." I heard the words from a group of Walkers near us.

It was more ominous than I expected. Almost as if they'd said, 'the beginning of the end'. I linked my right hand with Brace's and the left with Lucy's. I had to physically restrain myself from tracing away with my loved ones right now. Talina was close by as well, sitting alone, pulling out long strands of grass.

"They're being overly dramatic because this is the first time Walkers have had to face their own mortality." Brace kissed my cheek. I sensed his need to calm my racing heart. "Since those two dead Walkers were discovered, the clans have been a little crazy, but no one is going to die today."

"I'm with you, Abbs. I've got a bad feeling about all this." Lucy's words had my heart racing again.

The hard facial planes and jet-black hair that Que sported was the first thing I noticed as they stepped through the doorway. He was followed by an army of Walkers. While we had maybe fifty between our two clans, he looked to have equalled that.

"I still don't understand. If this is a battle with rules, why bring such a force of Walkers?"

Brace laughed without any humor. "Sometimes Walkers decide that they don't like a decision. Sometimes they decide they know better. On those occasions it helps to have a little clout behind you as backup."

"I'm guessing you say that from experience," I replied.

"Yes. Que has on more than one occasion won these battles by simply showing up with the biggest army. It starts as an intimidation tactic, and ends as a cheat-to-win tactic. Que is the only Princep who keeps very close ties with all of his clan. Therefore, he always has them under his control and ready for battle. The rest of the clans are ... free. No one really controls them, and it's a rare occasion that we gather in large groups."

Great. This was going to end in disaster.

"Bracelional, I need you to join the member of your clan."

Que and his crew were about fifty yards from the rest of us. They stood in strict formation. There was no relaxing of their robot expressions, or, as Lucy would put it, removal of the sticks up their butts.

"I am with the members of my clan, Que," Brace said, not moving an inch.

His father smiled. "We will see, son."

And on that ominous note, it began.

Josian stepped away from Lallielle. "Let's not waste any time. I'm ready to call my team for battle."

It was in that moment I sensed a feeling of satisfaction. I shook my head. I was pretty sure that wasn't my emotion. But the feeling persisted. I ran my eyes over the crowd of Walkers and noticed that Que had a smug, self-satisfied expression. I focused on him for a moment, studying his features.

A flash of light slammed my eyes closed. I clutched at my head as I tried to figure out what had just happened. Despite my scrunched-up eyes, the flashes continued. It took me a few moments to realize they weren't just light but flickers of thoughts and images crossing my mind. Again, not my own.

"Are you okay, Red?"

I opened my eyes to Brace's concerned features. I managed to smile enough to semi-reassure him. With one last look, he turned back to watch the proceedings.

Que had just waved a hand for Josian to get on with it. Suddenly I knew. I knew what my mind had been trying to tell me. I dashed for Josian.

"Stay with Lucy," I yelled to Brace as I ran.

He ignored me, of course, but I noticed he gave me a few seconds' headstart.

"I call Grantham of –"

I grabbed Josian's arm, interrupting his speech. "Dad."

He paused.

"Baby girl? This isn't the best timing." His eyes were bright, golden in the sunlight.

I leaned in closer to him. "You can't call Brace. He has to leave; he has to get away from here."

Josian's features fell for the first time into lines of confusion.

"We need Brace, Aribella. I know you're worried, but I promise I won't let anything happen to him."

"I'm sorry. Are we interrupting your family time with this little inconsequential battle?" Que's tone was mocking, and I wanted so badly to punch him.

Ignoring this for now, I kept my pleading face locked on my father's.

Josian held up one hand to Que to indicate we needed another minute.

"Dad, listen to me. This is not about keeping Brace safe; it's about keeping everyone safe. You tell me he's the most powerful Walker and Que wants him on your team. I think I just picked up his thoughts – well, kind of his feelings – and he wants you to choose Brace more than anything."

This was the moment, the bad feeling I'd had since the announcement of this battle. Josian examined me for a few silent moments. I held my breath, hoping he would believe me. Brace finally reached our side.

Josian took that moment to face Que. "And I call Tolialth, my second-in-command."

I sighed in relief.

"Do you accept that which has been challenged of us? To protect and claim the half-Walkers Aribella of Doreen and Talina of Abernath?"

Brace controlled his features, although I could feel his confusion. I needed to get him away before Que called him to battle.

Leave, Brace. Now. Open a doorway, and get far enough away that Que can't call you, I ordered him with my mind.

He looked at me once, and then without any hesitancy opened a doorway and was gone. A shocked silence filled the green space. I was surprised that he hadn't argued. I guess it was good to know that under all of his over-protective crap there was an honest trust in me. I just hoped it was justified today. Grantham stepped forward to stand with Josian. His generally jovial expression was serious.

"I accept this challenge."

One of the reds also stepped toward my father.

"I accept this challenge." He echoed Grantham's words.

And if he was surprised by his sudden inclusion in this battle, he hid it well.

I noticed Que's expression, and for the first time he looked unsure, as if he didn't understand what had just happened. Of course that lasted all of two seconds; I doubt anyone else even noticed. He glared in my direction and, if looks could kill, I'd be in trouble. Fury poured off him.

"I call my second and third lieutenants, Marcus and Lional."

Two large Walkers stepped forward. They looked like twins to me, with their long hair, dark and pulled back in low ponytails.

In unison they spoke the words of acceptance. I wasn't sure that anything happened after that, but I could feel something in the air, a sense of ... officialdom.

"Let us begin." Que waved his hands, and the rest of his men stepped back to form a semi-circle enclosing the back part of the field.

A doorway opened again, and Brace stepped back through. I ran to his side, allowing him to gather me up.

"You better explain to me what just happened, Red."

His words were muffled in my shoulder as he hugged me close.

Que wanted Josian to pick you. It was part of his strategy. I just knew you couldn't be involved; it was going to end badly.

I really hoped I was right, and that I hadn't just sentenced my father to battle without his most powerful weapon.

Don't let Que get in your head, Abby. He'll twist your perception of everything. Don't let him have any control there. If it happens again, block it out. Don't encourage him.

I couldn't tell if he was angry with me or not. Either way, our bed had been made, and now we needed to see what resulted from this battle.

Chapter 15

The six Walkers were motionless in the center of the field. Everyone had filed back to form a circle with a diameter of at least a mile. I threaded my hands through each other over and over, but my habit was doing nothing to stem my nerves. Brace reached over to separate them and kept hold of my left.

For some reason no one spoke. I don't know what the signal was but the fighting started without any visible warning. I swallowed my gasp, though a small whimper escaped. I was probably squeezing the life out of Brace's hand in my panic.

Josian will be fine, baby; he's strong and has good men at his back.

Despite everything, my heart still fluttered when he called me baby; he didn't do it much and

I really liked it, which surprised me. I had never pictured myself falling for the cutesy name.

The fighting started to move rapidly. Walkers zipped around the field, testing each other. Josian and Que came together and again they went hand-to-hand combat-style. The other four kept each other occupied. I watched as Grantham crouched close to the ground, placing his palm flat on the green grass, and wondered what he was doing.

"Is he having a rest already?" I finally broke the silence.

"His affinity is for natural elements. Minerals, dirt, rock, and stone, all of those found in the base of planets," Brace answered me.

And then I could see it for myself. A huge crevice was spreading through the area, surrounding the second and third of the Abernaths. I knew it wasn't much more than a distraction, but it was still impressive.

I turned back to watch my father and Que. I'd had just enough training to see that Que was in a class of his own as a fighter. It was apparent where Brace got his ninja smoothness. The man flowed from one movement to the next without pause. I was relieved to see that Josian was holding his own, but he couldn't keep it up against that unwavering onslaught for long.

391

"Josian knows Que's weaknesses. We've practiced for this," Brace reassured me, probably hoping I'd stop chewing my nails to the bone.

Lallielle stepped up next to me. I hadn't seen her much lately, and I wondered how she was handling the stress. Using my free hand, I gripped hers tightly. She smiled but didn't take her eyes from Josian.

"He's just so good," I said, caught up by Que's amazing fight.

"He'd want to be; his sole focus in the last few thousand years has been becoming the supreme commander of this star system."

I'd thought my life sucked growing up. I'd bet having a father like that made mine look like the ideal childhood.

"Your father will be fine, darling. He's not without skills of his own." Lallielle ran a comforting hand over my curls.

"I hate this. I never imagined that upon finding my parents I'd be thrust into a universal battle. And that I'd be the reason for all this fighting –"

I let my whining drift off as I caught sight of Talina standing alone. Damn, I needed to be grateful for the gifts in my life. Talina had just lost everything.

"Sorry," I muttered. "I'm actually happier than I've ever been. I just feel guilty."

"It's not your fault that you were born, and that's all it comes down to. The circumstances of being a half-Walker have dictated this heartache in your life," Lallielle said, her voice breaking a little at the end.

She sniffled once, but I couldn't see any tears. I let her tuck me under one arm. Brace had to release my hand so I could hug into her properly. She smelled of lilac and cinnamon, scents that had always been familiar to me, and before now I hadn't known why. Pulling back from her warmth, I forced myself to focus on the fight. For all the buildup and anticipation it seemed to be progressing rather slowly. It looked like there was more verbal and mental sparring than physical.

"They seem afraid to actually touch each other." Lucy piped up.

She had a point. The three on each team were staying close to their own side. Besides Grantham lobbing rock torpedoes randomly around.

"Yeah, that's why Walker battles happen rarely. We're too powerful. Many of them end before they even begin." Brace was our expert, and I hoped this fight also turned into a non-event.

Que and Josian separated from their groups again, stepping forward to meet in the middle. They were arguing, but I was too far away to make out any of it. Josian's head spun once in our direction, and the fury on his features made every hair on my body stand on end. I'd never seen him this angry, even when he'd destroyed stalker-Walker on the beach.

He struck out at Que, and not with fists, but with power. Energy blasted throughout the arena and everyone in the vicinity hit the ground hard. And we stayed down. I wasn't hurt, but I couldn't pull myself up from the floor. Brace had stayed standing, but he was the only one I could see from my semi-facedown position.

What's happening? I screamed at him, hoping something would get through all this energy surrounding us.

I felt as if I could see the streams in the air; it was heavy and strong and I was starting to feel very claustrophobic.

Well, Josian just dissolved Que's second and third lieutenants, and right now is directing an energy stream. We're just getting the residual side effects.

I thought Josian said he wouldn't do that again.

This is different to what he did on the beach. That was absorbing energy; this is simply blasting them apart, right down to the cells.

Brace reached down a hand and pulled me up, and the moment he touched me I could move through the pressure.

If you're stronger you can overwhelm them with energy and they can't hold onto their cellular shape any longer.

Then what happens? There seemed to be a lot of variances to this immortal thing.

They'll eventually be reformed back at our point of origin. But it takes a long time and is immensely painful.

It was something to keep in mind should I find myself blown to pieces, though I did have the disturbing sensation that my half-nature would prevent me from reforming. The energy surrounding us didn't appear to be abating. The air was still thick and cloying, making it difficult to breathe through. But I noticed Josian and Que were both standing.

"Josian's been holding out on me," I heard Brace say, with just a touch of admiration.

But before I could question him the fight re-drew our attention.

Grantham and the red Walker – what did Josian call him? Right, Toliath – were crawling through the energy to close in on Que. Now that the other two Abernaths were gone, Josian's men could surround the true threat in the battle. As the visible energy eased, the air cleared and finally I could breathe again.

I watched closely as Que moved around the other three, faster than I had ever seen. Before anyone could react he was at Toliath's side and, reaching out, he touched him. Josian's second-in-command wavered for a moment. The look on his face spoke of complete astonishment, and then he collapsed. I held my breath waiting for him to jump back up, but he lay motionless.

"Brace, what happened?" I clutched his arm, my panic increasing.

"I've never seen him use it before. He brags about his touch of death, but I thought it was just a scare tactic." Brace's confidence may have wavered slightly, and all I could think about was Josian.

He could not get touched by Que.

Que hadn't stopped moving. He dashed across the field toward Grantham. I gasped in worry for the jovial man. Luckily, the Relli Walker had had enough time to see what had happened to the other red, and managed to avoid Que's first touch. Then, using his abilities, Grantham erected a massive wall of rocks between them; they rose from the ground to provide a temporary barrier. Que punched through them, but Grantham was already gone, and was now standing side-by-side with Josian.

"You should have let me fight, Abby. This needs to end today, and I don't think anyone can take him out." Brace looked agitated.

I glared. "You just said you don't know how to counteract that touch-of-death thing. I probably saved your life."

I was angry and scared, and feeling immensely guilty that a Walker may have lost his life because of my weird premonition. On top of that I could lose Josian today, and I had no idea how to save him. Well, I had one idea, but no one was going to let me hand myself over. I needed to remember that I had to save the world from the Seventine, according to the missing member of our group, Francesca. And considering her recent unreliability, I wondered if we should even trust her anymore.

"Something is wrong here." I don't think Brace realized he'd said that out loud.

I grabbed his arm. "What, Brace. What's happening?"

"He's playing with them. He never does that in battle." His eyes were glued to the remaining members.

The three circled each other, Josian and Grantham staying side-by-side, never allowing Que to get the drop on them.

"It's as if he's ... " Brace said slowly, his head spinning around to observe the rest of the field. "Distraction." He bit out before I could demand again. "He's distracting them, drawing the fight out. But to what end?"

"Your father's aware of this. He wants me to check if Brace has any idea what Que's plan is," Lallielle said from beside me.

She was staying in touch with her mate.

"I don't know. I have no idea what might be coming that would be more powerful than Josian and Grantham together. Que believes he's his own greatest weapon."

"It has to be about you, Brace." I managed to keep my voice a decibel level under a shriek. "He wanted you in the battle, and he wanted you on Josian's side. There must be a reason for that."

Brace's eyes narrowed as he stared across the field toward his father. "I would never have defected to his team; surely he wouldn't think a sense of loyalty would turn me at the end. He knows you're my mate, and I'll always be by your side."

I felt it then. Something big was coming, something devastating that was going to rock my world to its core. Again, these emotions appeared to be coming from Que.

"It's happening now," I said, my voice tight.

But I was too late.

As the words fell from my lips, Brace dropped to his knees.

I spun around to find Samuel crouched behind us. I hadn't even heard him move. What was he doing? His eyes met mine for a brief moment, and the screaming agony there was so intense I gasped. Samuel had betrayed us. I turned back to my mate, dropping down beside him. I couldn't see what was wrong.

He didn't look at me.

His head hung low.

"Brace?"

He didn't look up. "Abby ... run." His words washed over me, their tone biting and intense.

I didn't move, my frantic eyes scanning him. My heartbeats slowed as a realization washed over me.

I couldn't feel him anymore.

I was distracted by a strange dot on his neck near his ear. I was just reaching over to touch the black mark when I was yanked backwards. I kicked and screamed but it was to no avail. The arms locked around me were strong and unforgiving.

I could see Brace still hadn't moved. I tried to contact him mentally, but he was gone, and it was not like those moments where he had blocked me – even then I could still feel his mind, I just couldn't access it. Now the space was empty.

Tears flowed unconsciously. My melded side believed that our mate was dead. Nothing else could explain this emptiness. A strange keening noise annoyed me, until I realized the sounds were emitting from my own throat.

"Baby girl." Josian's voice close to my ear let me know I was at least not in Que's slimy arms. "We need to get out of here immediately. We have to get away from Brace."

"No!" I shouted. "I can't leave him." The sobs burst free again.

I pulled my eyes from Brace long enough to notice that we'd made it across the field. Josian opened a doorway and ordered everyone through. I was passed to another set of arms.

"NOOO!" I screamed before kicking out at whoever held me.

Brace needed me; I had to get back to him.

With a groan, I was released.

I managed to duck around the group, before stopping mid-stride.

It seemed as if the moment I'd screamed, Brace had awakened. He stood in the same spot, but everything was different. His hair was longer, his skin darker, his marks no longer black but an iridescent purple and his eyes were a startling swirl of gold.

"You cannot leave." His words were low, but I could feel the push from each one.

Behind me the rest of our group made it through the doorway. Josian grabbed me again, and this time I let him, because the man standing there – he scared me more than anything I had ever witnessed in my life.

I wondered if he would let us leave. Something told me he had the power to stop us if he chose to. But he didn't. At the last moment, before Josian dragged me through the doorway, Brace raised his hands.

No, no, no, no, I chanted in my head, because I knew what was coming next.

The inky darkness started in slow swirls, before exploding from him in black clouds. This was his dream, and I knew that Brace, my heart-mate, my love, was gone, and I'd never told him. I'd never said those three little stupid, amazing, heartaching words. Maybe that was a crazy thought, considering everything that was happening, but there it was.

Even after the doorway closed, and I could no longer see the creature that was wearing Brace, I

401

was trapped in golden swirls. They danced before my eyes until eventually the pain eclipsed all else and darkness engulfed my mind.

***

Please, if you loved this book, could you do me a huge favor and post a review on Amazon and/or Goodreads. Reviews are so valuable to independent authors and I'd appreciate your feedback. – Jaymin ☺

http://www.facebook.com/pages/Jaymin-Eve/519939168016600

Or email jaymineve@gmail.com

About the Author

Jaymin Eve is a twenty-eight-year-old with the best job in the world. When she's not being a mother to two beautiful girls, you'll find her hammering away at her computer lost in her fantasy worlds, or traveling to far-off places for family fun and exploration.

She'd love to hear from you, so find her at
http://www.facebook.com/pages/Jaymin-Eve/519939168016600

Or email jaymineve@gmail.com